LEGACY
OF
DANGER
Hell's Valley

Book Three

Jillian David

Book and cover design by eBook Prep
www.ebookprep.com

October, 2018
ISBN: 978-1-947833-79-1

ePublishing Works!
www.epublishingworks.com

ACKNOWLEDGMENT

As ever, thanks to Gwen Hayes and her steadfast belief that I could write these crazy stories. I also appreciate Julie Sturgeon and her ability to take any manuscript and always make it better.

When my former publisher closed shop, it was amazing author Kathy Lyons who kindly shared information for me to use in getting this book to print. I'm not sure if I would have been successful in publishing this book without her support.

And finally, to hubs, who thinks psychic ranchers are almost as ridiculous as the fact that I still don't have a short, bald guy on the front cover: I'm nearly certain that one day you might possibly be on one of my book covers. Nearly certain…

CHAPTER 1

Vaughn Taggart's knuckles blanched as he fought to keep the loaner sedan from spinning out on the way up a snow-covered western Wyoming Forest Service road. His younger sister, Shelby, needed him.

Finally reaching the gravel parking area, he pulled behind her Subaru and his brother's horse trailer. He threw the car into park hard enough that the seatbelt locked up on his chest. Goddamn buckle. His fingers fumbled on the release; finally, he unfolded his frame from the vehicle and braced himself against the frigid, biting air. Scowling upward, he imagined the sun setting behind the thick, gray clouds. With any luck, the snow would hold off until he could check in with Shelby.

Pulling his sturdy insulated boots from the back seat and shoving them on, he unfurled his unwanted but sometimes necessary supersensory power. Like shaking out a blanket, he opened himself up and stretched his mind as if opening a gate on his tightly fenced consciousness, probing for danger. Sometimes he got prickles on the back of his head and could control his focus by squeezing his hands into hard fists. Sometimes, the sensation of danger just grabbed him like an invisible hand and yanked him toward the threat.

As he stood still in the silent forest, his power encountered...nothing.

For now.

A virtual finger of ice chilled his neck. He whipped around, his power flaring to life, trying again to sense the environment around him. Ouch. He rubbed his temple to soothe the headache that always accompanied a telepathic search as he peered into the cold forest. Woods. Light snow on the ground. A few intrepid animals foraging in the leaf litter. Nothing else.

Right now, he had to find Shelby and figure out why she was freaking out over the danger to their family. Needed to make sure she was okay.

She would have never called him and left a message unless things had gone beyond manageable.

A wave gripped him, blanketing him in a suffocating heaviness. His hands shook. This time, it wasn't his power that affected him.

Damn it, no. No way. Not today.

Plain and simple, he needed a drink.

Jumping neck deep into the suds had helped create the nightmare that ruined everything a year ago. Sure as hell wouldn't solve any problems now. Or ever.

His heart sped up until he forced a few big breaths in and out of his lungs. No time for regrets. No time to wonder what ass kicking waited for him back on the family ranch. Time to help Shelby.

Tracks from boots and hooves traced the route away from the vehicles.

Good enough. Vaughn buttoned his jacket, cinched the laces on his boots, and took off into the forest.

An hour later, as night fell, Vaughn stomped his cold and weary feet into Kerr's hunting camp. He spared a glance at three customers in brand-spanking-new hunting gear, huddled around a roaring fire. Only they weren't feeling hand-warming, s'more-roasting cozy, judging by the deep frowns on their clean-shaven faces. Interesting.

Then his kid brother emerged from behind a tent. Kerr had only a slight limp now. Good for him. Their quick hug and back slaps triggered a lump that Vaughn couldn't swallow past.

"How'd you get here so quickly?" Kerr asked. "Shelby called you this morning."

"Pulled a favor with someone who owns a private jet."

"Mr. Big Bucks."

"Not exactly. MMA connections." He cringed. He'd been used for those connections before, too. "Where's Shelby?"

"Wow, you're really here. Good to see you, too, Houdini. Long time, no see. You look, um, not exactly good. And you're still ugly." Kerr shot him a crooked grin, then raked a hand over his bright red hair before cramming the Stetson on his head. "Eric's with Shelby." He pointed into the quiet, snowy forest. "They haven't returned yet."

"What the hell do you mean, they haven't returned? She left me a weird message but no details this morning. What's going on?"

Damn, it was good to see Kerr's cold-reddened face. The shadows from the flickering flames made his youngest brother appear years older than, what, twenty-eight? A baby compared with Vaughn's thirty-five.

Kerr had aged far too much in the past twelve months, but everything else about him was familiar. Kerr appeared...healthy. Like before his accident. Before Vaughn had iced the cake on the disaster of his life choices and had to leave town, for his family's sake as well as his own.

Later. Vaughn would deal with the fallout of his return to Copper River later. For now, his sister needed him.

"They should be here soon. Not sure why they're still out there." Kerr's head whipped back and forth between the forest behind him and his hunting guide service guests in front of him. "We located a lost hunter," he lowered his voice and nodded toward the three guests, "this afternoon, but she found him. Of course. On the way back, Shelby wanted to check on something suspicious in the woods first. Why couldn't she just leave well enough alone? She found the missing guy. Mission accomplished, right?"

Yep, because of her supersensory power to become a human radar. She could find anyone, anywhere. That tool sure came in handy, but, like all Taggart powers, caused pain.

So Shelby had left her message before she headed here, at least six hours ago. Crap. That meant her other ability had fired up– sensing when something terrible was about to happen. When she got a hunch, a smart person listened. That was the exact reason Vaughn took her panicked and short message to heart and got his ass from New York to Wyoming in record time.

He frowned. "So you all found the missing guy?"

Kerr crossed his arms and leaned on a tree trunk. "Yes."

"Then why is she still out there alone?"

"I told you. Eric's with her." Kerr rubbed his leg absently, and Vaughn flinched in sympathy. "I had to take care of my clients."

"Of course."

Kerr and Eric's fledgling hunting guide business would be devastated if they lost a wealthy client.

Vaughn checked on the hunters huddled next to the fire. One guy looked like he'd seen a ghost, but his buddies were giving him a good dose of "atta boys" and something in a flask. Whatever they were drinking didn't improve the terror etched across the man's face.

Didn't improve Vaughn's stress levels either as he stared at the metal bottle and licked his lips until he dragged his gaze back to his brother. With effort, he tamped down the liquor cravings. Barely.

What the hell had his brother so freaked out? Vaughn rubbed his temples again. His ability to detect danger had gone on neck-prickling high alert in the past few minutes. He checked over his shoulder. Nothing there.

"Yeah, something about this situation feels...wrong." He tapped his head. "In here. You feel me?"

Kerr pointed at Vaughn's head. "Bro, when you get the danger heebie-jeebies, it's the real deal." He shifted from foot to...well, foot. One was prosthetic.

"Yeah. Damn it." Silence while his brother watched him. Ah, right back into the oldest brother role. Vaughn rolled his shoulders. Now wasn't the time to buck responsibility. Now was the time to man up. "Let's track down Shelby and then get the hell out of here before I crawl out of my own skin."

Vaughn curled his hands into fists. Damn, what he'd give for a solid punching bag right now. Or a huge sparring partner or two. Or a drink. Anything to burn off the unsettled, nervy sensation. "Something's sideways. With...I don't know...maybe with everything. I can't pin it down. Can you read anything from Shelby?"

"I've been checking every few minutes, and everything seems okay." Kerr tilted his head to the side, going into that faint connection he could access with his twin sister. He blinked his gold-flecked eyes, a family trait, and focused on Vaughn. "She's maybe nervous and...curious about something. That's all I can tell right about n—" Kerr dropped to his hands and knees, sawing air in and out of his gaping mouth. "Holy crap, dude."

"What?"

"It's Shelby. Something just happened. She's hurt. Oh, shit, the pain." Kerr reached under his long duster and grabbed his prosthetic leg.

Vaughn put out a hand. "What's happening?"

White lines formed around his brother's mouth, and he gasped in response.

"Screw this. We're going after them," Vaughn growled.

Kerr pushed himself to a shaky standing position. "Roger that."

The old Vaughn would run straight into the woods, guns a-blazing. But impulse control issues had gotten him nowhere except a long trip out of town for the past year. At least he could learn from his past fuckups. He took a deep breath and calmed his mind, like he did before a fight.

"What about calling the police and EMS?" Vaughn asked.

"We called several hours ago when my guest went missing. All emergency services have been occupied elsewhere but should be headed here any time now." Kerr yanked out his satellite phone and dialed. "Garrison? Call 911 again. Get their asses up here." A pause. "Yeah, I know you can't leave the ranch. I get it. Just have them park near us and follow the tracks into the woods. I'll have one of the guests direct them in." Another pause as his mouth tightened. "Don't know. Something with Shelby. Something bad."

Kerr turned the phone off, laid out succinct plans with his clients, and turned back to Vaughn. "Let's go. Hopefully, EMS won't be far behind. I have a feeling Shelby's going to need help."

Twenty minutes of pushing their skittish horses past the limits of safety and then hiking through the dark forest while following tracks in the snow from Shelby and Eric's last known location finally brought Vaughn and Kerr to a ridge.

Vaughn ran to the edge of the bluff. Two sets of footprints stopped there, illuminated by his headlight.

His temples throbbed. An invisible hand squeezed his head and cranked it until he peered down the rock face. Dimly, he registered Kerr's slower steps as his brother caught up.

"What?" Kerr panted.

Their flashlight beams bounced off the bottom of the bluff, about fifty feet down.

The whistling scream of Vaughn's ability blasted to redline levels and sliced through his skull. Like acid poured onto whip-raw skin. His vision went blood red.

Danger.

There, at the bottom of the cliff, lay his sister's broken body next to Kerr's business partner, Eric. They were partially buried under and surrounded by rubble and rock fall. And a weird, lurid, green fire licked over their bodies. Vaughn reared back as a blast of hot sulfur shot up the bluff.

A few feet away from Shelby and Eric loomed a cloudlike, dark shape, with two red glowing points of light where eyes should be. That green fire came from within the goddamned thing.

Kerr yelled, "Shit!"

"Is she alive?"

His brother froze and cocked his head to one side. "Yes. Barely." The words ripped out of his throat.

Vaughn's ability drove him as he half slid, half fell down the slope, the scree shifting underfoot. He didn't care if he joined the motionless mess of humanity at the bottom of the drop-off. All he wanted was to get between his sister and that…thing.

As he slammed into the ground, the air left his lungs. No matter. He didn't need to breathe to take care of that bastard creature in front of him.

His power ramped up as light and sound whirled then reconstituted into different forms. He stepped in front of the black creature that sucked up light and oxygen. Vaughn's head burned.

But this time, his power didn't want to protect Vaughn.

For the first time in his life, his ability indicated danger to another person. Shelby.

Then he mentally whiplashed, head snapping back, as pain clicked to a brand-new agonizing level.

A boiling mass of pressurized, pissed-off, super-charged fury grew out of his mind, expanding from Vaughn and toward the black figure that reached dark fire-coated claws toward his baby sister's limp body.

Get away from my sister.

With a roar, he stepped in front of Shelby's bruised face and battered body. Too long. He'd been away too long, and this was the price paid for his absence. No way would his sister die. No way would Eric die. Not today.

The creature emitted a horrible sound halfway between a dying wolf howl and a blast furnace. It grew larger, the fiery dots of what passed for eyes in its shadowed depths glowed brighter red.

More terrified of his sister's death than his own, Vaughn gritted his teeth, rolled his hands into fists, and his power followed, pushing out into a desperate sphere, creating terror to match the beast in front of him. Pure hell faced pure hell. He ignored the headache that ripped through his skull.

He pressed harder.

With a roar that turned into sucking vacuum of a sound, the creature receded, screamed once more, and disappeared, leaving hot sulfur in the air that stung Vaughn's nose. Desire to hunt down anything that threatened his family gripped him, but his sister's hoarse voice stopped him.

"Vaughn?" she croaked before she crumpled over Eric's body and the pile of rocks. Dark smears of dirt tracked over her face. Even unconscious, she maintained a death grip on the back of Eric's shirt. One of her legs bore a makeshift splint, but the angle of her limb beneath the straps seemed all wrong.

"Yeah, sis." When he gave an awkward pat on her head, she didn't move. "Shelby?"

Her eyes rolled back in her head. His heart stopped.

"Kerr?" he yelled.

"On it." His brother picked his way over rocks to reach them. "Shel?" He pressed fingers to her neck. "Still alive. Damn it, Eric's half buried. Is he…?"

"They're both still alive, but they don't look good," Vaughn said. "What the hell was that thing?"

"Probably the reason why Shelby tried to contact you. She had a feeling. And also, we've seen that thing before." He held up his hand. "Details later." Kerr whipped out the sat phone and mumbled then looked up. "Okay. Search and rescue guys are nearly at base camp. We are getting these two out of here. Now."

"Fucking A, you bet we are."

CHAPTER 2

A *BCDE ABCDE. For the love of little puppies. AB freaking C. Airway, breathing, circulation, disability, exposure. Concentrate.*

The trauma resuscitation mantra was for amateurs, and Mariah West was many months out of residency. But she would do whatever was needed to stay laser focused on the two patients in front of her. Sure, she could handle multiple patients at once, but it got dicey when they were in such critical condition. In the rural Bondurant Valley Hospital, the family doctor on call also covered the ER since the patient volumes and acuity were typically low.

Typically low. Except when she went on call. Then all flipping hell broke loose. Or so it always seemed, thanks to her doctor's superstitions about having a karmic black cloud.

Tonight, Bondurant Valley Hospital's small emergency department vibrated as nurses, doctors, and EMS personnel scrambled to stabilize these two seriously injured patients.

Staff threaded additional large bore IVs into the patients' arms. Both subjects were breathing on their own. No airway compromise at this time, although both had head injuries, so their status could change rapidly.

Mariah glanced over at the stone-faced man who had planted himself on the far edge of the room. According to a nurse's whisper, he was Vaughn Taggart, the oldest brother of the unconscious woman in front of her and son of Mr. Austin Taggart, head of a local ranching family and one of Mariah's regular clinic patients.

Vaughn had insisted on coming into the ER with the patients. But instead of getting in the way, he hadn't moved from his vigilant position against the wall. The intensity of his scowl made Mariah want to rub the back of her neck.

Or hide.

He observed the care team with a quiet grimness, but the tight lines bracketing his hard mouth made him look concerned, not terrifying. His Adam's apple bobbed, shifting cords of muscles around in his neck. He reminded Mariah of the guys at her brother's MMA gym in Salt Lake City. Always tense, clenched, and primed for a fight.

Shaking her head, she tried to ignore the man and concentrate on the secondary evaluation of her patients.

Right as she leaned over to reassess her male patient, the trauma bay door slammed open and she jumped, losing her grip on the stethoscope bell. Garrison Taggart stormed into the room. The second oldest Taggart sibling. Mariah had met him a few weeks ago; she'd cared for his girlfriend, Sara, and his only son, Zach, when they had been injured.

Wow. This family could not buy a break.

Garrison stalked straight over to the unhappy man plastered to the wall. Vaughn stood there like a bronze cowboy sculpture. In fact, with both men next to each other, it was clear that Vaughn was a harder, bigger version of Garrison, like the rough draft before the final product. Vaughn's face wasn't so much handsome as compelling. Dark brown, almost black eyes narrowed beneath thick brows. A crooked nose suggested this wasn't his first confrontation, and the tilt of his thick chin told her it wouldn't be the last. His dark brown hair had red glints, like embers in a banked fire.

Not breaking stride or momentum, Garrison lifted a thick, shearling jacket-clad forearm and slammed his brother in his chest, the boom reverberating through the trauma bay, making everyone freeze. How did Vaughn remain standing after such a hard impact? The two men glared at each other. Nurses' jaws dropped open.

What the hell? Sweat prickled Mariah's chest.

"You've got some nerve, coming back here now, after all this time. What I'd give to punch your lights out." Garrison's voice filled the room.

"So do it," his brother gritted out. His body was tense, but his arms remained down. Although, given his massive frame, he could likely fend off any attacker and then some.

Damn it. Were those two bulls going to go at it in her ER? Because she only had experience as a ringside doctor, not as an actual MMA fight referee. No way did she want to get between the two glowering men.

He reset his grip on Vaughn's leather jacket lapels, making the glass cabinet doors rattle. Then Garrison growled.

Yep. Definitely going to brawl.

Not happening. Not here and not if she had anything to say about it.

Rule one of trauma management? Make sure the environment is safe to care for patients. Control the situation.

Control? Safety? Funny, since the first half of her life had been all about a lack of safety and zero control of her situation. Well, then. Nothing like making up for lost time in a public forum.

She took a big breath and snapped, "Take it outside, guys. That crap has no business in here."

Everyone in the room pivoted and stared at Mariah. Even the machine beeps seemed to stop.

Attention. Damn it. Heat flowed over her chest and neck. She pushed her discomfort aside; patients' lives depended on her ability to maintain order and focus on their care.

Over Garrison's shoulder, Vaughn's gaze locked onto her until she shivered. It wasn't so much that the action was inappropriate. It was his blank, detached exterior that stole the air from her lungs. The coldness. Like he didn't care if Garrison beat the hell out of him. Didn't care if he made a scene. Didn't care what anyone thought.

If she had felt inadequate before, his cold assessment triggered too many memories and took her insecurities to a whole other level. Exactly what she could not afford today. And frankly, his opinion meant nothing. She had one job to do, and it didn't involve this hulk of a man.

With a flex to his massive shoulders, Vaughn pushed against the wall and lifted his hands, dislodging his brother's grip. He stormed out, followed by Garrison. In their wake, clods of sandy mud and snow dropped from their thick boots onto the trauma bay floor.

The air whooshed out of the room, and everyone continued to stand still for a few seconds.

Then with a ripple, like shaking themselves awake, Mariah and the staff all turned back to caring for the patients. The low voices and sounds of medical devices resumed.

An invisible band she hadn't realized had been cinched around her chest released. She could breathe again. A fleeting headache came and went across her temples.

Exhaling deeply, she turned back to her patients.

ABCDE. Airway, breathing, circulation, disability, expos

CHAPTER 3

Vaughn slumped against yet another wall while Garrison came unglued in the hospital waiting room. Not that he cared what anyone else thought about his brother's behavior, but the fact that no other person wanted to approach within thirty feet of them came as a relief. Hell, Vaughn didn't want to be within thirty feet of this damned hospital. He wanted to leave so badly that his muscles twitched and skin crawled.

Back in that emergency room, the sharp scent of rubbing alcohol and snap of gloves combined with the sounds of whooshing and beeping, blasting him with a memory of Mom's last days as she fought cancer. How many years ago had that been? Four? Five? For his part, Vaughn had been too involved in self-destructing via alcohol-fueled brawls to be fully present for his own mother. Couldn't fix the past, but no way would he make the same mistake again. No more hiding.

Which meant, at some point, he'd have to fess up and tell Garrison his real reason for leaving the ranch last year. Not now, but soon. If he thought Garrison wanted to kill him now for deserting the family, wait until he heard about how thoroughly Vaughn had screwed up his brother's life. Now that was a conversation to look forward to. Start the popcorn, kick back, and enjoy the shit-show.

"Son of a bitch, what are you doing here?" A vein. A real goddamned vein stood out on Garrison's wind-roughened forehead, visible even beneath the brim of his hat. His younger brother's hands curled into hunks of anger at his sides. It would come as no surprise if Garrison punched him into oblivion.

Vaughn tapped his own forehead. "Shelby left a weird message with me earlier today and thought I needed to be here. You know how she gets feelings."

"Of course I know about her feelings. And your feelings. And all of our goddamned feelings. We're all a bunch of fucking mutants with our brains wired crossways."

Garrison hadn't been left out of the strange power lottery. No, he could reach into someone's mind and detect if they were lying. Seemed like a great gift, until paranoia and distrust made him avoid everyone.

In the immediate family, the four Taggart siblings had these special "gifts." But go a little further out on the family tree and there was a mess of…odd…cousins in Montana, where Mom grew up. Nosing around a little more, Vaughn had found stories about his maternal grandmother from back east and the interesting things she could do.

For the most part, the Taggart kids kept their powers hidden. It was hard enough growing up in the fishbowl of a small town without being freaks of nature.

Garrison took a breath. "Why return now? Why not a month ago or two?"

"No one called me before today."

"Lame excuse. Try again."

"Gar, it's late—" He checked his watch. "Or rather, early. We don't need to work through all of our issues right now. Let's put our energy toward Shelby and Eric in there." And as a bonus, Vaughn wouldn't mind figuring out why his power had just flared around that ER doctor, right when her moss-green eyes had pinned him in place. Maybe whatever had changed in his head when he flipped gears and protected Shelby and Eric had fried his ability to detect danger.

Or maybe interacting with that nasty, stinking glob out there had changed Vaughn's power. What the hell was that thing anyway?

Later. He'd figure it out later and then get rid of the thing.

His brother rubbed his neck. "Look, Vaughn. Can you just go back to the ranch and stay there? I want to be here with Shelby and Eric. And now that Kerr has sorted out his guide service guests, he needs to be here with her."

Ah yes, Shelby and Kerr's extra "twin sense." Feeling his sister's injuries must have rattled the hell out of Kerr. Almost as bad as what Shelby had suffered when Kerr had almost died in that IED explosion in Afghanistan.

Vaughn glanced around the empty waiting room as a prickle of his power came and went. "Why can't I stay at the hospital, too? We can all three wait."

"Because there is some bad juju going on. Long story, but the Taggart family is having issues."

"Issues? Is Zach still…normal?" Garrison's young son. His brother's pride and joy. And his biggest fear, due to the uncertainty of whether Zach would also manifest a supersensory ability.

"Yeah, no powers yet, thank God. Maybe it'll skip a generation. But we've got much bigger problems. Not sure how much help to ask for"—worry lines crinkled around his eyes—"since I don't know how long you're sticking around this time."

That comment hurt. And was also well deserved.

He continued, "But right now, the rule is that one of us has to be at the ranch all the time, in case—"

"In case what?"

"In case something happens," he lowered his voice to a hoarse growl, "like that thing you saw out there. Not sure what the hell it was, but it has our number. Son of a bitch. Too much going on." He paused. "You going back to the ranch will also give you time to see Dad."

"How's he doing?"

Maybe he didn't want the answer, based on the downturn of Garrison's mouth.

"Poorly."

It was like an uppercut to the jaw.

"What do you mean?" Vaughn asked.

"He isn't doing well, okay? That's all you deserve to know right about now."

He opened his mouth again, but Garrison cut him off with a slice of his hand through the air. "Later. We'll catch up once I make sure that Shelby and Eric are okay."

Because someone had to take care of them went unsaid. *Because my oldest brother fell down on his job.*

Vaughn clamped his mouth shut. "Got it." He strode through the hospital doors. It was a still night, cold and harsh.

Colder, now that he was away from his sister and brother.

The separation shouldn't have been palpable, but their connection as Taggarts, as family, as individuals who shared a strange secret, all pulled at Vaughn like a tightening rubber band, painful and stretched to its limit.

When would it break?

The dirt road to the main buildings of the family ranch took far too long to travel, and the distance was more than he could measure in miles.

Early dawn glowed on the cloudless, cold horizon. The weather had cleared out, leaving a biting chill. Sparse snow failed to soften the wild rangeland Vaughn had called home for his entire life.

Until last year.

Until the biggest mistake he'd made in his life.

Unless you counted returning home, which might turn out to be an even bigger mistake.

His heart thundered in his chest. What had Garrison meant about Dad not doing well? Shelby hadn't mentioned anything in her tense, whispered message.

His gut churned. That might have been the last time anyone heard his sister's voice.

Christ.

As Vaughn guided the loaner car over a rise in the bumpy road, the wan light gave the ranch buildings a grim, flat appearance, like quiet ghosts rising out of the wild Wyoming land.

He blinked and rubbed his eyes.

The big barn was missing. In its place stood a skeleton of new lumber.

Off to the other side of the big ranch house and out buildings, cattle lowed in a small field. Wasn't it too early to bring them close to the house? There was still forage available on the grazing land. Too early for calving. What was going on?

Where were the three yapping dogs that usually ran amok–their family pets and working ranch dogs?

As the sky lightened right before the sun broke over the horizon, he caught a shadow of movement off in the trees beyond the field a few hundred yards from the house. A wince against the inevitable headache, a prickle on the back of his head, and his ability activated, senses on high alert. He didn't need to clench his fists to open his mind this time.

His power yanked his head around toward the tree line. He peered into the gray forest.

Nothing there. The ache in his temples receded.

Had he imagined it? Was he tired and hallucinating?

Since when had any of the Taggarts' abilities been wrong? Even when he and his siblings didn't want their powers to be right, no such luck.

He parked the sedan next to Kerr's old truck near the kitchen, where a window glowed with warm, yellow light. Waves of memories crashed over him: his mother and father fixing meals as they stood at the counter together, the cheery red-and-white tile floor, the loud chatter across the table while he ate with his three younger siblings. One time, there had been a food fight, followed by a terrifying walk to the barn that all the kids took with their father. The anticipation of doom was enough to set Vaughn and his sister and brothers back on the right path.

What about the hours of games, hiding in all the nooks and crannies of the ranch buildings? Or laughing their heads off at the worst tackle football games ever. Vaughn always won.

Despite the memories, nothing felt right. This wasn't a homecoming.

He had screwed up. He had taken the better of two rotten options and left all of this life behind more than a year ago. Done and done.

His own life had changed for the better in New York. Well, mostly. By using that power to detect danger, Vaughn's MMA star was rising quickly, although he'd declined to enter the UFC as a contracted fighter, because he had one or two ethics left. Extra ability equaled unfair advantage. But along the way, he had gained some wealthy friends.

And wealthy friends attracted women who wanted Vaughn solely for his connections. Damn it. Hadn't seen that betrayal coming. His danger detector hadn't made a peep when that particular Delilah walked into Vaughn's gym, embedded herself into his life, and then ripped it all apart when she spun around and sunk her talons into one of his wealthy friends.

Given why he'd fled the ranch, a woman betraying Vaughn was the most perfect karma the universe could dish out. After that disaster, he had stuck with what he did best: fighting and picking stocks.

Pair his ability to avoid danger with financial decision-making, and he'd developed a reputation as quite the financial advisor with a hell of a track record, even over the brief period of time he'd been in New York City. He cultivated many of the MMA managers and organizers as his personal clients. Succeeding in those two worlds guaranteed that he had money and well-placed friends.

So, hell yeah, when Shelby had called him for help, he had pulled a well-connected favor and hopped a private jet.

But aside from saving her life, it had otherwise been a mistake, coming back to Copper River and opening all these wounds.

He paused. Well, maybe returning hadn't been a complete mistake. In his mind's eye, an image formed of the pretty doctor with those quick movements as she worked on his family.

At least he'd met someone new in town. Well, not met, actually. Got yelled at.

So, *not meeting someone new* at all.

Slamming the car door closed, he strode into the kitchen.

Kerr sat at the worn wooden table. His head and shoulders drooped as he gripped a coffee mug. Car keys rested on the table.

A tall, sturdy woman Vaughn didn't recognize had three skillets on the stove, all emitting mouthwatering aromas. When she turned, he rocked back on his heels. Her hazel eyes glinted with the same kind of gold flecks he and his siblings had. The woman's auburn hair was pulled back into a no-nonsense bun. One corner of her mouth lifted.

Kerr cleared his throat as he waved a hand. "Vaughn? Ruth. Ruth? My brother Vaughn."

She closed the space between them with purpose and gave a firm handshake. "Ruth Turcot. I'm a nurse caring for your father until he…improves."

Vaughn reared back. Improves?

She continued, "You might see my husband, Odie, wandering around. If you do run into him, please tell him to stay out of trouble."

"Could someone tell me what the hell is going on here?" Vaughn's grip on his temper slipped.

The woman coolly raised an eyebrow and moved back a few feet.

"Better to show you," Kerr said, pushing to his feet with a grimace. He led Vaughn out of the kitchen and down the hall.

Gut churning, Vaughn whispered, "Who the hell is that woman? And what's the story with Dad?"

"A lot's gone on since you left, bro." Kerr opened the second to last door at the end of the guest wing hall.

Vaughn had always viewed his father as a powerful man, grabbing life by his two work-worn hands and forcing it to obey his steel will.

The only similarity between the father of his memories and the man huddled under the blankets? The thick, gray hair.

Vaughn's stomach muscles clenched like he'd been sucker-punched. He jerked his head back to Kerr, who merely shook his head.

Vaughn drew enough air to create words. "What the hell?" he whispered. Sure, Dad had been ten years older than Mom, but he'd always been the picture of health. The man in the bed looked…geriatric.

His brother's shoulder lifted and fell. "Stroke. Happened right after the barn burned and Hank Brand kidnapped Zach and Sara." At Vaughn's raised brows, Kerr added quickly, "Sara. Garrison's girlfriend. Anyway, Dad had a stroke."

Vaughn staggered into the doorjamb.

"Yeah," Kerr said. "And you know Dad. He didn't go to the hospital when he started having symptoms, waited too long making sure everyone else was okay."

Hesitant, he took one step, then another, toward the bed. "Dad?" he choked out around a tight lump in his throat.

The rustle of sheets and a creak of bedsprings pierced the silence. "Son?" One eye opened. The other remained half closed. "Is that you?" He reached an arm out. The other limb remained in place.

God, no.

"Vaughn?" Dad asked again, a quaver in that whispery-gravel voice.

Kneeling next to the bed, Vaughn gripped his father's forearms, the thin skin slack over diminished muscles. He swallowed. "Yeah. It's me."

"You're back." When Dad tried to reach out, he couldn't hold both arms up.

As an invisible dagger sunk into his heart, Vaughn leaned in and gave him a hug. Since when had his dad's shoulders gotten so thin? Since when had it hurt so much for Vaughn to pull air into his own lungs?

He inhaled. The familiar scent of Aqua Velva created a horrible churning in Vaughn's emotions. "How are you, Dad?"

"A little setback." The words came out hesitant, uneven. Slurred. "I'll be back on my feet soon."

"Sure you will." He pulled back and patted a bony shoulder. Suddenly, Vaughn needed to leave the room. Escape. "Uh, you get some rest now, okay?"

Dad's relaxed sigh sent him shrinking into the pillow. Melting. Fading.

Waves of nausea pushed Vaughn back to the door. Then he spun around. "Why didn't you tell me?" he hissed.

"Garrison said if you wanted contact, you'd call." His brother's face fell. "I wasn't kidding when I said a lot has happened."

"And now?"

Kerr eased the door closed as they exited, then pointed at the room. "Right now, that's Dad's condition. He talks a good game, but he mostly stays in bed. Although I have to say, Nurse Ruth has worked wonders motivating him."

"Who's paying for the in-home nursing?"

"Right now, the three of us are scraping funds together."

"Damn it. I wish I had known. I can pay for his care." Of course he could. Vaughn's meteoric rise as a financial advisor had netted him a six-figure salary and bonuses. If his power to detect danger created an unfair advantage, well, at least he could use the resulting bounty to help his family.

"Garrison said that you'd left for a good reason and would come back when it was the right time."

"If I'd have known…"

"Leave the past in the past." His younger brother scowled. "That's what I have to do."

Of course he did. "How's the leg?"

"Better. Almost ready to dance a jig." No smile. "You still fighting?"

Way to change the subject. "Sure am. Lots of MMA opportunities in the greater New York area."

"Still cheating?"

"It's not cheating. I'm using my full resources is all." He sniffed. "The headaches keep me from doing it too much."

A snort. "Well, that makes it all better, doesn't it?"

Vaughn followed Kerr back down the hallway, careful to keep pace with his brother's uneven gait.

"So what's the plan?" Vaughn asked as he inhaled the scent of hot, fresh breakfast—bacon and eggs—that drifted through the house.

"You stay here and protect the ranch."

"Why?"

"Because whoever burned down the barn—and it looks like the Brand family had something to do with that action—and stalked our family is still around."

"Stalked?" Another change in air pressure pushed Vaughn off-balance again. He resisted the urge to check his back.

"Yeah. Whatever that black…thing…was that was climbing over Shelby and Eric last night has shown up here as well."

"Wait. It's a separate problem from the Brands?"

"Think so. But who knows?" Kerr glanced around the empty hallway and whispered, "We're in a shit-storm over here, dude."

"Not good." Vaughn clamped down so hard his jaw ached.

Kerr ran a hand over his bright red hair, making it stick up. His kid brother's narrowed eyes rocked Vaughn back on his heels. "No, Mr. Obvious, it's not good. Between you and me, all I'm waiting for is the dust to settle and for Shelby and Eric to recover. Then I'm going after that creature myself."

"Alone? You sure about that?"

"If necessary. I have skills, too, you know."

Kerr's ability to never get lost, combined with his gift to literally disappear, could come in way handy in this situation. But kid brother solo versus that thing? Kerr might be resourceful and wily, but Vaughn had seen firsthand what that creature could do. No way would he let little bro go it alone. "Want help?"

"I want it destroyed." Kerr sniffed. "So, yes, I'd love some help."

"I'm on board with that concept." Vaughn spared a glance at the walls filled with childhood photos, starting with baby pictures and finishing with high school graduation portraits times four. "Garrison know you've cooked up this idea?"

A shrug. "No time to chat. I'm sure he'd be fine with it." The who-me? innocence didn't convince Vaughn.

"Got an actual plan?"

"Details are still in the developmental stage."

"Don't do anything if it puts more of us in danger."

"Danger?" Kerr leaned his shoulder against the bottom of the stairs bannister and studied him. "What? Are you feeling anything else threatening since being here?"

Besides the shadow sensation when he arrived at the ranch? And the impact of a certain doctor's beautiful green eyes that knocked him back a few steps? "If I did, I wouldn't admit to having fear. Makes me sound like a scaredy cat."

"No comment. However, you might want to take those instincts seriously. There's something bad out there. Everything is just...wrong here, man. I can't explain it. Nothing we're doing is working. Everything's broken."

"Like we're cursed?" Big news there. Vaughn had felt cursed his whole life.

Pausing at the entry to the kitchen, Kerr gripped the jamb and whispered, "Not exactly. More like we're being sabotaged or targeted."

"That's crazy."

"So you think." He entered the room and nodded to Ruth, who set a plate of steaming food on the table for Vaughn. Kerr kept on walking. "I'm going back to the hospital. Hold down the fort."

"What am I looking for? Stuff that is out of place?"

"No. That's small potatoes." Kerr turned at the back door. "Look for stuff that scares the holy hell out of you."

CHAPTER 4

A t the start of Sunday morning rounds, Mariah had her hands full of caffeinated survival and her mind full of test results for the critically ill patients from early yesterday morning. Or was it two nights ago?

Her days and nights ran together. She rubbed her face with her free hand as she trudged down the first floor hallway to the back stairs. At least a few hours' sleep last night and a good shower had helped. With any luck, the coffee would push her over the hump from marginally functional to semi-human. She rolled her neck.

What about her patients? Shelby Taggart, first of all. The orthopedic surgeon had cleaned out the open fracture and placed the external fixation device on her lower leg. Antibiotics were running, and she was afebrile. Normal CT scan.

So why didn't she wake up?

She had also reviewed Eric Patterson's case with the neurosurgeon in Casper. The scan had showed a skull fracture but no brain swelling, bleeding, or CSF leak. After Mariah had updated a calmed-down Garrison and youngest brother, Kerr, they'd made the decision to keep both patients here in Bondurant Valley Hospital.

Actually, no. They had *insisted* on both patients staying here unless there was no other choice. Not the reaction she was used to seeing.

And what about that fight in the ER between Garrison and Vaughn?

She shivered at the memory of Vaughn's hulking frame, his apparent refusal to fight back against his furious brother, and the way he searched her like she had the answer to a question he needed to know.

No. Not exactly an answer to a question. He'd looked at her like he could strip her bare with a mere glance.

Quit it. He was a stressed-out family member in an emotional situation, nothing more. People had all kinds of reactions to such experiences when their loved ones were injured or sick.

Time to look at probabilities. Had some random guy affected her confidence, or was her self-doubt the problem?

In medicine, the saying went: If you hear hoofbeats, think horses, not zebras. Same with weird feelings. In Mariah's case, the most likely explanation was that she had weird feelings because of her own neuroses, not because of some random guy.

With a sigh, she exited the empty service stairs to reach the back entrance of the patient floor.

Rounding a corner, she came within a sloshed drop of dumping her coffee on Wyatt Brand. She pulled up short as the large, wild-eyed man loomed before her.

The Brand family, like the Taggarts, was well known in town. Wyatt owned the local hardware and supply store. One of the Brand brothers was a principal at the school. Another one was the sheriff. Their mother was also a patient of Mariah's.

And a few weeks ago, yet another Brand brother, Hank, had kidnapped little Zach Taggart and Garrison Taggart's girlfriend, Sara.

Then Hank disappeared. Like, no leads for the investigation, no body parts left behind, no forensic evidence. Vanished.

Which left brother Wyatt to fill the void of bad behavior and even worse attitude. A baton he appeared to have picked up with gusto.

"Dr. Mariah?" That grating voice, combined with the typical leer, was enough by itself to make a gal want to kick him in the nuts. Not to mention, a few weeks ago, when he had accompanied his ailing mother to one of her appointments, Wyatt had made a pass at Mariah.

She carefully folded her arms as she kept her cooling cup of happiness between herself and the guy.

"No" apparently didn't mean "no" in his world, if his ten other advances since were any indication. Points for persistence, but enough was enough. She might have hang-ups from the traumatic experiences in her youth, she may have set the dating bar low due to her past relationship mistakes, and she may not have gone out with anyone in more than a year, but Mariah drew the line at dating co-conspirators in possible felonies.

He scratched at his unshaven chin and stretched to his full, burly height, causing her to crane her head back. Then he leaned forward, invading her personal space. "Have you thought about my offer to take you out for dinner?"

His stale breath of onion-laden hash browns made her eyes water as she backed up. "No, thank you," she sputtered. "What are you doing here? It's seven o'clock on a Sunday morning. I haven't been in to see your mom yet. After I round on her, I'll be sure to update you."

He waved the comment away, like his mother's pneumonia had nothing to do with his presence here in the hospital. Uh oh. Her heart didn't so much flop as go *splat*. That last sip of coffee turned to acid in her stomach.

He grinned. "Thought it might be a good time for us to talk."

Nothankyouplease. "About what?" Would it kill any other staff member in this hospital to use the back stairs this morning? She'd pay good money for a distraction right about now.

"Our future together."

Right about now, she'd take a fire alarm or a Code Blue. "Pardon?"

"It's simple. I want you. You want me. What else is there to say?" As his beady eyes raked her from feet to head, she fought the urge to yank the lapels of her white lab coat closed.

He pressed a meaty palm to the wall near her head. The thick scent of greasy male clogged her nose. His other arm rose on the other side of her.

Hauling air in and out of her lungs, she whipped her head from side to side. She gulped. *Oh no.* Her vision blurred at the edges and her head swam. Mariah so did not do confinement in any physical form. Not after…Damn it, she needed to step away from this situation before her flashbacks took over.

No help? No problem. She'd get out of this mess herself.

If only she didn't have a severe allergy to personal confrontation. She could assert herself if a patient's life was at risk, but any other situation? Not her comfort zone at all. But enough was enough. She peered down the hallway. No one in sight; all the nurses must be in morning report. Great.

She tried a test duck, but he slid that hand down next to her shoulder and blocked her exit. Then he smiled, the curl of his damp lips triggering a rush of bile up her esophagus. Too familiar. Too much like before.

The hospital linoleum beneath her feet shifted into plywood in her mind's eye as her memories turned this unpleasant situation into a past horror. She was stuck in that room all over again.

Air. She couldn't get enough air into her tight lungs.

No more nice doctor.

"Mr. Brand, I need to go see patients. Thank you for the offer, but I'm not interested." She forced herself to meet his too-avid leer. Damn it, she'd need a shower to wash away the taint of his gaze all over her. "At all. Ever." Her voice rose, the words coming out clipped and salty. "And do let me know if you'd like the answer provided in smaller words or interpretive dance. I'll do whatever is necessary to get the point across."

"Not possible." A red stain crawled up his neck and face.

As she slid under his big arms, she got a weird tingle over her skin.

Safety. Like a cocoon.

God, how she wished. She peered around. A stairwell, an empty public restroom, and the dead end of a long hall. No safe haven here.

"Okay. We're done here." She edged farther away from Wyatt.

In a burst of movement, the coffee mug flew out of her hand with a crash. A painful pinch on her upper arm, and suddenly she stopped flush against the wall. Air left her in a coughing whoosh, and her pulse skidded out of control. His face loomed inches away.

What the hell? This gorilla had actually put a hand on her.

"I'm not good at taking 'no' for an answer, Mariah. We'd be so great together. Give us a chance." He gripped her arm; her past and present slammed together in nasty juxtaposition. "You saying that you're too good for me?"

Her ears buzzed. This entire situation was surreal. Couldn't be happening. "No. No, I—" She should scream. She should run. She shouldn't freeze like this. Like she did before...before. She opened her mouth. No sound came out.

His fingers dug into her bicep. Tears burned her eyelids. "Then I don't see what there is to discuss," he said. "Unless maybe you like the chase or making the man work for it. Or maybe you like rough stuff? Okay. I can play that game, little teaser." He raised his empty hand.

And just like in that nightmare from long ago, she flinched away.

A low growl nearby, and the hairs stood on her arms as a large man entered her tunneled field of vision, sucking up the light behind Wyatt.

Vaughn Taggart slid in front of her and wrapped his hand around Wyatt's wrist until the man let go of Mariah. Then Vaughn walked, one big man pushing another back, step by slow step. Wyatt gave a guttural grunt as his eyes widened, then narrowed.

"This is none of your business, Taggart," Wyatt spat, leaning forward but going nowhere.

Vaughn radiated strength and confidence out of the back seams of his form-fitting gray Henley shirt and faded jeans that stretched over his muscled thighs. He did the best impression of an impassable obstacle she'd ever seen. His stance widened, almost like a fighter at the beginning of her brother's MMA bouts, and then he took another step forward, forcing Wyatt to shuffle backward or fall on his ass.

Good.

"Have a nice day, Wyatt." Even though Vaughn's tone remained low and calm, its intense power rolled through her bones. She actually sagged against the wall.

"But, I was only—" the jerk sputtered.

Vaughn continued to hang onto Wyatt's wrist. To a casual observer, the grip was light and easy. The tell? Tight sinews and blanched knuckles as Vaughn clamped down on those bones. "She doesn't want to talk to you."

Hello? She's right here and can hear you. But maybe now wasn't the time to interrupt the glory of Vaughn Taggart bullying the bully.

"How would you know?" Wyatt seethed, trying to pull away.

"You're right. Maybe I misread the situation." Vaughn made a quarter turn and locked onto her with a dark, narrowed stare. A whiff of shaving cream and vital, warm male made her take a deeper breath. It was a lovely scene, watching Vaughn hand Wyatt his ass. "You want to talk with him?"

She crossed her arms and glared at Wyatt. "Nope."

"Works for me." Vaughn turned back to the incapacitated jerk. "The good doctor has work to do, like take care of people who need her help. She doesn't want to waste her time talking with morons. She needs to check on my sister and friend."

Wyatt grinned. "Yeah. How are they doing?"

"Now it's my turn to say none of your business." He released Wyatt's wrist like it was toxic slime and continued to walk forward, imposing his body into the guy's space.

Wyatt slipped on the pool of coffee on the floor and landed square on his butt. Scrambling to his feet, the sweating man craned his head around. Rage played across his contorted face. One of his eyelids twitched. A red glow came and went in his eyes, along with a weird whiff of burnt sulfur. Had to be a trick of the light along with a chemical smell. She didn't move.

"You've made yourself an enemy, missy." He pointed at her before facing Vaughn. "And you, Taggart. Mark my words. Everything is about to change. You've only seen a tiny amount of what's to come. We've nearly completed—your family will soon become extinct." He spun on his feet and stomped down the hall, the squeaks of wet boots on linoleum fading away.

For several seconds, she mutely stared at the broad back and shoulders in front of her. Then the thermal-clad torso fully rotated until she came nose to chest with one of the best sets of pectoralis muscles she'd ever viewed beneath cloth. What would those muscles feel like under her fingertips? Would his skin be as warm as she imagined? She only wanted to know for clinical data, of course. No other reason.

After too long of a delay, Mariah stuck her hand out, determined to salvage her unprofessional lapse. "Well, thanks for that..."

"Vaughn Taggart."

The same hand that had incapacitated Wyatt now enveloped hers, somehow generating a physical sensation of safety. She frowned as a swift headache throbbed for a few beats then dissipated. As his thumb moved over her skin, a jolt of interest headed from her chest due south and arced between her ovaries. Wow.

Oddly, his big frame and presence took up a lot of space, but she didn't feel threatened.

Eyes with irises the color of gold glitter swirling in dark coffee locked onto her, and her cheeks warmed.

Okay, she didn't feel exactly *safe*. But whatever the sensation, it didn't scare her.

"Mariah West. I've been taking care of your sister and Mr. Patterson."

"I know who you are." The hard slash of his mouth formed words in an economy of movement.

"Okay, then. Thanks again for the help." Her hand rested in that warm paw of his, and she tugged.

Nothing happened. His fingers remained locked around her hand. Not painful, not intimidating, but firm. Unmoving. Making it clear: he would let go when he chose to do so.

Her heart fluttered, a bird banging around a cage.

After studying her for more long seconds, a line formed between the thick, nearly black brows.

"What the hell?" he breathed, almost to himself.

"Pardon?" She pulled on her hand again. "Um?"

"Sorry."

He released her hand.

In a vacuum-like sensation, the feeling of safety receded, leaving her reeling on her heels with what probably passed for a dumbstruck expression.

He rubbed his chin with the heel of his hand. "Weird."

"What?"

He shook his head, the hall lights catching glints of auburn in his dark brown hair. "Before I forget. My apologies for my behavior in the emergency room."

"Well. Okay." She licked her lips. "Family members are often stressed out in those situations."

"Anyway. Yeah. Sorry." He shoved a hand into the front pocket of his jeans, accentuating areas she had no business contemplating without being board certified in urology. "So what's the deal with that Brand asshole?"

"Wyatt? He can't take a hint."

"I didn't like how he looked at you."

"And it's your business because...?" How fabulous would her life be with someone like Vaughn who cared about her wellbeing?

The lines of his uncompromising face became harder. One curt dip of his hard chin. "No reason."

Right. Because she had totally read into every bit of the tingly feels she got around him. Not like she didn't have a track record for misunderstanding men. Case in point, last boyfriend. Two years invested, mountains of disappointment, ending in the statement that she didn't fit into his vision of a future. Oh, and don't forget his ultimatum about her career. Hell of a blind spot, not seeing that one coming.

What about her over-the-top reaction to Wyatt's encroaching on her personal space? Always came back to how that damned horrific past haunted her. One day, maybe her experience in that awful place wouldn't color every part of her life in shades of brown plywood. Not today, though. She sighed, tugging at the stethoscope hanging around her neck.

"Uh, thank you for taking care of my family," Vaughn broke the awkward silence.

Her head whipped up at the sudden warmth in his tone. All right. He could ricochet from intense and brooding to appreciative. Fine, she could keep up. "Sure thing. So…I should probably get this mess cleaned and then go check on my patients."

"Let me help. I'm the morning shift staying here today, so I don't have any place else to go. We can chat more when you see Shelby."

Great. Exactly what she did not want: him monitoring her every move as she examined his family member. Even now, his proximity felt like a hand resting an inch from her shoulder. Not touching her, but present.

Not exactly threatening, though, was it? More like…waiting.

CHAPTER 5

Vaughn tried not to stare while Dr. West bent down to pick up the shattered pieces of her coffee mug. Truly, he tried.

The way the strands of warm brown hair fell forward made his fingertips itch with his desire to feel if those strands were as silky and thick as they appeared. He could imagine that hair spread out on something totally random like, oh, maybe crisp white bedding.

Which sent his libido sprinting to the finish line of his racing thoughts: what the petite doctor herself would look like on *his* crisp white bedding. Maybe wearing only a white coat.

Strike that. No white coat.

Fuck him sideways. Had he not learned *any* lessons from his past? And had he truly lost all grip on his sanity that he would now fantasize about any woman in front of him?

No. Not any woman. *This* woman.

A weird tingle of his power ran through his gray matter like a sewing machine needle pricking a path. What the hell? The sensation made zero sense given the context—he was safely standing in front of her in a perfectly unthreatening hallway.

So was his ability to detect danger trying to tell him something else? Amplifying his interest in her? Or maybe his desire had somehow triggered his power. The cause and effect still didn't add up.

Well. At least his interest was focused on someone unmarried this time.

Yeah, he'd checked. A discreet question posed to the hospital receptionist confirmed that the good Dr. West was at present, unattached.

Not that he had any business asking. The combination of his track record with women, plus with the fact that he would blow out of town in a week or so, hopefully never to return, sealed the decision on any interest he might have wanted to explore. Not going to happen.

He got another strange tingle in his mind.

Damn it. Why the hell would his power choose now, of all times, to change? For years, he was the Taggart kid who had the ability to detect danger to *himself*. Simple. Came in handy with high school scuffles, stock picks, and his MMA bouts.

He waved off a nurse who hurried toward them. Then he dashed into a nearby bathroom and pulled out fistfuls of paper towels from the dispenser.

Returning to the spill, he knelt next to Dr. West. Mariah. A scent of coffee and mint wafted over him, making his mouth water.

Because he wanted coffee and a mint?

Hell no.

As he laid the towels out on top of the spill, the tan paper turned dark brown, like old blood on an octagon mat. He swept the lump of damp towels and ceramic chips into a big wad. His hand brushed against hers, and a zap of warmth shot up his arm and into his chest.

Damn it, he'd sworn off women since last year's disaster.

Since he'd betrayed his brother. Which reminded him that he hadn't talked with Garrison yet. Hadn't laid all of his sins out on the table.

Frankly, Vaughn never imagined he'd return to Copper River, much less talk with his siblings again.

An image of Shelby's unconscious form, chest draped in electrodes and arms poked full of IV's, rose in his mind. There was one sibling with whom he still couldn't talk.

"Well, that should take care of it." He stood and grasped Mariah's fine-boned forearm to help her up. A few brown dots marred the hem of her white coat. Holding out the towel bundle, he gestured toward the remaining pieces of mug in her hands. "I'll take that."

He disposed of the entire mess in the bathroom garbage can, returned with a few more towels, and scooted them around the floor with his boot until the area was dry.

"Thanks for cleaning up and also for stepping in back there," she said, her voice somehow mellow and sharp at the same time. When she chewed her full lower lip, a rogue wave of heat urged him to do the same exact thing.

Offering her a clean paper towel, he paused and shrugged. "Wyatt Brand's an idiot."

She dried off her hands and then stepped to a nearby dispenser to get a glob of antibacterial gel, and he followed suit.

Her nose scrunched, making stupid birdies flop around in his stomach. "Tell me how you really feel about him," she said.

"My real feelings for most of the Brand family are not fit to express in polite company."

"Aw, you think I'm polite? That's so sweet." Her raised brows over sparkling green eyes threw an upper cut at his libido.

That foreign feeling in his face, like half-dried clay cracking apart? It was a real, honest-to-shit smile. "Most people would have told him off or decked him."

A pause. "Well, I didn't want to mess up the fancy manicure." She waved perfectly normal, buff and trimmed nails, devoid of all polish, in front of him. Great. Now he wanted to know how those fingers would feel trailing over the skin of his chest, his belly, and lower.... "Besides, I hate showing off." She brushed off imaginary dust from her shoulder.

"Wyatt wouldn't want to get his ass kicked by a five-foot-nothing woman," he said. Damned if the corners of his mouth continued to creak upward.

She tucked her hands into the coat pockets and frowned at the floor. "Well, that's a crappy start to the morning. No coffee plus jerk. Nowhere to go but up, right?" A brief grin transformed her pixie face from impish to radiant.

His tongue went dry, and it took him two attempts to form words. "Maybe I could make it up to you?" The second those words left his mouth, he wanted to take them back. On the one hand, hell yes, he wanted to spend some time with Mariah. What guy wouldn't? But on the other hand? Christ, he had only to review his entire body of work in the field of Mistakes With Women to know his request was a bad idea.

A red flush flew up her neck. "What?"

What a great look on her. Blush. He smiled even wider, despite his misgivings. "What if I took you out for coffee and a bagel sometime?"

"Out?"

He had committed. Wouldn't back out now. "You have to eat sometime, right?" Stupid silence filled the space between them.

She blinked and frowned.

That weenie smile of his dropped like a lead balloon. *Mission abort. Pull the damn cord.*

When the flush reached her cheeks, it made her beautiful emerald eyes glow. "Of course I have to eat. It's just that…it's generally not something I do with company." Then she cringed.

"Maybe it should be something you do more with company," he tried one more time, like a desperate pirate digging one more hole, hoping to find the treasure.

"Well." She chewed her lip. "Sure, I guess that would be okay."

The world started spinning again, and the invisible pirate did a jig. "Sounds good to me," he chuckled.

Sounds good to me? Since when did stick-in-the-mud Vaughn become Mr. Yuck-It-Up? And how un-cool did a guy have to be for *sounds good to me?*

"Any time in your schedule tomorrow?" he blurted out. *Real smooth, man. Not desperate at all.*

"Monday? Well, I have rounds in the morning then I'm off for the rest of the day because I was on call this weekend. Maybe a late breakfast?"

Warmth spread out from his chest and flowed into his limbs. Maybe he had a tiny chance to have a normal conversation over a meal with a normal woman and not make a mess of it. This wasn't a life decision. This meet-up could be a way to get back on the proverbial bike but with training wheels. So he wouldn't be hurt again. Simple enough. "Bring your appetite. We'll go to the Hungry Moose. Ten?"

"Sure."

"Good." He stood there like a real, live dope, watching her. For what? Praise? To see if she would spontaneously burst into flames?

God, man, say something. Quit staring. Too much silence.

A frown formed as she toyed with the stethoscope around her neck. "So, um, if you'd like to wait in Shelby's exam room, I'll check on Eric and then her. I can update you then if you like." She clamped her mouth shut, spun on her heel, and hustled down the hall, her white coat providing cruel cover as she disappeared into a work area.

As he dragged his sorry, un-suave ass down the hall to Shelby's room, he craned his neck to get another glimpse of Mariah, but she was deep in discussion with one of the nurses.

Back to business already.

And why not? She had a job to do, which didn't involve mooning over Vaughn.

He stretched his fingers, working his wrists in circles. Kerr had told him that Vaughn's old punching bag in the main barn had burned up in the fire several weeks ago. It had been three days since he last trained, an eternity for a routine-driven guy like himself. His muscles ached to get back to the gym, lift weights, and then pound the hell out of something. He needed to work out to keep those liquor demons at bay. Needed to punish his body to remind him of the pain he caused other people.

MMA training had been the only thing that saved his life, too. Without the discipline of his training, Vaughn would be permanently pickled. Or dead.

His love for MMA wasn't really about the fights. No one outside of the northeast had ever heard of him, and he preferred it that way. No, what he loved about MMA was the regulation of the activity, the way he could become stronger, how he could use the mind-numbing hours of punches and kicks to work through his baggage and come out better both mentally and physically on the other side.

If time permitted, he could take a trip down to his old gym down in Rock Springs this afternoon and do some sparring.

But what would satisfy him more than a good workout or winning a big MMA bout? Taking down a grade-A asshole like Wyatt Brand.

At the door to Shelby's room, he paused, hand on the door handle.

Kerr sat, crammed uncomfortably into a chair positioned right next to the motionless figure drowning in wires and electrodes and tubing. Their vibrant sister had become a still-life piece of decorated medical art.

Like his mother had looked, years ago, before she died in this same hospital.

Damn it, his family needed to catch a break.

"Any changes?" Vaughn asked, entering the room.

Kerr's light brown and gold eyes flicked up and then back to Shelby. "No." He stood in a slow, stiff action, shifting from foot to foot. "Stable, so not worse."

"Doctor's coming in after she sees Eric."

He rubbed his thigh after a few steps. "I'll stick around for the report, then head out."

Vaughn paused. "What's the story with Wyatt Brand?"

"The lily-livered monkeyfucker?"

Vaughn choked on spit. "Nice image. Yeah. Aren't they all kind of assholes in that family?"

Kerr's expression twisted, and he shook his head. "Not all of them. But the Brand men are royal pains in the ass."

"I just had a bizarre run-in with Wyatt."

"Really?" Kerr shrugged. "Seems like I heard that his mom has been sick in the hospital here recently."

"What he was doing had nothing to do with visiting hours."

Kerr ran his hand over his short orange hair. "He was an accomplice to Zach and Sara's kidnapping."

"So you had mentioned. Why isn't that sicko in jail?"

"Did you get knocked out in a fight and forget that this area has some real close-knit ties? They have family members in law enforcement, school, and one uncle is a judge. We'll never get a charge to stick against any of them."

Of course Vaughn knew about the judge, given how many times he'd stood in front of the man for sentencing, no thanks to Sheriff Tommy Brand. What a winner, Tommy. That particular jackass had taken great pleasure in hauling Vaughn's butt to the county jail, over and over. The Sublette County sheriff's department probably had to reduce their workforce after Vaughn left town.

"Convenient, isn't it, how all of our concerns about crimes on and off the ranch have been swept under the proverbial rug."

"The fuck you say," Vaughn spat.

"Why, yes, as a matter of fact, I do like to talk during sex. Thanks for asking." Kerr's mouth quirked upward. "But no, I'm not lying. Wyatt may end up getting off scot-free."

"Not okay. Can't we lawyer up or get a private investigator?"

"With what money, bro?"

That statement nailed him right in the guilt complex, somewhere near his liver. "I heard that Wyatt helped Hank kidnap Sara and Zach." The skin of Vaughn's neck prickled.

"Sure did."

"What happened to Hank?"

"Disappeared in an explosion. Like a fart in a stiff breeze. Blowing up that shack in the woods effectively destroyed any evidence. *Kaboom.*"

Vaughn shook his head. "Not buying it."

"None of us are, but that's the only explanation we have at this time. Supposedly, law enforcement is still investigating but…"

"The Brands own the police."

A curt nod told the tale.

What he'd give to punch something. Or someone.

Before he could ask another question, Mariah entered the room, along with that mouthwatering hint of mint and mocha. With a glance that seemed to linger on Vaughn—or was that wishful thinking on his part?—she turned and performed her exam while talking to Shelby like she was awake. Like she anticipated a reaction. A movement. Anything.

Hell, they all wanted Shelby to respond.

Turning back to Kerr and Vaughn, Mariah looped the stethoscope around her neck. "She's stable. Breathing on her own and without any need for additional oxygen. Labs are good. No evidence of infection in the leg. That's all good."

"But?" Kerr scuffed a boot on the floor.

Fine furrows appeared between her brows. "Well. She should be awake by now. Anesthetic from surgery has long since worn off."

Vaughn's ears began to ring. "Do you think there's been…damage to her brain?" Not his baby sister. God, no.

"Well. Possibly. Time will tell." Damn, but the woman was direct.

"What about Eric?" Kerr asked.

"Similar but with a worse head injury with that skull fracture. I've been on the phone with neurosurgery in Casper several times in the past twenty-four hours."

"And? Anything *they* can do to help?" Vaughn snapped. He wanted to take the words back the second they left his mouth. He didn't miss her flinch.

"According to the specialist, no further treatment is needed right now. I redid the CT scan on Eric this morning, and the swelling is going down. He doesn't need surgery." She bit her lip. "I'm happy to transfer him to Casper if you'd feel more comfortable."

"No!" Kerr sliced the air with his hand. "They both stay here."

Vaughn's head snapped up.

Kerr ran a hand through his orange hair, making it stand on end. "I meant that it's better for them to be close to family if possible."

Mariah exhaled. "All right then, I'll stay in touch with the neurosurgeon and we'll continue to care for them here. Our orthopedist will come in later today to check on Shelby." She walked to the sink and washed her hands, then turned back. "I'll be on call through tomorrow morning. If anything changes, we'll let you know." She didn't mention the Hungry Moose date. Of course not.

Vaughn watched her retreating back, all the while feeling like a dog watching his favorite toy leave the room.

"Dude. You need a bib for that drool?" Kerr grinned and made a kissing face.

"It's not like that. Besides, she's the…"

He inspected his nails. "Cute doctor who saved Shelby and Eric's life?"

"Maybe," he mumbled.

"Someone you'd like to perform a physical on you one day?"

"Damn it. No." He rubbed his chin. "Doesn't matter." And that was a problem, wasn't it?

The real problem had nothing to do with Mariah at all. It had to do with the fact that Vaughn had no business even thinking about a relationship with anyone. Not after what he'd done. And certainly not when he planned to stay in Copper River for as short a period of time as possible. Once things were back to normal with his family, he had a life to continue elsewhere.

He had cut ties, started over, and created the life he'd always dreamed of.

Right?

His head snapped up as Kerr groaned and walked around the foot of the bed. He stretched out his back and picked up his feet. No, foot. With a tired slump to his shoulders and a halfhearted wave, Kerr left, pulling the door closed behind him.

Vaughn sat his sorry ass down into the uncomfortable chair and rested his hand on Shelby's slack arm as his daytime shift at her bedside began.

CHAPTER 6

Vaughn went ramrod straight in the chair as Garrison stomped into Shelby's hospital room that evening. They still had unfinished, unpleasant business to discuss. There was the status of the ranch, the supernatural creature stalking their family, the feud with the Brands, Shelby and Eric's uncertain health, Dad's stroke, and, of course, the 800-pound gorilla: Vaughn's fuckup.

"Any change?" The lines on his brother's face had deepened since last fall.

"No. Stable. It's a waiting game now." He tried to meet Garrison's narrowed glare but couldn't.

Garrison laid his hat on a rolling bedside table. "Well. Take off, then." The way he said it sounded like taking off was Vaughn's forte. He wasn't wrong.

He pushed to his feet to meet his brother eye to eye. "Garrison. I need to explain about your wife."

"Ex-wife," he spat.

"Okay." Sweat collected on his lower back, making the fabric stick. "Look, I need to take responsibility for my part in what happened last year."

"Not necessary." Garrison's words came out low. Controlled. It would be easier if he'd just yell and get it over with.

"Yes, it is. I screwed it all up for you, man. Your marriage. Everything." Damn it, Vaughn was the oldest. Supposed to be the rock. Instead, he'd been a betraying lush who went terra incognita.

"Not all of it." The smile barely creased Garrison's tight mouth.

"Huh?"

"Tiffani had checked out of our marriage long before she started making passes at you."

Vaughn's jaw dropped. "You knew? Back then?"

"Suspected. As it turns out, she'd had several extracurricular activities."

"No way." He shifted his weight from one foot to the other in the silence. Scuffed the vinyl floor with a boot.

"You weren't the only one she..." Garrison muttered.

Vaughn shook his head. "Not sure if that makes me feel any better."

"It shouldn't. And I hope you're haunted by what happened. I hope it motivates you to...be better or some crap like that." Garrison crossed his arms with a creak of material, not bothering to take off the shearling leather jacket. He planted his legs like he wanted to tackle Vaughn.

Carrying out an uncomfortable conversation wasn't easy for the best of communicators. But for two dudes like he and Garrison? Wasn't pretty. But by God, Vaughn would keep going, even if it hurt.

"Every day I think about what happened." Vaughn sucked in a lungful of air. "If it makes you feel any better, I was drunk when it happened. With Tiffani."

"No, it does not make me feel any better."

"Right."

Garrison rubbed the back of his neck. "There's more. She was involved with Hank Brand shortly after you left."

"That asshole? Talk about fucked up." Vaughn clamped his mouth shut for a solid ten seconds in case he said something else stupid. "Sorry."

His brother's lips twisted. "You have no idea. Then she sent me divorce papers, threatened to take Zach if I didn't sign, drained the bank accounts, and disappeared. Turns out she left Hank, went to Salt Lake City, got mixed up with some sketchy folks and ended up dead."

"Shit. I'm really sorry."

"I've dealt with it." The negligent wave didn't match Garrison's haunted expression. "In retrospect, she was unhappy for years. Unhappy with me, with being tied down to the small town, and probably unhappy with herself."

"Wow." He rubbed his chin with the heel of his hand and tried not to fidget. "Still doesn't excuse that I didn't stop her advances."

Garrison dropped his hands to his sides. "No, it does not excuse what happened." Vaughn had to strain to hear his low voice. "I would have hoped for more from you."

Yeah. Time to come clean. Might be the end of his relationship with his brother. Hell, how much worse could it get? But he had to tell the entire story. "She'd tracked me down a few times in the barn, making suggestive comments. Little touches that were not consistent with *sister-in-law*." When he gulped, it was like swallowing glass shards. "One night, you were down in Rawlings working cattle sales. I'd been drinking, as usual. When I woke up, she was in my bed. Naked."

"Son of a bitch."

"It looked like we'd been...yeah." He paced in the too-small room, a comatose sister serving as second witness to his confession. "I don't remember any of it. I still can't believe that I did anything. With her. But I just don't know. She had taken pictures of us in bed together. Told me she'd use those pictures to break you and little Zach. Shit, it's my word against a dead woman's. But I think it was staged." His tongue tingled with the desire for something liquid and high proof to roll down his throat. "You don't have to speak to me again. You can punch me out cold, if it will help. But, God's honest truth, that's what I think happened."

Garrison sank into the vacated bedside chair and rested his elbows on his knees. "Damn."

"Yes. And no, I didn't encourage any of it. I might have been a drunken idiot, but I didn't lead her on. I swear."

His brother remained silent for the longest minute of Vaughn's miserable life.

"Do you still drink?"

"Nothing for over a year now. Not that I don't want it every single day."

Garrison flicked invisible dirt from his denim. "So you up and left. Because you were too chickenshit to deal with what had happened. Without explaining anything to us. To me."

"Figured it was better to cut myself off from this family than hurt it more. I'm sorry."

"Well, your leaving hurt us." Garrison's grim and lost expression when glanced up would haunt Vaughn for a long time.

"Damn it."

"I need time to deal with this new information, on top of the normal piles of crap waiting for me back at the ranch."

"I'm sor—"

"Stop saying that."

"Got it."

He shoved back to his feet and paced. "It's going to take a long time for me to trust you, man."

"I know. And I need to earn that trust back. I get it."

He welcomed Garrison's dude-hug and fist on the back like he'd been starved for this moment.

Vaughn went boneless as adrenaline seeped out of him. He wasn't innocent. Garrison wasn't over what had happened. But they were on the right path.

After more than a year of self-imposed exile, damn, it felt good to be at peace with his brother.

Long may it last.

After he left the hospital, Vaughn headed to his old gym, Bar None MMA, in Rock Springs, Wyoming. The ninety-minute drive in Kerr's truck did little to clarify his churning thoughts.

But once he went through a killer workout, those stress levels dropped. Sure took the edge off the hooch cravings. After an hour of beating up inanimate objects, he paced circles on the mats, cooling down.

"Man, you're cut," said one of the guys who had high-fived him when he entered.

"Good to see you, too, Marcus. Still fighting at lightweight?"

The wiry guy grinned. "Moved down to the featherweight trenches, 145 pounds or bust. I have a fight next weekend at the Owl Creek Casino in Lander. You want to come along?"

"Sure love to, but it depends on stuff going on back at the home front."

As the seven o'clock session got started, a few other acquaintances wandered over and shook hands or slapped Vaughn on the back. The gym. Hell, he loved the easy camaraderie. Like he had never left.

Strike that. It was better than before he'd left. At least now, every workout session didn't involve spending the first hour sobering up.

"Where have you been?" One of the older fighters and gym owner, Earl, crossed his zero-body-fat arms. "Heard you're all uppity now. Big-shot city guy, fighting in the concrete jungle. Too good for the common fighters out here in the boonies?"

"It's not like that at all. I had to leave town for a while."

He sized Vaughn up. "How long are you back?"

"No idea. A week, maybe more."

"You stay fight ready?" Earl nudged one of the other men, and they snickered.

What gave? "Sure, why?"

"Want to take a fight on short notice up in Lander?"

A surge of adrenaline made Vaughn's heart thud. He hadn't fought on the local circuit for several years. Being in jail repeatedly put a cramp in his training regimen and fight appearances back in the day. But now, with the opportunity to pound the crap out of a real live human being? Hell, yeah. He'd take that fight any day of the week ending in the letter Y.

Vaughn's power to avoid danger buzzed. "Depends. What weight?"

"Light heavyweight." Earl pinched Vaughn's nonexistent love handle. "You're soft, like butter. Can you make 205 by this weekend?"

Fifteen pounds in five days? Wouldn't be a problem. "Sure. Who am I fighting?"

"Looks like you'll fight Lincoln McDowell, the regional champ."

"Linc."

"You know him?" Earl asked.

The opportunity to flatten that asshole's face almost gave Vaughn a hard-on. "Yeah, we've fought before. Many years ago. He's a dirty bastard." Split decision in Linc's favor. One of the few fights Vaughn had lost. But call a spade a spade: Vaughn didn't do himself any favors by rehydrating with Jim Beam after weigh-in. If he almost beat the guy while sloshed, imagine what he could do sober.

His hands curled into eager fists.

The owner grinned. "That's why you two would be a match made in heaven."

"Why doesn't Linc have a bout lined up?"

"His opponent got injured last week and had to pull out of the fight. Angelo Martinez, the fight promoter, would give anything to keep that card filled. If I send him a replacement, he'll be more willing to put my gym's guys on fight cards in the future."

"Are you certain of the fight?" Angelo was the shrewd promoter for most of Wyoming. The guy worked hard to elevate fighters to the next level of MMA. He worked even harder to make bank on every event, too.

"No. This is secondhand information. But I'll tell Mr. Martinez to call you ASAP. I bet he'd be very interested."

"Fair enough." He shook Earl's hand. "Well, I have work to do. Can I take a bag home for the week?" He motioned to one of the Everlast punching bags hanging by a chain.

"Don't see why not." Two of the men took the bag down and left to stow it in the back of the truck. "You also want something for ground and pound work?"

"Yeah. Give me the heaviest grappling dummy you can spare. I'm going to need it. Hey, maybe I'll see you guys this weekend in Lander."

Marcus hollered, "Hey, pansy, make sure you bring your A game. Linc's gotten better over the past few years. That bastard is scary as shit."

"Understood." Throwing on a sweatshirt, Vaughn pushed through the front door and into the bracing night air.

No more snacks for the next week, then. So be it. He curled his fingers around the steering wheel as a smile pushed the edges of his face. A live fight. This trip back to Wyoming was turning out to be therapeutic as hell.

CHAPTER 7

T he next morning's rounds had Mariah up bright and early.
    Well, at least early.

She cradled her cup of sanity like it was priceless crystal as she shuffled to the nurses' station. No one was going to deprive her of her drug of choice this morning. She rolled her shoulders. Thank God for low census in the hospital. She had only seven patients to round on, then she was off to brunch with a certain guy who made her uterus quiver.

A woman in flower-patterned scrubs strolled over.

With reluctance, Mariah set down the cup. "Good morning, Amber. Any changes with Ms. Taggart and Mr. Patterson?"

"Ms. Taggart woke up a little while ago."

"As in, awake-awake?" The unspoken question of mental status hung heavy in the air between them.

"Alert and oriented." The nurse looked at the floor then back up, triggering a sinking sensation in Mariah's stomach.

"But what?"

"Her vision is gone. Can't tell when the light is on. No sight at all."

"Oh, wow." Mariah racked her brain for stroke syndromes and head injury complications causing isolated blindness. Occipital lobe injury? Funny, the CT scan didn't show any abnormalities in the woman's brain. "Okay. I'll check on her. How about Mr. Patterson?"

"Still in a coma. No change."

"That's the damndest thing. I'll give the neuro guys in Casper another call to see if there's anything else we can do. Thanks." After a sip of the coffee, she trudged down to Shelby Taggart's room.

Before opening the door, she peeked through the narrow slit of glass. Sure enough, Shelby's eyes were open. Even though her patient's head was turned in the direction of her twin brother, Kerr, the unfocused gaze supported her nurse's assessment.

Mariah rested her hand on the door, but her muscles refused to work. The intense bond between brother and sister was obvious as he patted Shelby's shoulder and talked to her. A painful vice sensation developed around Mariah's ribcage.

Damn, she missed Kevin. Sure, Mariah and her brother chatted or texted a few times every week, but it didn't take the place of being near each other. They'd stuck together despite injury, struggles, and parents who had all but abandoned them. They had been each other's biggest cheerleader, the person each could call in their deepest funk. She and Kevin had escaped that awful situation together, years ago. Something no kid should ever have to deal with.

So, no question, Mariah knew all about the bond between brother and sister.

Sliding her hand off the door handle, she backed away.

She'd evaluate Mr. Patterson first. She brushed a hand over her eyelids.

Must be some pieces of lint irritating her eyes.

Copper River's famous Hungry Moose diner was nearly empty in the post-breakfast, pre-lunch lull on this cold weekday in December. After checking with Kerr to make sure Shelby was still awake and improving, Vaughn had decided that it would be okay keep his appointment with Mariah. Then he'd take a shift at the hospital, sitting with Shelby. His sister was awake. Thank God.

Vaughn took off his leather coat and adjusted his neatly tucked thermal shirt once more.

He checked the parking lot for the tenth time in the past three minutes. Not that he cared if Mariah showed or not. Might be better if she canceled.

As his growling stomach attested, having a meal date while trying to make weight was one of the more boneheaded decisions he'd ever made. The aroma of bacon and hash browns? Torture.

A prickling sensation at the back of his head signaled his weird radar awakening.

Ah, speaking of torture.

He gritted his teeth as he mentally unfurled the control he had over his ability, trying to ignore the headache that came with it. The compulsion to make sure Mariah was safe overrode all other instincts when he got close to her.

She pulled up in a black Mini Cooper, complete with little racing stripes. Seriously, who drove a car like that in this town? It looked like a toy parked next to his ranch truck. Then she hopped out of her car without any difficulty, and he understood why she had such a ridiculous ride. That tiny car fit her to a T.

He snorted, then froze in place.

A shadow flitted behind her car. A glint of ember red shone within the darkness of the shadow.

His headache spiked.

As she glanced up toward the diner, she pitched forward and her foot slid on the ice.

His power surged, and he jumped in her direction, nearly traveling through the glass storefront. At the last minute, he rested a fist on the window and sucked in air until the urge passed. She hung onto his truck handle but didn't hit the ground. He checked again. No shadow visible. Head aching, he vibrated in place but managed to stay put. What the actual hell was going on with his ability?

Entering the diner, she looked around and shot him a sheepish grin. "You didn't see that, right?"

"I saw nothing." He couldn't quite pull off the lie.

Damn it all if her reddening cheeks didn't made her green eyes sparkle.

Damn it all if her green eyes sparkling didn't make his stupid toes tingle.

Toes tingle? He must be hypoglycemic from the weight cut.

"So…?" she said.

"Yep. Let's." He caught the attention of a waitress, who waved them to an open booth.

Mariah paused to remove her wool coat, and he took it from her, hanging it on the hook next to their seats. The material gave off that minty scent he associated with Mariah, and he inhaled deeply, hoping she wouldn't notice.

He hung his coat as well and slid in across from her, wincing when his knee banged the center metal table post.

"Busy this morning?" he asked.

"Yes. Shelby's back to what I'm told is her snarky baseline."

The smile moved unused muscles on his face. "Good luck to us all, then. That's great."

Mariah nodded, then leaned back and stretched her shoulders; the knit fabric of her sweater briefly outlined her breasts. Christ, they were perfectly proportioned to her body. His tongue turned to sand. Time did a weird warp thing for a few seconds. Or was it minutes?

Finally, he figured out something to say. "Are you done with work now?"

"Barring natural disasters or other emergencies, I should be off for the rest of the day." Flicking a finger along the edge of the menu, she asked, "So, were you, uh, working on the ranch this morning?"

"Morning chores. You bet." And an hour's worth of sweating out some pounds before the chores. "So where are you from, Mariah?" *Great intro, man. Way to dive right in there.*

"Utah originally." Before he could ask another question, she said, "How about you? From Copper River?"

"Yeah. Born and raised here, along with my crazy brothers and sister."

A quick crease flitted across her forehead. "You've been gone for a while, right?"

"How did you know?"

She indicated in the general direction of the diner front door. "Small town."

Not good news. If she knew that he'd left, she might know why. "I've been gone for a little over a year. New York City."

"I've never been there. How do you like it?"

"It's a different world. Lots of suits, faster pace, folks climbing corporate ladders."

"You didn't answer the question."

Huh. Okay, he'd bite. "How do I like it? Obviously, well enough to set up shop there." Damn, that came out too sharp.

She rolled her lips together and stared over at the empty tables.

Impulse and anger. Two things he needed to work on, pronto. While he was at it, he should also knock down his defensiveness a few notches.

Smiling at the waitress who filled her coffee cup, Mariah wrapped her fingers around the mug and sighed as she took a sip. What would it be like if he ever earned a sigh like that from Mariah, say, a few inches away from his ear? His groin had the answer. Hand up, so to speak.

She gave the waitress her order. "Pancakes, sausage, and hash browns. And an OJ."

"Impressive. Hungry?" He chuckled.

Ducking her head, she gave a sheepish smile. "Hey, I don't miss any chances to eat. Old habit from medical school and residency. 'Eat when you can, sleep when you can,' as they say."

"Not sure where all that food will go, but best of luck to you." He turned to the waitress. Damn it, this week sucked. "Two egg whites, scrambled, with veggies. And an apple if you have it."

A dark eyebrow quirked. "For a big guy, that's a pretty dainty meal."

"Maybe I'm on a diet." *Shut up*, he commanded his hollow stomach.

"Why would you need to diet?"

And just like that, without his conscious thought, his chest puffed out. "Naw, it's a joke," he mumbled. "Ate earlier this morning." Lie. He didn't want to get into the MMA stuff. Because then he'd have to go into the *why* of MMA and field more questions he wasn't ready to answer. Later. If there was a later.

For right now, he wanted to learn more about the woman in front of him, but she had some serious verbal judo skills deflecting conversation away from herself.

"So, how'd you end up in Copper River?"

A shrug of a small shoulder. "Loan repayment."

"I don't understand."

"I'm with the National Health Service Corps."

"What's that?"

"It's for poor medical students." That little nose scrunch nearly did him in. "As a student, if you commit to work in an underserved area, NHSC will pay off the medical school tuition. It's a good deal when you have to pay off school loans."

"That does sound like a good deal."

"Sure, until you figure I still have to pay off college. No one helps with that part. But yes, the program is good for medical school loans."

"How long will you stay here?"

"I'm obligated for four years, but, obviously, they hope physicians will stay longer. Put down roots." She chewed her lower lip.

And? Would she stay?

He had no business asking the question.

"So, tell me about the Taggart ranch," she said, too brightly.

Why did the question about her loan obligation bother Mariah so much?

She wasn't ashamed of needing help with her debt from medical school.

No, what bothered her most about Vaughn's innocent question was the "putting down roots" part of her answer that she blurted out.

Most NHSC students served near their hometowns. If they were adventurous, they fulfilled their obligation elsewhere, but often returned to where they were from.

But Mariah didn't have a home, did she? Well, she did, technically, but no way would she ever go back there.

As she listened to Vaughn chat about his childhood, growing up on the ranch with loving parents and pesky siblings and getting into trouble in school here in Copper River, he painted a picture of what she had missed. A home base. A place where she fit. Even though Vaughn had moved to New York City, he still saw this place as home.

Even gone for a year, he was part of this town and the people in it.

Where did she belong, truly?

Not with her last boyfriend, whose view of a future wife's role didn't involve an independent, smart woman. And that future sure as heck didn't include a woman who moonlighted as an MMA ringside doctor. To him, nothing could be more lowbrow. In retrospect, forget him. She was better off alone than with that guy.

But the slice her ex made about her not fitting in with his big, wealthy family because of her past and her career? That comment cut deep. Too deep.

"Am I boring you?"

She startled, her cheeks warming. "Of course not." Vaughn, boring? It was a testament to how unsettled those thoughts made her that she couldn't concentrate on the intense guy sitting on the other side of the table.

"Good. Because…just good." His brown and gold gaze raked across her.

Her heart thumped under the intensity of the space between his words.

For some reason, she couldn't stop looking at the sensual slash of his mouth, oddly soft in his hard face.

The food arrived. Thank God for something to do other than gape at the guy. She dove right in, enjoying the pop of bacon and starchy fried goodness of the hash browns.

Vaughn finished his tiny meal in a few bites and then watched her in silence.

She paused, fork halfway to her mouth. "You want some of mine? That look you're giving my plate…it's like you want to telepathically eat the whole thing."

He leaned back, eyelids half-mast. Vinyl booth material creaked as his weight shifted. "Not what I was thinking at all." With a quick buff of the apple on his shirt, he bit into the fruit with a too-loud crack, all while keeping his focus on her. The way the muscles in his jaw moved as he chewed shouldn't have looked sexy.

But it did.

Oh.

Was it warm in here, or did she have too many layers on? She tugged at the neckline of her sweater.

Nope. No layers.

In for a penny. She set her utensil down. "Care to share what you were thinking, then?" Could he see her sweating? Man. This brunch was higher pressure than an interview.

He took another bite. "No." A bit of apple pulp clung to his firm lower lip.

"P-pardon?" If he didn't brush that piece off, she'd do it herself. With her mouth.

Stop it.

"No." Abruptly he sat forward, arms on the table, leaning close to her. He licked his lip. Apple piece gone. "No. As in, what I'm thinking as I watch you polish off a delectable breakfast should best wait for a second date. Or maybe a third."

"Oh?"

"Yeah, oh." He gestured with the apple and leaned back again, resting the same arm over his broad chest. "Don't let me interrupt your meal. The sooner you finish, the sooner I can ask you out again."

Hungry? Sure, she was hungry, but for something other than the food on the plate in front of her.

Her phone rang, making her jump. Sliding out of the booth, she fished the phone from a coat pocket. "Sorry," she said.

With another laconic crunch that made her jealous of the fruit, he waved for her to go ahead.

Ten seconds was all she needed for the nurse to give her the information. Time to head back to the hospital.

"I'm so sorry to cut this short, Vaughn."

"Natural disaster?" His brows drew together.

The guy had a great memory. "No, this falls in the category of 'other emergency.'"

"So you're bailing on me."

"No. Yes, but." She pointed at the phone. "The hospital."

The slash of his mouth hardened. "I see." Did he think she was blowing him off? Because, no way.

"Um, thank you for the meal. Can I pay for mine?" She glanced at the half-eaten feast.

"Of course not." He set the apple core down on his empty plate, tossed some bills on the table, and stood next to her while she shrugged into her coat. The scent of his shaving cream made all the blood rush out of her head.

"Thanks again." Why couldn't she catch her breath?

"Maybe we can do this again?" he asked. Why did it sound like a formality? Like he wanted nothing to do with a second date now.

"Sure. I can give you my number..."

"No need. I know where you work."

CHAPTER 8

During Tuesday morning rounds, Mariah skidded to a stop halfway down the hall. She rubbed her eyes.

Because what she saw couldn't be happening.

Garrison pushed Shelby—the patient who had only awakened from a coma yesterday—in a wheelchair, flanked by none other than a fierce Vaughn. As a matter of fact, his scowl seemed to create a bubble around the three of them. Nurses and techs gave him a wide berth.

The good feelings from their pleasant but odd brunch yesterday drained away in an instant.

She hurried to the trio. "What are you doing?" It was unfair how she had to tilt her head to glare at Vaughn.

He crossed his arms over a tight-fitting, gray thermal shirt and smiled. Like he had some kind of power over her, with that...chest. Or like he had leverage, since they'd had a date? Not really a date-date. More of a meal together.

Not really a full meal, either, more of a quick snack before she had to leave early. Did he always eat apples like that? Because she could go for watching him demolish a Red Delicious again.

Okay, so not a date. More of an apple-viewing party interrupted by a phone call from the hospital.

Damn it. How long had she stood here, staring? For Pete's sake, she was a professional.

She rocked back on her heels. How dare they move her patient?

Fair enough. Shelby looked pretty fit right now, which significantly lowered Mariah's fear for her patient's life, freeing space to think about things like Vaughn's pecs. She mentally shook her head. But still, Shelby's condition had been critical not twenty-four hours earlier. Her vision was only just now returning. That woman needed to rest and recover. In bed. Where she could be flippin' monitored. By medical devices to keep her from being dead.

She shouldn't be out on a stroll with her brother. Brothers.

Vaughn's spine snapped straight as he locked his glitter-swirling irises onto Mariah. A shiver worked its way through her, but regardless of how he made her feel inside, she would remain in control of this hospital situation.

"You guys. What the heck?" she tried again.

"We're taking our sister to see the patient in that room." Vaughn tilted his annoying chin toward Eric Patterson's ICU bed. Today, his words came out ice cold, a totally different man from yesterday. As if they'd never had a date...meal...apple together.

Fine. She could play this game.

"This may not be safe. I didn't give permission for her to be moved." Mariah spaced her legs shoulder-width apart and fingered the bell of her stethoscope that hung from her neck.

"We didn't ask your permission." Vaughn crossed his arms over that damned chest.

Garrison did a land-based fish impression as he stared at his brother.

Her pulse pounded in her ears.

From the wheelchair, Shelby jerked her head up toward Vaughn. She squinted, but her expression held an air of concentration, like she sniffed the air between Mariah and Vaughn.

For his part, Vaughn opened his stance and leaned forward, like a fighter about to begin a round. A physical contest would end badly for one of them, Mariah had no doubt. Where had the nice guy gone who took care of the bully, cleaned spilled coffee, and then nibbled a Weight Watchers breakfast?

Beneath his narrowed gaze, she fought the urge to pull her lab coat tight around her. No, she needed to assert some control to preserve the safety of her patients. Damn it, she was responsible for their recovery.

"You sound familiar." Shelby said.

To put a hand on Shelby's arm, Mariah had to brush elbow to elbow with Vaughn. He moved not at all. Damn the heat radiating from his hard body.

"I'm Mariah West, one of the family doctors. I checked on you yesterday morning, but you were still pretty groggy. I'm also the ER doctor who has been seeing far too much of you Taggarts over the past several weeks."

"So why are you working here and not the ER, then?" Vaughn raised his hard chin again, tempting her to put a fist into it.

Would a simple *thank you* be too much to ask?

Best recovery was a good offense.

All right, Mr. Grumpy Expert. Let's play ball.

She popped a fist on her hip. "*Mr.* Taggart. Being that you live in New York City and all, you're probably used to big city medicine, but this is a *rural* hospital." She emphasized the word with the perfect amount of snark balanced with professional confidence. "We're not exactly flush with specialists, so we all wear multiple hats around here."

"Well, then how'd you have an orthopedics guy around for Shelby?" Vaughn lifted his chin. "He's a specialist."

On the edge of her field of vision, Mariah spied dual horrified expressions on Shelby's and Garrison's faces. Really? They were surprised that big brother was a surly mess?

Time to educate.

She stepped close enough to feel his heat and smell that clean scent of shaving cream that made her mouth water. And no, she didn't miss how he stuffed his hands into his jeans pockets. The tight, worn jeans fit so well on his lean hips.

Not caring about things like pride, she went on tiptoes and pinned him in place with some surliness of her own. Emotions from the hectic pace of work, the fear of practicing far outside of her comfort zone, her personal carry-on baggage that she lugged around every day, and the stress of caring for critically ill patients with little backup all wadded into a messy clump. Might as well smear her own issues on top and bingo! Crap cupcake, complete with rich and tasty defensive frosting.

She forced a slow, deep breath in and out of her lungs and tried to count to ten. Made it to five. Close enough.

"We were very lucky," she bit out, somehow managing to stay this side of professional. Barely. "Our orthopedist happened to be in town after his outreach day in the clinic. He canceled his weekend plans so he could stay and patch Shelby up in the OR and then check on her over the weekend, and we appreciated him doing so. Didn't we? Yes. You're welcome."

She lifted her hands as a warning for him to keep his mouth shut. "Anything else you want to discuss, like how I schedule my day? Or maybe how we obtain prior authorizations from insurances? Please let me know." Swiping her palm over her cheek, she tried for another count of ten. Nope. Still couldn't get past five. "No requests? Then let me tell you about the way we pulled together every last damned resource in the county to keep your friends and family alive. What? Big talker suddenly has nothing to say?"

She didn't miss how Garrison exhaled the word *shit*.

For Mariah's part, her lower back was damp with sweat. But way to go with the standing up part.

"Uh, no. Nothing else," Vaughn mumbled as he broke eye contact. The sensation of being hit with a wall of danger ebbed away, along with that stupid stress headache.

Shelby grabbed Mariah's hand. "Even if my boneheaded brother is too stupid to say it, thank you for making sure we all got patched back up. This time and also a few weeks ago when my nephew came in." She peered at Mariah. "And thanks for taking care of our dad when he had the stroke."

"And taking care of my girlfriend," Garrison added.

Vaughn's mouth twisted like he'd sucked an entire lemon. Good.

"My pleasure." She managed to smile sweetly at Shelby and Garrison but slid an almost-snarl past Mr. Big and Suddenly Silent.

"So, how's Eric doing?" Shelby asked.

Mariah stepped back and let go of the woman's hand. A foot away from Vaughn, the temperature dropped ten degrees. "Stable. I've been in contact with the specialists in Casper, and we've done all the tests and treatments they recommended. We talked about sending him to Casper, but neurology said it's more a matter of giving him time to wake up."

"How much time do they think he needs?" The shimmering worry in Shelby's eyes triggered a lump in Mariah's throat.

"It varies from person to person."

Shelby pinched the bridge of her nose. "He should be awake by now, right?"

"Well. Yes." She added, too quickly, "But every patient is different."

"Geez. Okay."

The men studied the floor while Shelby sniffed.

Finally, she looked back at her brother. "Garrison, could we go in now? If it's okay with Dr. West."

Mariah paused and studied Shelby for a few seconds, weighing the woman's very human need to be close to a loved one against taking a medical risk. "All right. But after you're done, I want you resting again." She stepped aside.

Garrison propelled her forward as Vaughn followed, like a big, docile puppy.

That is, if a big, docile puppy radiated barely restrained danger and smug satisfaction.

Thirty minutes later, a booming male voice echoed down the hall. "We need some help in here—now!"

Mariah leapt from her seat in the work area and ran down the hall. Before she registered that it was Vaughn who had called out, she was in Eric Patterson's room.

She froze.

Eric was awake. Despite the dark purple bruises and cuts covering most of his face, he appeared exceptionally lucid as he gestured toward a motionless Shelby, who was slumped forward, half out of her wheelchair and half lying on the hospital bed.

Garrison and Vaughn sported wide-eyed expressions of disbelief. But something about the way they stared at each other didn't seem right at all. What the heck?

No time to figure them out. A nurse and a respiratory tech ran into the room.

"Get more help," Mariah said, circling the bed and easing Shelby's slack body back into the wheelchair, keeping her neck in line and protecting the airway. Vaughn rushed to help. "She's breathing." With pressure of her fingers on Shelby's carotid, Mariah held her breath for six seconds, counted, and multiplied by ten. "Heart rate one hundred." Glancing up at the respiratory tech, she asked, "Could you put a pulse ox on her? And get a set of vitals."

Damn it, she needed to figure out why Shelby had suddenly gone unconscious, several days after the initial injury.

She froze.

Only one medical condition she knew of could cause this pattern: subdural hematoma. Mariah's pulse thundered in her ears. The timing didn't fit, but she had no other explanation. And if a brain bleed had occurred, time was slipping away for Shelby. After a window of lucidity, a patient with a subdural would become unconscious again, followed quickly by death. If it was a subdural. If.

Sweat broke out on her upper lip.

"Call radiology and clear the CT scanner, *stat*," she called out to the ward clerk standing at the door. "We're taking Ms. Taggart down for a head scan now."

"Shelby?" Eric called in a hoarse, dry voice. He reached out, his face contorted into a rictus of pain and horror that chilled Mariah's blood.

"What happened?" she asked.

The three men in the room looked at each other. Silence. Shrugs. Not exactly guilty, but they knew *something*.

Staff wheeled a gurney into the room, and they eased Shelby onto it. Vaughn stepped back next to Garrison at the edge of the room. As Mariah followed the bed down the hall, she heard the rise of angry male voices flowing out of Eric's room.

No time now. She'd sort that mess out and re-evaluate Eric in a few minutes.

As the bed rolled, she asked, "Are her oxygen levels okay?" The respiratory tech nodded. "Good enough. Can you grab portable oxygen and meet us in radiology?" He ran off to get the supplies.

As Mariah took over pushing the bed while a nurse pulled at the foot of the bed. To maneuver a corner, Mariah yanked on the heavy, unwieldy gurney, leaning against the handles to turn the piece of equipment. The sudden presence of a warm body behind her made her jump. Vaughn covered her hands with his big ones.

"Let me. It's my sister. I can help." Gone was the pissy giant from half an hour ago. In his place, this serious rock of a man exuded competence.

And judging by his posture, God help anyone who got in his way.

At this point, she'd take any reasonable assistance, even from a guy whose behavior whiplashed between flirty and hostile. She ducked out from under his arms.

Dashing to the elevator, she held the door while he and the nurse maneuvered the bed through the doors. Squeezing in next to him, she pushed the down button. Vaughn's hip pressed against hers in the cramped space between bed railing and elevator wall. The guy took up an impressive amount of space. The ride down one floor took an eternity.

Fifteen agonizing minutes later, and she had the answer: normal head CT. No subdural hematoma.

Made no sense.

In the radiology work area, Mariah covered the mouthpiece of the phone and asked the nurse and radiology tech to take Shelby back to her room.

Slouching in the office chair in front of the monitors, she clutched the phone to her ear. Had she misunderstood the radiologist on the other end of the line? Maybe he had read the wrong scan. She asked again.

Normal.

She sat there, boneless, staring at the screen.

So if the loss of consciousness didn't come from the subdural, what caused it? Infection? There was no fever. Normal white count.

Once again, she called the neurologist in Casper. He had no other ideas or explanations for the change. No evidence of increased intracranial pressure on exam or on CT findings. Give it time, he said.

Damn it, Mariah was fed up with giving it time. She needed to get some answers from the people who were present when Shelby lost consciousness.

Shoving on the arms of the chair to stand, she slammed down the phone's hand piece and sped into the hall.

And ran smack dab into a rock-solid wall of heated male.

CHAPTER 9

Vaughn grabbed her out of instinct but loosened his grip when he felt Mariah's delicate frame stiffen beneath his palms. The top of her head with that glossy chestnut hair stopped a few inches below his chin.

He tried not to notice how perfectly she fit next to him, how that white coat couldn't totally hide her figure. His traitorous arms twitched with the need to wrap around her. A ridiculous notion, given the situation brewing with his sister. Hell, he still needed to hunt down and destroy that fucking creature that had put his sister in this hospital in the first place.

He had no time and no business thinking about anything besides professional matters when it came to the woman in front of him.

Okay, maybe another brunch date. Where he could watch her eat large quantities of food.

Christ.

Through some miracle of whatever gods still had his back, Vaughn managed to hold his shit together. What he really wanted was to back Mariah flush against the wall and press every inch of his body hard against hers, from her black pants to her plum-colored shirt that made her green eyes glow. But he didn't move a muscle.

Instead, he inhaled her mint aroma, which made his mouth fucking water, the craving stronger than when he wanted alcohol. Her scent also fired up his power again, and he gave in, mentally throwing the latch as he grimaced against the headache when the damned ability reached out to surround her and protect her.

Protect her from what? Danger? Only person here was...him.

Well, crap.

"Sorry there," she said.

Her breathy voice erased all rational thought, but he couldn't help himself. His biceps flexed, drawing her into his chest. Like she belonged there. So right.

So wrong.

No one belonged this close to Vaughn. Hell, he was practically radioactive. Everything he touched went to hell, and he'd be damned if Mariah would be hurt because of him.

Also, they were in a professional situation here.

Her small palms seared him through his shirt as she pushed back.

Pushed back.

Of course she did.

Faster than when the bell signaled the end of a fight round, he let go of her.

Damn her wide eyes and open mouth, but he wanted more of her, from the bow of her fuller upper lip to the tip of her pert nose.

His power flowed from him in a wave of crushing need to keep her safe, sucking the air from his lungs. That damned gift wanted to cocoon Mariah as surely as his physical arms. This was more than familiarity from their date together yesterday.

His head ached.

He swallowed a lump of what felt like gravel mixed with failure. "So, did you figure out what's going on with Shelby?" Mariah flinched. Time to tone down the angry voice. It wasn't her fault his brain waves fritzed when he was around her.

The inward roll of her lips had as much of an impact as if she'd dragged them over his skin. Fuck. Then that soft, pink mouth was moving.

"...no bleed in the brain, which is good. But I don't have an explanation for her loss of consciousness."

Eric had filled him in on what had happened back in that hospital room. Shelby had used her power to pull Eric back to the world of the living, but the cost was that she went into another coma. Whether she would recover this time was anyone's guess.

Unfortunately, no one in the family would ever spill the secret about the Taggarts' strange powers. Which left one doctor very frustrated and worried. Not that a medical professional knowing what Shelby had done would be able to help. According to Garrison and Kerr, their sister's ability had grown a few weeks ago. No one knew the price of that power changing.

Icy terror crystallized in his veins. Maybe this was the end game for his sister. For all of them. What if the Taggart kids could tolerate only so much of a shift in their power, and beyond that, their heads imploded?

A horrible thought, considering he was talking about his sister.

A fist formed way down deep in his chest. Damn. It wasn't fair. None of the bullshit his family had to deal with was fair.

He must have mumbled something marginally coherent, because Mariah answered, "That's it. I'm going to call Casper back and get Shelby transferred."

"No!" he said, grabbing her shoulder.

"What? Why not?"

He gave her the two inches it took for her to slide free of his grip. "I mean, you said that we just need to give it time, right?" *You call that a recovery line?* Lame. Why not put up a billboard that read: *unstable freak, steer clear*?

"Sure, but I'm not a neurologist, and what's going on with her, I can't explain." When she swallowed, the movement of her throat froze him in place. He couldn't stop staring at the graceful line of her neck. "Whatever is happening to your sister is way out of the scope of care for any doctor at this hospital."

"You saying you can't hack it?" *Damn it. Stop saying stupid shit.*

Her pale skin went ashen. "What?"

How'd that foot taste, shoved into his mouth?

Christ, she didn't deserve to be the target of his ping-ponging moods. Didn't matter that his fear of screwing up any relationship with a woman drove those hot-and-cold responses. But it sure seemed like every time he dared to hope that he could have a normal relationship, reality reminded him why hope was a crappy plan. And without a filter stopping these knee-jerk verbal reactions to his warring desires and fears...no one deserved to be treated like this.

"What I'm saying is, you took care of Shelby and Eric in the ER and when they were critically ill. That's pretty good. Uh, good skills. What services can be done in Casper that can't be done here?"

Her mouth opened and closed. She tugged on the stethoscope around her neck. He recognized it as her nervous tic by now. "I feel that we aren't making any progress, and in fact backslid this morning, for a reason I can't determine."

"Eric's awake."

"Sure, but why?"

"Time? Patience?"

"Maybe." How badly he wanted to run his fingertip over the skin to smooth the furrows between her dark brows.

"We'd really like to keep our family all here in Copper River." Keep them close. Protect them from whatever was stalking the Taggart family.

"Even if it's not optimal care? That doesn't make any sense."

Smart woman, trying to put pieces together, even if the pieces didn't fit. He needed to shut that activity down, fast.

"That's our family's decision." He tried to cap the statement with as much finality as he could muster but remain civil.

"Well. Okay, then."

She chewed her lower lip; what he wanted was to crush his mouth to hers. That decision would be yet another in a long string of mistakes on his part.

So he settled for a half measure. "I'm sorry to be so short with you. Now, and earlier yesterday. It's just"—no way could he explain the real reason—"uh, I'm worried about my family."

Her shoulders lifted and fell. "Understandable." The woman had more grace in her right pinkie than he ever could hope to possess. Maybe he could repair the damage. Maybe he could get a second chance.

Or maybe, instead of mooning over the woman in front of him, he should act like a big brother and focus on his sick sister.

"All right. I'll go sit with Shelby." He tried to soften his stupidity with a passable smile that felt all wrong. When had he truly smiled last? Well over a year ago.

Except for the coffee incident with pretty doctor the other day. And at brunch yesterday. She'd made him smile, and for those brief moments, his life had been filled with light and happiness.

The muscles in his neck tensed with an effort to hold back any more inappropriate statements.

"Okay." She didn't meet his eyes. "I'll be back in a bit to check in on her again."

Her quick steps faded down the hall. As Mariah turned into the stairwell doorway, he caught one more glimpse of her glossy brown hair as it slid over her shoulders with the movement.

Then she was gone.

The air went stale, lifeless.

CHAPTER 10

Mariah lost all hope of ever catching up after her third train wreck of a patient visit in as many hours at the rural clinic attached to the hospital. Normally, a patient with ten major medical issues and a laundry list of concerns to discuss? Bring it on. She loved the challenge. But today she was too distracted to delve into the long, complicated appointments.

Didn't help that the face of a certain man kept popping up at inopportune times, pulling her concentration in directions it shouldn't go. Crazy how she kept thinking about him and his changing moods. Explainable by his worry for family, sure. But whenever she talked with Vaughn, it felt like he held back important information. Or secrets.

She was a fine one to talk about secrets. She had a roomful of them.

She took in a big breath and blew it out slowly. *Focus on work.*

Last patient of the day would be a doozy.

After a pause, she knocked on the room holding Patricia Brand, the widowed matriarch of the Brand family who Mariah had just yesterday discharged from the hospital for aspiration pneumonia secondary to multiple sclerosis.

"Hello, Mrs. Brand," she called as she shut the door behind her. "How are you doing today?"

"What's it to you? You're late, by the way," the woman in the wheelchair snarled and sniffed. Made perfect sense to Mariah. Unfortunately, not all of Mrs. Brand's bad attitude could be chalked up to a long battle with multiple sclerosis with increasing complications and the resultant depression. Some of that bearish temperament was simply…her. Maybe some of the attitude had to do with her family, too.

Well, most of them.

The other woman in the room, her daughter, Izzy, shook her head and mouthed *sorry*, her face drawn and lined. Her long, blonde hair hung in limp, unkempt waves. Her blue eyes flicked up briefly, then she stared at the floor.

"You're right, and I'm sorry to make you wait." Mariah plowed ahead. "My goal is for you to feel better, Mrs. Brand. And I have to say that you look better than a few days ago."

"No thanks to you. Would have gotten better on my own anyway." The woman's atrophied hands flopped on her lap. When she inhaled, the on-demand portable oxygen tank gave a puff of air into her nostrils.

"Mom, please," Izzy whispered.

"Hush up. This is my visit. I don't even know why you're here anyway."

"Because you can't drive. And you need someone to push your wheelchair while the power chair is in the shop."

"Besides that."

Izzy clamped her mouth closed and peered into space, away from her mother.

At least Izzy had a mother present. A twinge caught Mariah between the ribs and she mentally shook it off.

Mariah plowed ahead. She refused to calculate how many more minutes of work remained in this never-ending day. "Has your breathing changed any since you left the hospital?"

"No. It's crappy as usual." Mrs. Brand sniffed. "Not sure why you couldn't fix that particular problem while I was in the hospital." A wet cough punctuated her words.

Izzy grimaced.

Mariah groaned to herself. The reason she couldn't completely fix the woman's lungs was due to equal parts an incurable underlying health condition and the fact that she kept smoking two packs per day.

No problem. Mariah could handle grumpy, ill patients all day long. "Any other issues like palpitations or chest pain?"

"No."

"Good. How about ankle swelling or fevers?"

"No." She waved her thin fingers near her face. "I must be perfectly fine, then. Good job, super doc." The harsh laugh held zero humor.

Mariah rolled her neck as she exhaled. "So I know that having multiple sclerosis makes it more likely to get certain health problems, like pneumonia. But also having a chronic illness can cause depression or anxiety."

Mrs. Brand grimaced. "What are you, a rocket scientist?"

Keep trying. "Sometimes being ill can make people angry or lash out at people they love." She paused. "Have you ever noticed yourself doing that?"

Izzy studied at the floor.

Mrs. Brand sneered, "What business is it of yours?"

Taking another calm, centering breath, Mariah answered, "My business is your health. I want you to be as healthy as you can be, inside and out."

"How about a total body transplant?" There, a flash of fear and vulnerability flitted over the woman's lined face. Getting closer.

"Boy, do I wish." Mariah smiled. "But until I can order a complete overhaul, how about we fix the things that we can?"

Mrs. Brand shifted, bumping the foot peg of her wheelchair. "What are you saying?"

"Well. I'm saying maybe you want to talk with a counselor or psychiatrist. They can give you good tools to deal with the frustration that comes along with chronic illnesses. Might help avoid hurting the people around you."

"That's not an issue," she snapped. And just like that, they were back to the irascible woman Mariah knew well. "Not sure why it matters, anyway. No one can fix what's wrong."

"Well. You matter. And my job is to help you as best I am able."

"Whatever that's worth." She sniffed.

"Mom! Please." Izzy leaned forward.

Mrs. Brand rolled her eyes.

"Come on, now." Mariah walked over and listened to the woman's heart and lungs, anything to redirect the negative emotions. She palpated her abdomen and checked her legs for swelling and adequate circulation. "Lungs sound better today. Let's continue with the antibiotics and steroids. It would be good to recheck you by the end of the week."

"Easy for you to say. Do you know how hard it is to get out here for an appointment? Especially when it's so cold out." The woman motioned toward the door.

"Mom, we'll get you here. Don't worry." Izzy patted her mother's arm even as she waved her off.

"Can you do anything that doesn't involve me leaving my house?" Ms. Brand said.

Mariah turned to the computer next to her and reviewed her work schedule for the week. The weariness worming through every inch of her body made her want to curl up and take a nap. Last weekend's call, a full workweek, and a scheduled ringside physician gig in Lander this weekend. At this point, adding one more item to the schedule could be the straw on the camel's back. But she had a job to do. "You know, I could probably do a home visit Thursday late afternoon if you'd prefer."

Izzy shook her head. "No. We can't ask you to do that. We live pretty far out of town."

"It's okay. I sometimes do home visits for patients who are homebound or it's a hardship for them to make the trip in for appointments."

"Are you sure?" Izzy asked. Her eyes locked onto Mariah, like Mariah was some kind of life buoy.

Mrs. Brand shook her head. "No way. I don't want her snooping around the ranch."

"Mom, come on. Dr. West is trying to help you."

"Fine, but she comes straight to the house and then she has to leave." Mrs. Brand struggled into her winter coat. "Let's go."

Izzy dropped her forehead onto her palm.

Mariah smiled. "It's decided, then. I'll see you Thursday." Glancing at her watch, she said, "Did you want some help getting out to the car? It's almost six, and most of the staff are gone."

"You don't have to—" Izzy started.

"'Bout time I got something for free," Mrs. Brand said, zipping her coat and pushing on the rims of the wheels, almost running over Mariah.

Jumping out of the way, Mariah got behind the wheelchair and maneuvered Mrs. Brand down the hall, waving at her medical assistant to leave. Then Mariah, Mrs. Brand, and Izzy went through the empty reception area, through the automatic doors, and into the cold night. This time of year, the sun went down early, and full night had fallen. Mariah hunched into her lab coat, a poor substitute for an insulated jacket.

Gloves would have been nice, too. The chilly wind cut right to her bones.

Above her, stars twinkled in the stark, clear sky. Temperatures were forecasted to be near zero tonight. Welcome to winter in Wyoming.

An uneasy sensation settled in her bones. Deeper than the chill. The feeling made her shoulder blades twitch. She glanced behind her, expecting to see something lurking there.

Nothing.

In the empty parking lot, they accompanied Mrs. Brand to a minivan in a handicapped spot. A bright parking lot light illuminated the vehicle from above. Rust bubbled the wheel wells, and dried mud and frozen slush coated the running boards.

Beneath the unending barrage of her mother's criticisms, Izzy heaved open the side door. She struggled to extend the heavy iron ramp.

"Sorry." One corner of Izzy's mouth rose. "Automated gate no longer automates."

"Technology, huh?" Mariah grabbed the other side of the large metal square and helped pull it down and fold a section out with a creak and a clank.

"Took you long enough. I'm freezing my venison off out here," Mrs. Brand grumbled as she tried to wheel herself onto the ramp. She made it a foot and rolled backward. With a grunt, Izzy pushed her mother's chair into the van.

A truck pulled up nearby, and the driver got out, his duster catching in the wind. He walked over with a slight limp.

"Hi Izzy." Kerr's face was half hidden beneath his hat. "How's it going?"

"Good, um. Nice to see you. We gotta go." Izzy turned her back on him to stow the ramp. Her attempts resulted in more clanks.

He frowned and reached down. "Can I help?"

She froze, then looked back over her shoulder. "Yeah. That would be great," she breathed, a smile lighting up her face for a moment.

"Who's out there? Is that one of those dirt-grubbing Taggarts?" Mrs. Brand hollered from the van, the dome light giving her face a skeletal, spidery appearance. "Get the hell away from my property."

"You can pick your nose, but can't pick your family," Izzy muttered.

Mariah and Kerr both covered laughs.

"Here, Iz, I've got it." Kerr hefted the solid ramp back in place like it weighed only a few pounds. He grinned at the car's occupant and tipped his Stetson. "Nice to see you, Mrs. Brand. You take care now." He slid the door closed on her profanity-laced response and brushed off his hands.

Izzy peeked up at him. Her exhausted expression transformed into one of exceptional beauty. "Thanks, Kerr. You, um, doing okay? With, the, uh…?"

He rubbed his thigh, almost as an absent motion. "Missing limb? Yep. Peachy."

A hand drifted to her mouth. "I didn't mean—"

All of a sudden, Mariah felt like a frigid third wheel as she stood there shivering. Behind her, she heard the front door of the hospital whoosh open.

Muffled epithets filtered from the depths of the van in front of her. The shadow of a raised claw fist inside the vehicle completed the surreal image as the van rocked.

Izzy scraped back her hair. "Man, my family puts the 'fun' in dysfunctional, huh?"

"Nothing in life is perfect, Iz." He stared at her, then shoved his hands in pockets. "Hey, if you ever want to grab a bite to eat, let me know."

"You…what?" she asked.

Kerr's smile fell. "Or not. No big deal."

"No. That sounds great, but I can't."

"Because of…?" He gestured generally toward his lower body.

"Geez, no. You're fine. I mean, of course you're fine. You're more than fine. Oh, heck. But we can't. Not because of your leg. Missing. Or not. Crap." Izzy palmed her forehead.

"Stressed much?" Kerr sucked on a tooth.

Out of the corner of Mariah's eye, a large man made a direct path from the front entrance of the hospital. The temperature on her skin dropped ten degrees, and the temperature in her chest rose twenty. She couldn't deal with another uncomfortable confrontation.

Vaughn strode toward her, his big work boots crunching snow and asphalt. Her heart rate sped up, but her stomach clenched, like she braced for a punch. Meanwhile, Romeo and Juliet were still flirting.

Let's go already, people.

"Iz, let me give you my number." Izzy held out the phone; Kerr punched in numbers. "Call me if you want, okay?" His casual smile turned into a tight grimace.

Izzy headed around the van, keys jingling in her hand. "See you Thursday, Dr. Mariah." She opened the door and a thick flow of invectives spilled out.

"G-good night," Mariah called.

"What's Thursday?" The sound of that deep male voice behind her slid straight down her spine to her...libido.

Izzy shut the car door and the cursing abruptly ceased once more.

Shivering harder, Mariah wrapped her arms over her chest and hurried back to the clinic, Vaughn keeping pace. Kerr trailed behind.

"Thursday?" Vaughn asked again, more gently. Like he was trying to be nice.

"That info is really HIPAA p-protected." Her teeth chattered. Icicles were probably forming in her eyeballs. God, it was cold out.

For his part, Vaughn wore jeans and a thin shirt, topped by his hip-length leather jacket. Unbuttoned, of course. And he didn't appear to be shivering at all. "You can't tell *me*?" he asked. But still with a calm tone and a disarming half smile. Like maybe he *was* a nice guy who had just had a bad couple of days and was trying to make up for it.

Mariah could appreciate someone who tried to be better. To be fair, she had seen how careful he was with his sister and how he'd stood up to Wyatt Brand on Mariah's behalf.

She, of all people, understood second chances.

Could she take another chance on him, after their rough beginning? She studied his earnest expression, crooked nose, hard jaw, and dark, intense eyes. Another shiver rippled down her spine, but it had nothing to do with the temperature.

While she owed him nothing, Mariah could at least keep an open mind. Frankly, she was intrigued. It was okay for a woman to want to know more about a guy. No rule against that at all.

"I c-can't tell anyone." At the main clinic entrance, she swiped her badge and the doors opened with a *swoosh*. She sighed as the heated air rushed over her.

"Bro, here are the keys." Kerr pointed toward the door to the main hospital. "I'm going thataway for the night shift with Shel. Anything new to report?"

"No. She's still sleeping. Nothing new, right?" He glanced over, brows raised.

"Not yet," Mariah said. "But she's stable."

"Stable." Vaughn's mouth pressed into a line. "Let me know if anything changes, okay?"

Kerr tipped his hat. "Will do."

In the low-lit reception area, Vaughn appeared tired and much older, like the weight of the world fell on his broad shoulders. She studied the strong lines of his frame, and the easy way he clasped hands with his brother.

"Night, Doc." Kerr smirked at her perusal of Vaughn's broad shoulders.

Her cheeks warmed. "Sure thing," she said to his retreating backside.

Which left Mariah and Vaughn alone in the empty reception area.

CHAPTER 11

T *hink, asshole. Come up with something intelligent to say to this woman.*

Hell, Vaughn had been salivating all day in the hopes of seeing her again. And now that he had his wish?

His mind went blank.

Why had he left Shelby's room to meet Kerr in the parking lot? Because Vaughn's power urged him to protect Mariah from something out there. Only there wasn't anything there except Izzy Brand. And her grumpy but harmless mother.

A lingering headache was all that remained of the power surge. He rubbed his chin but stopped when Mariah's gaze locked onto the movement. A slow spiral of interest worked its way down his belly. Maybe he could atone for his behavior. Start fresh, or at least backpedal enough to give him a chance later.

When she chewed her lip with those even, white teeth, the situation in his groin grew critical in a hurry.

Simmer down, there.

"So, uh, can I walk you to your car?" he managed to say. With luck, he could make up for his tactless comments earlier today. And yesterday. And the day before. Christ.

She pulled her chin back and frowned. "Excuse me?" Pointing a thumb at her head, she smirked. "Thought you weren't a fan."

Heat crawled across his chest. "Well, crap. Look, I meant it–I'm real sorry about being short with you. It's just that…it doesn't matter why. Please accept my apology for being a jerk at the restaurant."

"And?" Those arms stayed crossed over her chest.

Man, she was going to make him say it. "And for snapping at you about Shelby. I shouldn't have taken out my stress on you."

Rocking back on her heels, she peered at him until sweat prickled under his arms. This woman might be five-foot-nothing, but she drove spikes of terror into him. He toed the clinic carpeting.

And waited.

He couldn't stand it. "Truce?"

"We weren't arguing. Besides, not everything is a fight."

Huh. "I…yeah, good point. Anyway, I'm sorry." He stuck out a hand and tried not to flinch as a wave of his power fired up when her palm met his. Then he tried not to hang on longer as a second wave of pure interest flowed through his arm into his ribcage. What the hell? His power was now getting mixed with straight-up lust. And while on the subject of not making sense, would it be too much to ask for him to act normal?

With effort, he stepped back, their hands dropping to their sides. "So. Walk you out?" Because his power needed him to do so.

"Well. Sure. I guess. You don't have to, you know."

"It's late and dark out." A prickle came and went over his temple. "I'd feel better…"

Another squint, and she shrugged. "Sure. Come on back for a minute while I grab my things." Motioning for him to follow her through the door to the clinic hallway, she added, "Everyone's gone home. I was running late all day today."

"Okay."

Okay? All you have to say to her is okay?

He followed her quick, efficient steps into a small office.

Her office contained a desk with a typical rolling chair behind it and two vinyl-covered side chairs in front. A corkboard on one wall had a million documents thumbtacked over every spare inch of space, and then some, judging by papers peeking out from under each other. On one corner of the desk rested a stack of energy bars and an empty coffee cup.

One picture on her desk showed Mariah, same shoulder-length brown hair and green eyes, her arm thrown around a male with facial features similar to hers. In the picture, she had on a black and red graduation gown with a green velvet sash around her neck. The happiness in those two faces shone right through the picture to taunt Vaughn.

Had he taken any picture like this with his siblings? Not in years. Life kept intruding. First his mom dying, then Kerr's return from Afghanistan, Vaughn's colossal fuckup with Garrison's wife, Dad's stroke, and now Shelby's coma.

"Penny for your thoughts?" Her cool mountain-stream voice banished his dark thoughts.

"No pictures of your parents?" he blurted.

A quick intake of breath and wide stare. The corners of her mouth drooped. Damn, it was amazing how quickly he could step in the manure. Like he was going for accuracy *and* speed.

He touched her shoulder, stopping her as she shrugged out of her white coat. "My bad. Stupid thing to say. Sorry."

"All right." She didn't offer an explanation, and it wasn't his business to ask for one.

When she hung the white coat on a hook behind the door, the flash of her work slacks and blouse on her petite frame distracted him from his frustrating thoughts of the past and instead grounded him firmly in the present. The definition of disappointment was when a thick wool coat hid her from view again.

"Ready?" She paused and glanced at him before she grabbed a pile of papers. Some slipped to the floor. Did her hands shake as she picked up the papers and replaced them on the desk? Not that it mattered to him.

"Of course." He motioned for her to precede him out the back door of the clinic.

In the dark, empty lot, he scanned the surrounding area, senses on alert. His gift flared again, and he didn't fight it, bracing against the headache and unclenching a fist as the ability reached out. Something dangerous had to be out here, but what? Maybe his power had gone haywire, like how Shelby and Garrison's abilities had changed. Would he end up in a coma, like his sister, if his power shifted enough?

Mariah's key beeped to unlock that stupid mini Cooper. He peeked inside the open front door and groaned, imagining his knees up to his chest in the seat.

She tossed her satchel into the passenger seat and turned back around.

"So, interested in another try for a meal together?" The words burst out of him.

Dark brows flew up, and she sucked in a breath. "You sure? Because...things were a bit..."

Right. He had been a real prince.

Damn it, this woman wasn't like the others. She wasn't out to use him and betray him like his sister-in-law. Wouldn't get to know him because of his connections. Vaughn needed to deal with his past mistakes, move on, and quit taking out his gun-shy state on Mariah. Starting now.

"Have I mentioned that I'm sorry?"

"Yes, about three minutes ago. Hey, people have bad days, especially when someone they love is ill. I get it." The quick grip of her hand on his arm meant more to him than he cared to admit.

"Would you be interested in the bagels and coffee idea I originally proposed after our run-in with Wyatt Brand?"

She took a breath, making her coat fabric shush. When she exhaled, a plume of vapor drifted up into the cold night.

"So?"

"Oh." Crossing her arms, she leaned a hip against the edge of the vehicle. "I could go for a bagel and coffee. Any snack, really."

The woman had thrown him a golden opportunity. *Don't mess it up.* "Well, I didn't want to be too forward with food choices."

"Bagels *are* pretty extravagant." Her scrunched nose made his heart flop. "Hope you're a big spender, because I might get an everything bagel. Oh, and if it's your treat, I'll definitely order super fancy coffee."

The breath he had been holding finally released. He could play along. "Hold on a minute. We might need a spending limit on the drinks." What the actual hell? Vaughn attempting to flirt was like watching a grizzly bear perform ballet.

"All right, then. Fine. Super duper fancy coffee and bagel can wait until another time. I'll stick with the basics." Was that a flush on her cheeks or a response to the cold air? Hard to tell with the parking lot lighting.

"It's a deal." Hell, he'd buy her imported Irish coffee where the plant grew only on the shady side of the hills and was picked by left-handed leprechauns, if that's what she wanted.

"How about tonight?" she asked.

Damn it. Bad enough that he had to miss training time to be here with Shelby today, but he also had to avoid eating junk like bagels and sugary coffee. He still had another ten pounds to lose by Friday night. Even thinking about it made his stomach growl.

"Sorry, no."

"Tomorrow night?"

"Um, can't."

"How about Friday?"

Damn, he had weigh-in for the fight that night. "No. I have plans."

The corners of her mouth dropped, and so did his stomach. "Saturday?"

"Plans again."

She uncrossed her arms and stuffed her hands in the coat pockets. "Pretty tight social calendar, there."

"Mariah, no. It's not like—"

She held up a hand. "Hey. I get it. My bad for misunderstanding the situation. I should have known."

"What?"

Pressing her mouth into a line, she said, "How many women do you string along at any given time?"

"The hell?"

"It's okay." She shifted from foot to foot. "I totally understand. It was a mistake for us to go out in the first place, what with me treating your family."

"No, I—"

"You don't have to sugarcoat anything, Vaughn."

Boy, did his name sound good coming from her mouth. What he'd give to hear her say it again. Preferably in a whisper. While they were both naked.

For the love of all that was holy, stop thinking about that stuff. Concentrate on the fully clothed woman in front of you and try not to make things worse.

"I'm not sugarcoating anything. This happens to be a bad week."

"So, let me get this straight. You just asked me out, knowing that you were fully booked?"

Well, sort of, yes. But she could lay off him already. Christ, she didn't have to push all of his buttons at once.

The muscles in his legs bunched like he wanted to tackle something. Or someone. He locked his spine into a rigid line. And damn him if an image of Garrison's wife waving those incriminating pictures didn't pop into his head. Yes, this...whatever it was...was a bad idea. Best offense was a good defense, as they said.

"You seem somewhat sensitive about being stood up."

"I think we have to have a date actually planned for someone to stand up the other person," she spluttered.

Semantics. "What about how you bolted out of our brunch yesterday?"

She raised a hand. "Whoa. The stand-up occurs before a date even begins. What I had was a hospital emergency."

"You think that gives you a special pass?"

The jut of her chin spelled trouble. "You bet it does. And if that's too much for you to deal with, then we should probably keep our interactions strictly business."

A wise man would tap out. "Business?" No one would ever accuse Vaughn of being wise. He went into a wider stance, more in control, more comfortable in a sparring situation. "You're not a little controlling, are you?"

"Gosh, no. How can I be, with my crazy life and unpredictable work hours?"

"Uh. That's kind of a good point."

"So, anyway. Sounds like I need to be going. You have a booked schedule." She fished the keys out of her pocket. "And I am not going to be played."

"What do you mean?" he asked.

"Well, because…"

Now to knock her on her ass.

"Do you honestly think I would want to see someone else?" He put as much sincerity as he possibly could into the words. Show her that he meant it. Anything to try and fix the mess he'd made. Continued to make.

Even in the shadows from the halogen parking lot lights, he could tell she looked everywhere but at him. "Well. Sure." Her hair fell forward, partially hiding her graceful jaw.

He rocked back on his heels as the blood exited his head. Whoa. Stop the bus. What the hell had just happened? "Are you crazy?"

She spun away. "All right. That's enough. This conversation is over. Good night, and thank you again for the meal yesterday and for walking me out here."

He grabbed her upper arm and rotated her toward him. "No way you can doubt my interest in you." Then he let go and stepped back.

"Frankly, I don't know what your deal is. One minute you're growly and the next minute you're…not. My neck hurts from the whiplash."

Rubbing his chin, he stared down at her. "Not that I want to go into details, and not that it's any excuse, but I've been burned before."

"You're in good company. Along with many other people in this world, I'm sure. But you can still be polite, you know. Or at least not go all over the place with your reactions."

"I know. And you're right."

"So…" She shoved her hands in the coat pockets and jiggled her keys.

"One more chance for me not to stick my foot in my mouth?"

Her eyes flicked to the ground. "It's a big foot."

Keeping his hands at his sides, he nodded. "I have a big mouth."

"Not going to argue there."

"You're tough."

A pause. "You have no idea."

It took effort to keep his distance, but he wouldn't crowd her, by God. "Oh, I have a very good idea of your toughness. I've got the invisible scars from the tongue-lashing to show for it." He lifted a hand. "Not that it wasn't deserved." When he exhaled, a puff of vapor drifted away, taking some of his past misgivings with it. "Your call, Mariah. Any chance we can try to line up our schedules and have a nice bagel and coffee like two regular people?"

"Simple?"

"Of course."

"And it's not a date, right?"

"Yes. I mean, no, it's not. If you don't want it to be a date."

"And no getting mad if the hospital calls me while we're not on a date."

"You got it."

Her bright smile chased away the cold, dark night. "I can manage that."

He barked a laugh. "You can *manage* it? Like it's a chore?"

"No. It's just bagels. And coffee. Coffee is never a chore." A little wrinkle of her nose and he relaxed.

A rare chuckle rumbled through him. "Then it's a not-date?"

She tilted her head to the side. "Deal."

"And Mariah?" His heart pounded in his chest.

"What?"

"You have to know that I *am* interested in getting to know you. There is no one else in my life, relationship-wise."

"Well, thank you for saying so." She chewed on her lower lip, capturing his attention and stealing his ability to form a sentence.

The low rumble of the hospital HVAC cycling from the rooftop filled the silence between them.

His heart thudded loudly enough to be heard two counties over.

It would hurt like hell if he failed, but he needed to take a chance right here, right now.

"Mariah?"

"Yes."

Shit, he wasn't used to asking for anything. But he was too terrified to make a move without permission. Big, strong Vaughn Taggart, paralyzed stupid by his past. "I'd, uh, like to maybe give you a hug."

"Because of your sister?" Was she making fun of him? No. Open sincerity was written on her fine features.

"No. Because I'd like to give you a hug." He plastered his palms to his hips. "But only if it's okay."

"Are you asking me for permission because you were a jerk earlier?" The breathy voice with that hitch in it weakened his knees.

He swallowed. "No. Because I don't want to make another mistake."

Mariah trembled. Honest to God trembled.

The thought of stepping fully into the circle of his massive arms took her from having a few palpitations straight to emergent supraventricular tachycardia. The first time her last boyfriend hugged her, she had screamed. Great way to start a new relationship. Couldn't wait to see how she reacted out here in the Wyoming night to a hulking guy who sported an expression like a dog who had been kicked.

Worst part? Vaughn wasn't the problem. Actually, he made her want to use his embrace to help overcome her horrible past. She wanted to touch him. To feel the warmth of his body against hers.

But what if he hugged too tightly? Or not tightly enough? Or didn't let go? What if she had a flashback when he touched her?

God, the two of them were a hot mess.

"Okay," she whispered, not moving.

Vaughn lifted his arms slightly away from his body and took a half step toward her. "Your call."

"Everyone has a past, you know." Where had that comment come from? She glanced up at him.

A curt nod. "I'm not in the past right now."

A rough sigh ripped from her as she bridged the foot of space between them and pressed her cheek to his chest, between the sides of his unzipped jacket. Solid. Warm. His pulse…about ninety beats per minute. Regular. Steady.

His arms stayed out to his sides.

She relaxed into his torso by slow degrees, the heat from his frame seeping into her skin.

"Mariah." The timbre of his voice vibrated through the bones of her face and down to her toes.

As she slid her hands under his jacket, the muscles under his shirt tensed and rippled.

She wasn't confined at all. Running her hands as far around his torso as she could reach, she melted into his frame. A weight on her head told her he'd rested his chin there. And it felt right.

The gentle pressure of his hands on her shoulders didn't make her flinch. It made her want more. An unsteady breath shifted his chest.

Leaning back, she looked up into his dark, shadowed eyes.

Then he brushed his lips over her forehead. Just the lightest press of skin against hers.

The muscles of his back clenched into iron rods beneath her hands.

A headache flickered across her temples, followed by that cocoon sensation. A bubble of safety. She wanted more.

His rough palms brushed over the wool coat as he encircled her frame. Not too tight. But present. Solid. Safe.

A low growl came from his throat, triggering a frisson straight down her body into her pelvis.

Okay. Maybe not completely safe.

But not scary.

His lips descended again, this time sweeping over her temples and cheekbones, leaving behind tingling, hypersensitive skin. "Mariah." His hoarse voice sent her heart into another pattering rhythm. "Can I kiss you?"

"Yes," she breathed.

The virtual cocoon warmed several degrees as he bent his head down. She stood on tiptoes to meet him. She had wanted only a tiny taste. Mostly to make sure she was okay.

The second their lips touched…heck, she was more than okay. Her internal BTUs went from zero to spontaneously combusting.

His arms tightened around her as he slowly kissed her. He changed angles, drawing shudders and sighs from deep inside of her. A wave of headache came and went again. Must be the cold air.

The headache was a distant memory when he nipped at her mouth.

And when his tongue lightly traced the seam of her lips?

She stepped back.

He froze, his dark gaze locked onto her face.

Then she reached up and laced her fingers behind his neck, stretching to reach his mouth again.

With another guttural sound, he clasped her flush to his chest. As he swept his tongue across her lips again, she opened to him on a sigh. A throbbing between her legs grew, and she pressed harder against him. The friction created a little sparkle of stars at the edges of her vision.

"I want…," he breathed. "Christ, Mariah."

Another gentle onslaught of kisses stole her breath. The rasp of his stubble against her cheek turned her insides to warm liquid. And when her tongue tangled with his, she actually wobbled. But she knew that she wouldn't fall. Not with his arms around her and his solid frame supporting her.

"You're amazing," he whispered as he nipped over her lips.

As he rocked his pelvis against the cradle of her hips, his erection hardened. His fist tightened on her wool coat, like he wanted to tear it to shreds. Given the size of his hands, he could probably do it, too.

Breaking off the kiss, he lifted his head. "Shit."

One by one, though, the stars faded away, leaving two individuals standing on cold asphalt pavement in the hospital parking lot.

Air rasped in and out of his mouth. His nostrils flared.

"This isn't a fling," he said, as if talking to himself.

When he stepped away, a wave of vertigo made her stumble. Vaughn grabbed her elbow, steadying her. But he didn't pull her back into his embrace.

And she felt empty because of it.

"This isn't a fling," he repeated. Although he stared at her, it was as if he looked through her.

"I know this isn't a fling," she said, her own voice none too steady.

"No, you don't understand. You deserve so much better."

"Because of your past? We covered the fact that we both have some demons."

He rubbed his jaw. "That's not it."

"All right, then what?"

"This was a mistake."

She flinched, and her heart took a zero-G drop.

"Mistake?" she gasped.

"Not mistake, like what you might think of a mistake." He wet his lips. "Well, yes. Kind of a mistake." He held up a hand as she took a breath. "It's all my problem, not yours. You're fine."

"That's the lamest line I've ever heard."

His mouth gaped open, no words coming out. Good, because she might just punch him if he said something else stupid.

Rubbing a hand over face, she nodded. "Fine. I might be slow, but I finally get it. This time, for real, I'm going to take what shreds of dignity I have left and exit this situation."

"Mariah."

She blinked several times. "Don't say anything. Please." She straightened her shoulders and set her expression into what she hoped was a professional appearance.

His face went blank. That lack of emotion iced her blood. Something more than a simple kiss had happened. A connection had been formed, and breaking it hurt like a beast.

Better now than later. She turned her back on him and slid into the driver's seat. "Good night."

"Damn it. It's not your fault."

The burning behind her eyelids challenged her tight control. "Of course it's not." She turned the key in the ignition. "Your issues are your own. Good night."

"Mariah?"

"Unless you plan to yank my chain even more, I'll ask you to move away from the car and leave me alone." Cold. Final.

She had never talked to anyone like that.

He did as she asked, and she closed the door and drove off into the chilly night.

CHAPTER 12

Four solid walls, clean furniture, some knickknacks, and a few pictures did not a peaceful sanctuary make. Didn't matter that Mariah's house was located smack dab in the middle of Copper River, with pleasant neighbors all around.

Late into the evening, she paced circles on her living room carpet.

Right now, in her mind, she wasn't in Copper River.

No, in Mariah's mind, she was back at the compound in that desolate corner of Utah, trapped in the unfinished plywood room, pacing across rotting subfloor. Every circuit, she'd had to avoid a black section of moldy wood or risk crashing through the floor. Every circuit, she passed by the locked door.

How many times had she been trapped in that building, held there by men with guns who threatened her brother's life? Meanwhile, the closer Kevin had come to reaching his teenage years, the more beatings he endured.

Sweat beaded her brow, even in the winter climate.

Keep walking. Just keep walking.

Tonight's episode with Vaughn had rattled her down to the bones. He didn't trap her. Didn't confine her. Hadn't pressed. Maybe he'd manipulated her emotions some, and whether it was intentional or not was a subject for debate. But she could deal with that question. Hey, sometimes guys could be a mess.

To be fair, she had participated equally in this evening's parking lot interlude. He'd given her plenty of chances to step away. In fact, he had let her take the lead.

The intensity of her desire for him scared her—not because of the possibility of success but for the chance of failure.

Time to stop trying to diagnose herself.

She sank into the rocking chair, picked up the phone, and hit a number from her contact list.

"Hi, sis," came the voice on the other end.

She gripped the phone. "Kevin. How are you?"

"You called me. What's going on? Everything okay?"

"Yes. Just needed to hear your voice." The tension inside of her dissipated like a boiling pot removed from the heat.

A pause. "Did something happen? Do I need to come up there?" That was Kevin, always willing to drop everything and help.

"No. Of course not." Her voice faded away. In her mind, she was that fourteen-year-old girl, looking out a cracked window over the desolate terra cotta rock and sand terrain, desperately plotting a way to save them both. "Tell me how your training is going. When's the bout? January?"

"Yeah. This might be my big break, moving up to the next level. There'll be scouts from the UFC present. I've been working on jujitsu skills the past few months, and I think it'll pay off."

"Awesome. But are you staying healthy? Nutrition good?" Normal, safe topics. The bad memories faded away as she ran her hand over the solid, real, wooden arm of the chair. The present. Not the past.

"You bet. The gym here has a guy who helps with diet. Shouldn't be an issue to cut weight next month. I'm feeling good going into this one."

"Still fighting at 135?" Her brother might not be a big guy, but pound for pound he was one of the fiercest competitors she'd ever seen. He'd stand up to people twice his size, especially if it meant defending his older sister. That fierceness had drawn far too much negative attention and subsequent pain.

No. That's the past. Stay in the present.

"Yeah. It's a tough division, but if things go well, I might get a contract. Oh man, that would be awesome, fighting on the big stage. Maybe compete internationally." It sounded like he took a sip of something. "What about you? Working any fights coming up?"

"Just a few local matches lately. This weekend I'm going to Lander. Want to come up?"

"Can't. Gotta work to support my MMA habit."

She laughed. "You're a junkie."

"And you're enabling me by helping with the costs." He blew out a breath. "If I haven't told you thanks lately…thanks. I used that last check to cover my trainer for the month. You don't know how much those extra bucks help."

"Are you getting mushy on me, Kev? You might be my larger little brother, but I can still kick your butt."

"You can't kick anyone's butt, sis. And that's okay." His laugh warmed her soul. "But hey, I gave you got lots of free practice over the years. Also gave you practice patching me back together after fights."

Patching him up after other injuries, too. But she would not say the words out loud.

"Is that a glowing reference for my ringside doctoring skills?" Her neck and shoulder muscles relaxed.

"You don't need me to say a word. You did great here in Salt Lake the last year of your residency. And the local folks keep asking for you to work more fights here. That's compliment enough without giving you a big head."

"You're right."

The pause this time as he sipped on a drink wasn't uncomfortable. It was familiar. Easy.

"Hey, how's work?" Kevin asked.

Except for a certain man she kept running into at the hospital? A man who twisted her heart and mind into knots? A guy whose presence dredged up gritty memories she never wanted to explore again? Super duper. "Busy but good."

"But there's more."

She leaned her head back on the wood and rocked the chair. "No. Nothing more."

"Do you wish there was more?"

"No."

"You sure? Because I think you're not telling me everything."

Welcome back to her bratty little brother, poking until she lost her cool.

"Quit prying."

"I want only the best for my sister. Is he nice?"

"*He* doesn't exist, Kev."

"Nuh uh. I know your voice." He clicked his tongue. "And I think he does exist. Just make sure he treats you better than what's his face did, or I'll kick him into next week."

"Oh yeah?"

"Like that prick you dated in residency. He's like something I want to scrape off my shoes. No offense," he added quickly.

"None taken and good riddance." Sure, she would have been a good wife for her wealthy lawyer fiancé, but it wasn't worth yielding to the point where *Mariah* disappeared completely.

"So is this guy nicer than that pinhead?"

A groan of frustration, half for the dead-end conversation and half for the remembered kisses from Vaughn, escaped her lips. "Enough. There's no one. I just wanted to hear your voice, not get grilled."

"We don't always get what we want." His voice took on a prim and proper tone. "Sometimes we get what we need."

"Thanks for that, Mr. Helpful. All right. Get back to doing whatever you were doing so you can build more muscle or skills or whatever meatheads like you do."

His laugh on the other end made the corners of her mouth rise.

"Stay out of trouble, sis."

Bam. Bambambam. Each impact came with a hiss of air as Vaughn beat the holy living hell out of the punching bag hanging in the back of the barn.

Bambam. Pow. Fifteen pounds off by Friday's weigh-in. No problem at this rate.

Shelby's horse, Bob, rolled his eyes and flared nostrils in disdain.

Vaughn had started his training session at nine, after finishing the last of his chores this evening. That was when his father had gone to bed. Nurse Ruth said Dad needed to rest.

But sleeping for twelve hours per night wasn't normal.

The memory of his father shuffling down the hall with his walker this evening, one leg dragging, accompanied by ever-present Ruth, turned an invisible knife in Vaughn's gut. He'd never expected his old man to be laid low by a damned stroke. Getting run over by cattle or thrown by a horse, sure, but not something like a stroke.

At least Dad got out of bed now. According to Garrison, the first week back from the hospital, Dad had made zero effort and was dwindling right in front of everyone. Enter one tenacious nurse, accompanied by her laughing Cajun husband, Odie, and Dad had turned to putty in their hands, eating better and participating in daily physical therapy sessions.

What would Dad do when Ruth and Odie left?

What would happen to all of them when Vaughn left? That life back in New York, the one with the successful professional and MMA career, waited for him.

He pounded the bag with merciless upper hooks and jabs.

Damn it.

Shit. He also tried to pummel away the memory of Mariah's soft lips and the way her small form melted into his. His perpetual hard-on persisted, despite the attempts to exhaust himself with a wicked training session. Parts of his body wanted her, no matter how tired he got.

Wanted.

Needed.

His mind—a damned gerbil spinning on a wheel—tried to figure out Mariah. Tried to figure out his own fucked-up self.

He might have cleared the air with Garrison, but Vaughn still carried a boatload of shame for what had happened with his brother's wife. *You're not in the right headspace for a relationship with a quality woman like Mariah, man. You don't deserve her, and she doesn't deserve your baggage.*

And she sure didn't deserve a quick roll in the sheets followed by his inevitable departure from Copper River. Unfortunately, that was all he had to offer.

But wow. Her eyes. Her mind. Her body.

Pow. Bambam. Sweat soaked his T-shirt. It should chill him to the bone, but his blood boiled with the need to taste more than her sweet mouth. He wanted her under him, moaning in pleasure. Then his power surged with its own list of needs. Vaughn would slay anyone or anything that threatened her. Plain and simple.

After that damned kiss, it took an act of God for him to step away from her. At least his brain retained some small control. If he got her in his arms again, there was no guarantee that he could let go if things got hot and heavy.

Maybe. Barely. Probably not.

Christ.

"Snack?"

"Holy fuck!" He jumped at the low, feminine voice, then peeked at his tented shorts and scooted over so that the punching bag hid the evidence. "Sorry. Hi, Ruth. Odie."

"We thought you might want a snack." One corner of the nurse's mouth rose, but her face otherwise remained impassive.

The woman should be a poker player.

For his part, Odie couldn't tear his gaze away from her. Even though she was easily six solid feet worth of woman, Odie treated her like a priceless treasure. Vaughn didn't need Shelby's gift of reading emotions to figure out that the guy was utterly in love with his wife.

"How is the training, my friend?" The man's southern lilt sounded so strange here in Wyoming. His short beard and moustache fit right in, though. A Cajun cowboy. Who would've thought it?

Vaughn laid his cheek against the bag while praying that parts of his anatomy would deflate already. "Fine. This Saturday should be a good bout."

"Will you be ready?" Ruth asked, holding out a glass of what smelled like fruit and protein. Man, she was perceptive. Too perceptive.

Weirder still, when Vaughn saw Ruth, he got a flash of the recurrent dreams he'd been having for the past few months: a woman's arm. Lava. Heat. How did it relate to Ruth?

He bent and swigged water from his sports bottle, then took the drink she offered. After a sip, he held up the glass. "Wow. Thanks. This is really good."

Odie's eyes glinted as he grinned over at Ruth. "She's always good."

She giggled and blushed.

Nearly snorting the thick drink, Vaughn laughed. "TMI, you crazy kids."

"Ah, no one is ever too old for *amour*, isn't that right, *chérie*?"

Odie hadn't moved an inch, but Ruth's eyes glowed and her cheeks flushed even more. Wow. What Vaughn wouldn't give for that man's suave moves.

Odie pointed and whistled. "*Mon dieu*, my friend, but those are beautiful markings."

Vaughn glanced down. His right bicep was covered in a spiral of thorns. His upper chest and back had thick scrawls of Latin and more thorns. Themes of pain and self-control. Permanent reminders of bad choices. A warning to keep history from repeating itself.

"Thanks." Trying to soften the harsh tone, he raised the glass. "For the drink, too."

Focusing those odd but familiar eyes on Vaughn, Ruth asked, "Is everything all right with you? Here, being home."

Wiping sweat from his forehead with the glove, he took another gulp of the protein drink. "Sure. I'm just helping out here for a bit."

"Then you're gone?"

Why did she want to know? "That's the idea."

With a strange tilt to her head, she tapped her lower lip. "Sometimes—" She paused, like she thought better of what she wanted say. "Sometimes, life happens when we're making other plans. Or so I've been told."

Odie snorted and grinned. Like he knew something.

That smiling Cajun knew nothing when it came to the Taggarts.

"Well. Sure, I guess," Vaughn hedged.

Ruth continued, "And sometimes when life happens, we are changed by it."

What was this woman, some oracle on a mountain?

No, she was a nice person who brought him a protein shake and helped to pull his father back from the brink of fading away. Vaughn could at least listen to what she had to say.

"All right," he said, resting a hand on the punching bag.

The silent exchange between Ruth and Odie was blink-and-you'll-miss-it. What was going on here? Vaughn's skin prickled, and not only from the cool temperature on sweat. An undercurrent of familiarity and fear passed between the three of them.

Her gold-flecked eyes, so much like Vaughn and his siblings.

She pinned him with a placid hazel gaze. Ruth couldn't be more than a year or two older than him. Yet she possessed an air of age and wisdom.

"Have you personally noticed any changes since coming back home?" she asked.

A sensation, akin to when his power activated, zapped him in the temple. But this felt different. External. Like a puff of warm air over his skin or a featherlight brush of a hand over his mind. Familiar. Friendly.

No.

His head shot up toward Ruth, looking for clues. But the woman was like the love child of the Sphinx and Mona Lisa when it came to hiding her emotions. Impressive.

"Like what?" he asked. "Weird stuff on the ranch or personally?"

The sensation of that soft presence continued. Comfortable pressure, like the split second right before getting a warm hug.

What the actual hell? He must be dehydrated from the workout, and hallucinating.

"Either, I guess," she murmured. "Never mind my asking. It's not my business." She waved off Odie's hand from her shoulder.

Her voice faded away as another tingle began in his mind. This time, though, insistent terror swept like a flash fire through his veins. Without his releasing the latched control, power flared to life. Pushed him. It wanted his ass outside the barn. Now.

That meant he had to get Ruth and Odie out of here.

"So, uh, thanks for the drink." He patted the bag, giving an Oscar-winning casual act. "But I really need to get back to work here."

"Sure," Ruth said, brows drawing together.

Fighting to keep the tone nonchalant, he said, "Hey, when you get in the house, would you ask Garrison to come out here?"

Odie smiled. "Will do." He guided his wife out of the barn, hand on her back.

Damn it, could those two move any slower? As the door closed behind them, a sulfur scent permeated his nostrils. Like when Vaughn had found Shelby in the forest that night. Shit. His skin twitched.

His power had gone from a warning chime to a screaming klaxon blasting into his skull.

"Oh crap." He let go of the punching bag and crumpled to his knees, holding his head together as his power expanded outward, seeking danger, blaring an alarm.

Gritting his teeth, he planted his hands on the hay-strewn floor. Then he staggered to his feet and sprinted out into the night, ripping off his training gloves on the way out of the barn.

Against the backdrop of the clear, wide, star-filled night sky stood a dark object, one hundred feet from the ranch house.

The only light from the thing came from two glowing dots passing for eyes.

Fighting to stay conscious through the intense stab of pain through his skull, Vaughn focused on repelling the blast of hot rage coming from that thing.

The two red spots locked onto Vaughn.

The creature consumed more and more of the night sky as it drew closer.

Between the roaring in his head and the weird howl that warped sound around the creature in front of him, it took all of Vaughn's strength not to assume the fetal position on the ground.

He didn't know what this thing was, but he would be damned if he'd let it reach the house.

Who was in the house? Garrison, Sara, Zach, Dad, and, hopefully, Ruth and Odie.

Danger. Vaughn detected danger coming right at him.

Shit. Anyone with half a brain cell could figure out that this thing meant danger—it didn't take a fancy psychic ability to put those sick puzzle pieces together.

Yes, this was the thing he'd seen hovering over Shelby's broken body at the bottom of the bluff. The same creature that had threatened Sara and Zach a few weeks ago here at the ranch. Thank God Garrison and Shelby had been here to protect them.

Now it was back. What the hell did it want, and how could Vaughn eliminate it with extreme prejudice?

A slither of sound like a dry lizard tongue brushed by his ear. "Ah yes, the prodigal son. The last piece of the legacy."

"What?" Vaughn's ability pounded against his mind, urging him to get away from this thing. Against the will of every cell in his being, he stayed put.

What passed for a chuckle came out as concrete grinding glass. "Soon, my son. All of my love's legacy will be together. Then you will all join with me in the holiest of communion."

"Whatever, Friar Fuck. Get the hell off my property," he gritted out.

The darkness didn't so much come closer as it absorbed more space in his field of vision. Stinging sulfur-scented heat, like standing way too close to a fumarole, sent a blistering wave across Vaughn's face. Bonus: it flash-dried his workout shorts.

"I will leave when it is time. You will listen," it said, pausing like it prepared to deliver a dissertation.

Fuck. That.

The porch light came on, streaming brightness out into the night.

And the thing absorbed the light. Freakin' sucked it up like an ungodly ShamWow.

Garrison flung open the front door, braced his feet, and took aim with a shotgun.

The thing's voice hissed like a hot acetylene torch "The two eldest of the legacy children. Soon it will be four, and I will return to walk upon this Earth." What passed for breathing sounded like a whistle made of chalk and fingernails. "Then you all will be destroyed."

Vaughn had heard enough. An angry pulse pushed his ability outward, expanding outside the bounds of his mind. Shit, his head would explode into a million pieces if he grew any more.

But his power increased. Kept pushing forward.

No longer did his gift protect him, no longer did it detect danger to others, but now it turned Vaughn *into* danger, like when he'd found Shelby. It wanted to shift the ability outward. To hurt. To destroy.

Two red dots glowed before him. And inside of it, an outline of a...human form? Vaughn squinted in the porch light and shadows. No. Not possible. "Your days are numbered," the creature seethed.

In that case, hurting that bastard cloud monster sounded like a great way for Vaughn to pass his numbered days.

He grabbed a lungful of air and bore down as he shored up the bubble of pissed-off power that formed inside of him. The effort made him stagger, but he kept at it, unsure of what to do, but determined to do something useful.

What he had felt a few minutes earlier in the barn, the sense of a friend's touch, close to his mind boosted his power even further. No, it didn't quite boost the power—it helped focus it.

Why? How? He glanced at Garrison. It didn't seem to come from him. His brother's grim gaze rested solely on the phantasm trying to kill them both.

Vaughn visualized his power as a round, thick balloon. He shoved as much pressure into it, inflating, expanding. The crucible-hot press of it threatened to crack his mind. But he needed more. He wanted that thing away from the people he cared about.

With a great snap of energy, he blew the rubberized force at the creature.

A howl of a wounded animal combined with a very human-sounding wail of pain rattled the glass in the window casings on the porch.

The glowing twin embers dimmed.

"Not possible." More star-dotted sky appeared as the shape receded. "This result will not stand. You will bend to my will."

The crack of a shotgun blasted across the space between them. Garrison reloaded once again, his jaw set in a grim line. "Sorry, gave at the office. Whatever you're selling, we don't want it."

The creature howled. "I will destroy anything and anyone you hold dear." Red ember eyes glowed as it bore into Vaughn's retinas.

"That woman you lust after? Mine." It turned back to Garrison. "Your woman inside? Also mine."

Garrison nestled the butt of the gun into his shoulder and aimed.

Vaughn had had enough of this thing's bullshit. The creature needed to get the hell away from his family. A flicker of faces behind the living room curtains ramped up his pulse.

And that thing had better not even consider coming close to Mariah. His power cracked open into pieces, each shard focused on one goal: remove the creature. The ability changed, deepened, thickened. A picture of Mariah's delicate features floated across his mind's eye, followed by an image of her wounded body laying at the feet of this cloud-like thing.

No!

A hollow, split voice that came from deep within Vaughn echoed across the open ground as another bubble of pissed-off blasted the thing away once more. Sound faded as his ears buzzed. "We are stronger than you. You cannot have what is ours. *Get out.*"

CHAPTER 13

Jogging down the hall, Mariah shoved down the emptiness from last night's frustrating experience with Vaughn. Right now, she needed to focus on what had just happened in this patient's room. Yanking the door open, she pushed past a haggard Kerr.

And stopped.

Eric Patterson and Shelby Taggart shared the same bed, a concession Mariah had given in to yesterday. No decision, really. Eric was determined to remain close to Shelby one way or another.

But instead of the limp, unconscious woman from yesterday, Shelby rested in the circle of Eric's arms, bathed by the morning sunlight that filtered into the window. Awake.

Smiling, even. Nestled against his chest, Shelby's face relaxed in a picture of relief. Of belonging.

The intensity of that connection took Mariah's breath away, leaving hollow nothingness behind.

She couldn't begrudge them their emotions. Heck, they'd both earned happiness and then some after everything they'd been through.

So why then did the image of Eric, bruised and exhausted, holding Shelby like he possessed the best gift in the entire world make Mariah's chest ache?

Because she wanted what those two people had. Okay, maybe not the concussions and broken limbs. With a longing that brought tears, Mariah drank in the scene before her. Not the physical scene but the emotional one. Fitting with another person. Being cherished.

"Hi, Doc," Eric murmured, his smile uneven with the still-swollen cheek. "Look." He gazed down at the woman in his arms.

"Shelby, how are you doing?" Mariah moved over to the bed.

"I feel kind of hung over and can't see, but other than that, I'm terrific." The woman wiggled her legs. "Ow. And apparently my leg is still broken."

"I can't believe you're awake. Any weird feelings? I mean, not associated with the fracture."

"Believe it or not, I feel fine. When can I get out of here?"

Eric tightened his embrace and frowned.

Shelby's strange gold and brown eyes remained unfocused. She patted his hand. "Easy there, Tarzan. I don't want to run a 10K or anything. I'd just like to go home."

"Which home?" he asked.

She settled deeper into his chest. "Negotiable, based on your good behavior."

"Geezus," he said. "Coma for days, but the minute you wake up, you're back to being a pip."

The corners of Shelby's mouth quirked.

"Mind if I check you over?" Mariah asked.

"That's my cue to step out." Eric placed a kiss into the tangled orange curls on top of her head and extricated himself from their entwined limbs. "Don't go anywhere."

"Do I resemble someone who could make a quick getaway? Seriously?"

Mariah stifled a giggle.

"I'll be right outside," he said, motioning to Kerr to follow him. The door closed with a soft *click*.

Mariah checked Shelby's eyes with the ophthalmoscope. No pupil dilation. But no optic disc cupping or retinal hemorrhage. Eyes were a little bloodshot but otherwise had normal physical structures. What gave?

The woman simply couldn't see.

"I'm sorry about your vision. We'll get you set up with an ophthalmologist." She listened to Shelby's heart and lungs, then slung the stethoscope over her neck. "Hey. Looks like Eric's pretty happy you're alive."

"Took me going into a coma to figure out how much he means to me. Kind of like a control-alt-delete on the brain."

Mariah smiled. "Never thought of it that way, but okay."

"So. Is my brother being a jerk still?"

"Kerr?" She glanced back toward the closed door.

"No, Mr. Grumpy Pants. Vaughn."

"He seems to care a lot about his family," Mariah gave it her best politic response.

"Nuh uh. I might not be able to see your face, but I'm not deaf or stupid. He's being a moron, isn't he?"

"It's really not for me to say…"

"So, you mean, yes, he's a dumbass."

"Shelby—"

The woman plowed ahead. "He's had a lot of bad stuff to deal with, and, yes, he worries about us." She pinched the bridge of her nose. "I just want him to find happiness."

"Of course."

"And I think he should try to find it with you."

Mariah's mouth gaped open. "No, I don't. That's. Not appropriate. Um…"

"The only problem? That numb nut is too stupid to figure it out. Most guys are dumber than two bricks smacked together when it comes to women. Trust me, I know," she said with a raised brow and a nod toward the door.

"How in the world did you go from being comatose to analyzing nonexistent relationships?"

"It's a gift." Shelby's laugh lit up her whole face. "Seriously, when can I go home?"

Rocking back on her heels, Mariah said, "I'd like to run a few more tests today, then maybe home tomorrow. That would be Thursday, in case you've lost track of days."

"Works for me." A shadow of a frown came and went. "I can't wait to be back on the ranch."

"You do understand you can't do a whole lot, right? Your immediate future includes rest, more antibiotics, additional procedures, and physical therapy."

"I know. It's just…time to be home. Where I belong. With family."

Another twist of the imaginary knife in Mariah's chest made her cough.

Then the air changed. Became heavier, solid.

Secure. Warm.

A quick headache came and went, and she rubbed her forehead.

Vaughn stepped into the room. "Man, am I relieved you're awake." A leather jacket was draped over his arm, and he leaned against the doorjamb. But nothing else about his demeanor signaled *casual*. Every line in his big body was tense.

Mariah froze, her pulse pounding so loud that the others had to hear it.

Damn him, did he not own any loose shirts? It took all of her power not to auscultate the guy's heart sounds, just to get close to those pectorals.

"You sound tired." Shelby turned her head in Vaughn's direction.

"Little bit," he said. "I'm fine." He faced Mariah.

How had she not noticed the shadows under his cheekbones? He still filled the room with a massive physical presence, but it looked like the guy had lost weight. He appeared exhausted, even when he stared at her with that stark, tight gaze.

"Well, I'm going to go put in some orders," Mariah said, her face warming under his intense perusal. "I'll check back with you later."

Shelby sat up straight. "Actually, I want Vaughn to leave as well."

"What?" He pulled his chin back.

"Dude, I need to go potty and, no offense, but I do not want your participation or observation in the blessed event."

A splash of red colored his neck as he backpedaled to the door. "Got it. I'll be out here with Kerr and Eric."

She waved a hand. "Fine, fine. Hey, get me a nurse, would ya?" Laughing, she added, "And not Nurse Eric, either. I don't know how he ever got licensed, but he's terrible."

Mariah pulled the curtain as she followed Vaughn's broad back into the hall. The nursing assistant nearby ducked into the room to help Shelby.

Before Mariah could walk away, a warm hand on her shoulder stopped her. A jolt of adrenaline shot through to her toes.

"Doc?" Damn his rumbly, sexy voice, especially after…

She would remain professional or die trying. "Yes?"

Rubbing the stubble on his chin, he said, "I need to apologize for last night."

She shook her head. "No need. An error, and not one I will make again." Her insides quivered like Jell-O. *Stay calm.*

"It's just—"

"Please stop. You'll only make it worse." She stuck out a hand. "Friends?"

The fire glinting in his dark eyes spoke of anything but friendship. He wrapped her hand in his large, warm one. "Fine. Friends."

Why would friendship made her weak in the knees?

* * *

"So, got a thing for the doctor?" Kerr needled him after Mariah walked away.

Vaughn groaned. "Just friends." They walked down the hall to the family waiting area.

"Friends don't look at friends like a tasty rack of ribs."

"Man, for real? Drop it."

Despite the haunted circles under Kerr's eyes, he still grinned. "Tell me, am I getting warmer or colder?" He ducked Vaughn's jab. "Here, let's try another one. You think she's cute."

Vaughn clamped his mouth shut as he took a seat in an uncomfortable vinyl chair.

"I'll take that as 'warmer.'" Tapping his chin, Kerr stopped and studied Vaughn. "Oh, my. You *would* like to hook up with pretty doctor. I thought you were joking the other day."

"Okay. Conversation over." Because, hell yes, Vaughn wanted to think about things like getting a physical from that woman. He'd gotten a taste of her curves and her lips. God help him, but he wanted more.

"Red hot!" Kerr plunked down on a two-person couch.

Vaughn lifted a fist. "Enough!"

Kerr played the part of helpless younger brother perfectly, hands up and all innocence written over a face that was designed for the sole purpose of irritating the piss out of Vaughn. Kid brother hadn't lost his touch over the years. "Let me know if you need some advice. You know, in the woman department."

"Kerr..." It didn't help that Vaughn was tired, hungry, and grouchy. Making weight this quickly and then dealing with that...whatever the hell it was last night at the ranch...had drained his energy reserves. He was one more misplaced comment away from snapping.

Annoying brother crossed his legs at the ankles and laced his hands behind his head. "Advice is free."

"Isn't it time for you to leave and go back to the ranch?"

His brother's smile drooped. "You bet it is. I want to find whatever the hell you all saw out there last night. Garrison texted me a few details."

Vaughn lowered his face in his hands and scrubbed, trying to get the image of that evil creature out of his mind. Didn't work. "Same thing we saw with Shelby and Eric."

"Shit." He sat straight up. "How'd you stop it?"

"Garrison shot at it with a 12-gauge, and my power did something wacky and attacked it." His head still ached from the effort, and Vaughn's hearing had only this morning returned to normal.

"Really? That's weird. But it sounds like a good start to me."

"We didn't destroy it, though. That fucking thing is still out there. I'll be damned if it gets close to my family again." He leaned forward, anything but relaxed.

Kerr took a big breath and steepled his fingers. Uh oh. "First of all, way to go with making up for lost time, with that 'being there for the family' shtick." He held up a hand. "Second of all, you're not going out there half-cocked. God knows what that thing will do to you. Therefore, I'll go with you, as we discussed before."

"When?"

"As soon as we get Shelby and Eric safe and settled. Then you and I will go on a nasty-critter hunt."

"Garrison?"

"The less he knows, the better. While he'll probably be on board with the concept, Mr. Play It Safe won't like the risk."

"Guess that creature out there explains why our dogs are gone."

"Yeah, they disappeared a little over a month ago. We figured they ran off or coyotes got to them. But now…?"

"Understood." Vaughn rolled his neck, making it pop. "What do we do in the meantime?"

Kerr shifted on the vinyl couch, the material creaking under his back. "I recommend you get an appointment with a certain medical provider. You might need some treatment for whatever condition you have."

"Man, come on now." Damn his brother, but the idea had merit. Or trying again for that bagel and a coffee. He could keep his baggage well hidden for a brief not-date. Make sure the outing stayed light and breezy. What the fuck? Did the phrase "light and breezy" actually go through his mind? Christ.

A hand waved in front of his face. "Earth to knuckle dragger. You still in there?"

"Fine."

"Uh, that wasn't the answer to my question."

"Has anyone mentioned how annoying you can be?"

"It's a gift." Kerr leaned back again and crossed his arms over his chest. What Vaughn wouldn't give to knock that stupid grin off his kid brother's face. "Go on, now. Go to the ranch, do chores, punch stuff, continue not eating." He waggled his fingers. "Whatever you people like to do."

The growl burst out of his lips. "Jesus Christ."

"Most folks call me by my nickname, JC."

Vaughn shoved out of the chair and backed away. Leg or no leg, Kerr had pushed Vaughn's last button. If Vaughn didn't exit soon, his next action would be fratricide.

"Toodles!" Kerr winked.

CHAPTER 14

The professional concern that had weighed Mariah down for the past several days lifted at the sight of Garrison wheeling Shelby toward the main hospital doors Thursday afternoon. Next to her strode a recovered Eric, who had likely refused wheelchair transport. But Vaughn hovered next to him.

Avoiding eye contact with Vaughn, Mariah approached the group in the lobby. "This is so great to see."

"I'll say." Garrison's serious expression had finally relaxed into a brief smile.

"Thank you again, Doc." Eric's voice cracked as he rested a hand on Shelby's shoulder. "For everything."

Mariah shook her head. "A lot of folks pitched in to help. A massive team effort, and it was worth it. Now don't take this the wrong way, but I'm glad to be kicking you out of the hospital."

Shelby grinned in the direction of her boyfriend. "Ha. She couldn't wait to be rid of us. You think I was a bad patient here? Just wait 'til I get home."

"You're not moving off the couch or the bed or doing anything without help. Period." Eric crossed his arms and glared at Shelby, making Mariah laugh.

The smile briefly lit Vaughn's face. "Poor Eric. He doesn't know how stubborn Taggarts are when they want something." His glinting gaze lasered on Mariah.

Her heart stopped.

Cutting her eyes away from him, she bit her lip. She must have imagined the double entendre.

"Well, folks, I need to go on a house call before the snow flies tonight. You all get home safely and take care." Mariah waved.

Eric and Garrison wheeled Shelby out the front doors.

Vaughn remained behind, a large, quiet figure in front of her.

"Where's your house call?"

She peered around him at the heavy, gray skies. "I can't say. HIPAA protection and all."

"Where?" It was almost a demand. "I don't want you going somewhere unsafe."

A pique of anger sparked along her last nerve. "Okay, mister. Look here." She came within an inch of poking him in his solid chest. "You can't flash hot and cold like this, going from the caveman act and then indifference and then back to the caveman. It's not fair. We're friends, right? So you need to back down."

His thick, dark brows shot up. That big smile only increased her frustration. "I only meant that if the call is out in the boonies, not only could I help you find it, but I have a way better vehicle than your Mini to manage dirt roads." He hooked his thumbs in the waistband of his worn jeans, drawing her attention to a very un-friend-like location. "I'd hate to see you break that pretty car."

"Are you being sarcastic?"

"Not really." Honest. Straightforward. "Well, a little sarcastic about your ridiculous car, but the rest of it, no. I just want to help. Because we're friends."

Her lungs deflated. She wanted to melt into a puddle on the floor before him. "Wow, my bad." She rubbed her neck. "I made a couple of assumptions. Sorry."

"Yeah. We all make assumptions." He blinked. "So where are you headed?"

"Brand ranch."

"No." A chill and a wave of discomfort accompanied that one word.

She stepped back. "Yes. And why is that your problem?"

"Number one, I don't trust them farther than I can throw them. Number two, you're not going out there alone. And number three, the road to their place is wretched. Your car won't survive the trip." He ran his hand through his dark hair, the light catching auburn pieces. "Fuck, I hate those guys."

"So don't come. I can get there on my own."

A muscle popped in his jaw. "No. I said I'd help, so I'll help. Get your stuff and let's go."

"Don't act so happy about your offer, Robin Hood." Without waiting to see if he followed, she stomped back to her office, exchanged her white coat for her wool one, and slung her satchel with basic home visit equipment in it over her shoulder. Spinning around, she went nose to chest with a warm, male scent.

Yum.

Not yum. Friends.

Besides, she was still mad. She stepped back.

"Can I carry that for you?" His low voice flowed over her like a caress, making her hips ache.

Tilting her head far back, she scowled at him. Damned corner of his sexy mouth twitched. Yeah. He was so busted for making fun of her.

"Fine." With one fluid motion, she slid the bag off, picked up a little momentum, and swung it into his rock-hard gut, triggering a muffled *oof*. She brushed her hands together. Good.

Ignoring the raised brows and whispers behind hands of the medical assistants and nurses, Mariah hurried out the side door and into the cold dusk. The frigid air smelled of impending snow.

"Where's your car?"

"Truck," he muttered.

"Okay."

"It's Eric's and it's not fancy."

"Who needs fancy?"

As they approached the old, beat-up Ford, her heart sank. She'd need a rope ladder to get into the passenger seat.

He opened the door. "Jump," he said.

"What?" She gave a lame bounce with her feet, and his hands clamped around her waist, lifting her in a smooth motion into the truck. Then the satchel hit her in the gut.

Oof.

He grinned as he closed the door.

Well played.

He climbed in with ease and pulled out of the parking lot.

"Do you know how to get there?" she asked after he steered the vehicle away from town.

"Unfortunately, yes."

"I know Hank Brand kidnapped Sara and Zach, so it's understandable that you don't like him. Hank disappeared, didn't he?"

"Yeah."

"But what about the rest of the Brand family? Izzy seems really nice. And her mom is kind of...interesting."

He snorted. "Let's see. You've met Wyatt, and he's a real piece of work, as you well know. He was tormenting Shelby a few weeks back. If he's switched over to bugging you full time, let me know and I will put a stop to it."

"Pretty sure I can handle Wyatt Brand."

He snorted again.

As the truck rolled down the highway, Vaughn flicked his eyes to her and back to the road. "What skills exactly do you have to handle someone like Wyatt?"

She crossed her arms. "I know you aren't making fun of me."

"How could I?"

"Precisely." She rubbed her neck. "Well, I can throw hot coffee like it's no big deal. And being a medical professional, I do know about ten good ways to kill a person and not leave a trace."

His head whipped around. "Really?"

"No. Just kidding." She flicked a nail with her teeth. "About the coffee, that is."

A real, live smile cracked his stone face and made her mouth turn upward in response. "Good one," he said.

"So why do you hate the rest of the Brand family?"

The smile fled. "The Brand family has been after our land for years. They likely burned down our barn and stole cattle. Probably drove Dad to his stroke."

"You don't know that's all true."

"We have enough proof," he snapped.

"Okaaay."

He opened his mouth and closed it.

"Is there more?" she asked.

His knuckles turned white around the wheel. "Garrison had an ex-wife, Tiffani. She betrayed Garrison with Hank Brand, drained the account, and left."

"No way." She studied his hard profile. He held his breath. "Wait. There's more to that story."

"What are you? Psychic?"

"Nope. Good reader of people."

"Damn." He sighed. "Before she left Garrison and fell in with Hank, she went for me."

Her jaw dropped. "You two had an affair?"

His long pause did not reassure her. He rested a fist on the wheel. "Depends on how you look at it."

"Seems like a straightforward question with one of two answers."

He didn't answer.

"So that's why you left?"

"Hell, yeah, I wasn't going to torment my brother."

"You sacrificed your life on the ranch, with your family, to save Garrison's marriage?" Why did she get the feeling he was leaving out important information?

"It's not as altruistic as it sounds." He signaled to make the turn onto a chip-sealed county road. "And it didn't work. Sounded like she was unhappy regardless of who she was with. Hank swept her off her feet, she did as he suggested and destroyed Garrison, and the rest is history." Another pause. "Only that's not all of it. She died a while after hooking up with Hank."

"What happened?"

"No one knows. Hank disappeared after kidnapping Sara and Zach, so by the time I got here, he was long gone. No Hank to question."

"Wow." She looked out at the gray, snow-swept landscape. This tormented and tough-as-nails guy had a real soft spot for his family—to the detriment of his own future. She studied his hard profile. "What about the rest of the Brands?"

"At best, they have been unhelpful."

"At worst?"

"We think they're dangerous and willing to do whatever it takes to get our land."

"Still doesn't make sense in a state the size of Wyoming. Free-range grazing and all."

"Goes way back to a conflict between now-deceased Mr. Brand and Dad." He rubbed his jaw. "But I thought that spat was long buried. Who knows? The Brands are vindictive. They're erratic and they're getting worse." He pulled the truck to a stop a hundred feet before a dirt lane. No street number or mailbox. "Sure you want to do the visit?"

Her scalp prickled. She toyed with the latch on the bag. "While I respect the background information, I still need to take care of my patient."

"Give me your phone." He held out his hand. "Please." When she complied, he punched in his number and handed it back to her. "If ever you need help, call and I'll be there." He squinted at the phone again and exhaled a curse. "Actually, the damn thing might not work at their house. We're out of bars on the phone here. Dead zone." Putting the truck into gear, he stared at her, raising the hairs on the back of her neck. "If something happens in the house, just scream really loudly. I will get to you."

A real shiver hit her as they bounced down the rutted dirt road. "Aren't you being a little melodramatic?"

"No. I have a shotgun on the rack behind us. I will use it if necessary."

Her heart rattled in time with her teeth as the truck bounced down the rutted lane. "You're not serious."

"Aren't I?" The muscle jumped again in his jaw, and his knuckles blanched as he gripped the wheel. "Look."

He braked twenty feet in front of a run-down, wood-sided ranch.

Two men approached, one on each side of the truck. They aimed their rifles.

CHAPTER 15

The image of a man pointing a gun at Mariah sucker-punched Vaughn. Escape plan needed. Now.

His ability tingled and sparked to life, and he clamped his teeth together, releasing the control over his gift. The urge to protect himself and Mariah surged, jackhammering his fucking skull.

He scanned the property still visible in the house lights illuminating the darkness. One main building and numerous large garages and barns. He stopped in a snow-dusted dirt and gravel open parking area.

There wasn't much cover.

Not only would he have a slim chance of protecting himself if Wyatt or—he squinted—damn it, Tommy Brand with his scarred eyebrow got a shot off, but no way could Vaughn keep Mariah safe as well. The two men still pointed guns.

Vaughn's vision went red.

Why hadn't he insisted that she stay away?

Because that stubborn woman would've gone with or without his help, all to do her job.

Before Vaughn could tap out a text and hope it would reach home, Tommy rapped on the window with the tip of his gun barrel and hollered, "Hands on the wheel, Taggart. Get out of the truck slowly." Vaughn dropped his phone to the floorboard where the guys couldn't see it.

Wyatt knocked on the passenger side; Mariah yelped. The color drained from her face and neck.

Now Vaughn needed to kill that man for scaring her.

He pounded again on the window, his face steaming up the outside of the glass next to Mariah.

Her hand shook as she scrambled to unlock the door. With a wide-eyed glance over her shoulder at Vaughn, she clambered down into the dirt and snow-covered parking area.

After yet another tap, Vaughn barked at Tommy, "Unwad your panties. I'm coming." He kept his hands where the man could see them, stepped out of the truck, and hurried around the front of the vehicle. Anything to get closer to Mariah.

But it wasn't close enough. He was stopped before reaching the porch.

"What the hell are you doing here, Taggart? Thought this was a goddamned doctor visit, not you taking a tour of our property." Wyatt spat on the ground and stood in his way. "Besides, you're trespassing."

At least the guys had set the guns down against the house. Still too close for comfort.

"I drove the nice doctor down your piss-poor excuse for a road, so she could do your family a favor. If you don't want her to care for your mother, we'll get back in the truck and leave."

"Suits me fine," Wyatt growled.

A third man exited the house. With that sleeveless shirt, the guy had his own bulging guns on display. Dread turned to concrete in Vaughn's stomach, and his blood pressure did a swan dive.

He would recognize those dead, ice-blue eyes anywhere.

"Linc," he gritted out. "What the hell are you doing with these losers?"

The hulking man sneered, "Helping out around the ranch. Aunt Patty's been sick and all."

Fuck. How had he not connected that Linc was related to the Brands?

Wyatt snickered. "Taggart, you must know my cousin, Lincoln McDowell. Linc, meet pansy-assed Vaughn."

The Brands just got better and better.

Linc flexed his arms. "Oh, we know each other. It's been, what, four years? Doesn't matter. We'll finish our discussion later." In the octagon. Of course.

Vaughn curled his hands into fists, eager to start the fight early.

Mariah glanced over at Vaughn with a frown, and he gave a tiny head shake. He needed to get her out of the worsening danger. And loose cannon Linc McDowell personified "worsening danger."

"Hi, Doc," Linc sneered. "Long time no see."

Her spine went ramrod straight.

What the hell? When had Mariah seen him before?

Christ, everything about this place screamed *wrong*. Even the air felt heavy, sour.

Vaughn's power begged him to stand between her and Linc. But even though the guns weren't actively aimed at them, he didn't want to do anything to endanger Mariah.

She clutched the bag and squared her shoulders. "Well," her voice cracked, "I should take a look at Mrs. Brand, and then we can be going."

"Right this way," Linc announced.

She took stiff steps into the house.

Linc leered at her backside as she walked past him.

Vaughn almost lost his mind. Permanently. He wanted to tackle the guy. The only thing that stopped him was the threat of Wyatt and Tommy's shotguns. He took a step toward the house.

"Stay right there, Taggart." Wyatt spat another glob onto the ground. "Linc will take good care of her."

Crossing his arms, Vaughn leaned against his truck. "So, he's your cousin?"

"Well, second cousin. From Laramie. In town for the big fight coming up." The barking laugh had the same effect as salt on Vaughn's raw nerves. "It's not too late for you to back out. Linc put his last two opponents in the hospital. I think one guy is still drinking through a straw." A sniff. "Such a shame, your face being so pretty to begin with and all."

"We'll see." He monitored the house, every sense straining for some clue as to how Mariah was doing. Was Linc being a jerk? Stupid question.

Hurry.

Time crawled as the snow fell more heavily. In the silence, he could hear the tiny *blap* of snowflakes on his leather jacket. His stomach growled. Damn it, in times like this, he sure did want something strong to drink with zero nutritional value and a hell of a kick to it.

Idle time took chunks out of his soul.

He propped a boot heel against the front bumper of his truck in an effort to act casual while Tommy and Wyatt hovered. The tingle in his mind remained at a low level. Not a three-alarm power eruption. Yet.

Somehow, he'd know if Mariah were in immediate danger. He hoped.

While he waited, he memorized the visible layout of the ranch and the hills behind the house, with flat fields on one side and thick forest stopping at the outbuildings on the other. The house was made up of a main structure where several additions appeared to have been tacked on in a series of drunken afterthoughts. Near a large, metal Quonset hut outbuilding sat three rusting vehicles on blocks and large equipment partially hidden under large tarps. Kerr had mentioned that the Brands were doing some mining. This likely confirmed the activity.

Every few minutes, Wyatt snickered.

"What's so funny, Brand?"

"Lady doctor doesn't know that it's dangerous to hang out with a Taggart." The idiot's eye twitched.

"All right, I'll bite. What the hell are you talking about?"

"Well. Garrison's girlfriend got hurt after she started seeing him. And that other pretty boy got messed up good and proper after dating Shelby. Coincidental. Don't you think?"

Like a spark hitting a hissing Bunsen burner, his power shot to full flame. Wyatt backed up a step. Good. "You wanna go on record? You taking credit for something?"

"Now why would I do that? Everyone knows I'm innocent. So says my brother."

"Sheriff Tommy?"

The asshole in question tipped an invisible hat and tapped the butt of his gun on the warped wood of the front porch. A scarred eyebrow rose. Just like old times.

"Convenient, isn't it?" Wyatt grinned, his face shadowed with the house lights behind him.

Vaughn shoved his hands in his front pockets and tried to ignore the flakes of snow melting on his head. "Yeah, real convenient. Like getting away with murder."

"I haven't killed anyone." The unspoken "yet" chilled Vaughn's blood.

The man snickered and darted glances around the compound, like he expected to see someone.

Or something.

The background rumble of Vaughn's power blunted his ability to focus.

Where the hell was Mariah? It was full dark. How long had she been in there?

Wyatt spat on the ground. "So you'd better steer clear of lady doctor. For her safety."

Vaughn closed the five feet between them, ignoring any risk to his own health. "The. Fuck. You. Say." No one threatened Mariah. He'd had enough.

As he grabbed the man's shirtfront, Vaughn's power began to expand again, like a bubble that searched for her, wanting to keep her safe inside the sphere. Wanting to repel Wyatt far away from Mariah. An ache formed over his temples as the energy grew.

Wyatt's mouth gaped and his feet slid away from Vaughn, as if pushed by an invisible impulse. "Back away, Taggart, if you know what's good for you. One day, you'll be at our beck and call. Soon. You'll see."

Damn it, as badly as he wanted to hand this bastard his teeth, Vaughn needed to focus on Mariah's safety. His ears buzzed as he fought a gut-twisting need to get her far away from these armed nut jobs. He stormed across the porch to the front door.

As he reached for the handle, the door opened. Carrying her coat over one arm and the satchel over the other shoulder, Mariah stepped onto the porch. Under the halogen light, her eyes swam in a pale face. Her chest rose and fell at a rapid rate.

Linc appeared right behind her, dwarfing her. Looming. Vaughn wanted to move her far away from that man. Now.

"Get out of here, lady," Wyatt growled and motioned at her. "You too, Taggart. Get right in the truck and leave. Don't help her. She can manage. Hands on the wheel after you close that door. No funny business."

Vaughn gritted his teeth and did as he was told, swinging up into his seat and slamming the door.

With jerking movements, like her limbs had locked up, Mariah walked to the truck and, after two attempts, opened the door of the truck. In a clumsy move where her foot slid off the bottom step, she finally managed to clamber in. When she shut the door, she stared straight ahead and didn't move.

He'd seen that blank expression last night, when he screwed up in the parking lot, but tonight it was a million times worse, like a complete void. His gut churned. What had Linc done to her? Half of Vaughn wanted to exit the truck and pound a confession out of the guy. The other half wanted only to remove Mariah from this place.

"Get out of here, Taggart. Don't show your face on our property again or we'll shoot first and ask questions later." Wyatt yelled, reaching for his gun.

He turned the key in the ignition, and sweat cooled on his brow when it took two tries for the truck to start. Mariah sat like an ashen statue, hands clasped in her lap, staring out the front window. She still wore the satchel. Her coat lay in her lap.

"Are you all right?" he asked, as he made a sloppy K-turn, the truck wheels kicking out slushy gravel.

"Fine," she whispered, not moving.

She looked anything but. "Put on your seat belt."

With one shaking hand, she reached back and tried to pull the strap around. She couldn't do it. Tried again. Failed and gave up. Stared out the window again. What the holy living fuck was going on with her?

He hauled ass down the ranch road like the demons of hell snapped at his heels, the back end of the truck whipping from side to side. Careening onto the county road, he put another few miles behind them before yanking the wheel and pulling off onto a shoulder. Hopefully, the truck wouldn't sink in the soft earth and snow, but he needed to figure out what was going on with Mariah.

He smacked the dome light on, illuminating the moisture that glistened on her pale cheeks.

"God, Mariah, are you all right?"

She opened and closed her mouth. No sound came out. She stared straight ahead.

What was he supposed to do?

If Linc had so much as touched her, Vaughn would trek back there and start a title fight early.

"Damn it." He slid over to the middle of the bench seat and pulled her sideways onto his lap. The coat and satchel fell to the muddy floorboard. *Please, let this be the right thing to do.* Tremors racked her delicate frame, enough to shake his own bones.

"Talk to me. What happened?"

Trying hard not to startle her, he worked his arms around until he surrounded her stiff body and clutched her tightly to his chest. He rested his chin on her head. Shudders continued to rack her, and he had no solution other than to hold her.

Something bad had gone down. This woman saved lives for a living, faced down death, yet here she sat, quietly going to pieces in his lap. Every inch of her radiated sheer terror.

The contained suffering tormented him more than loud weeping ever could. With a wince, he released his ability. It bubbled up and settled over the woman in his arms. He breathed easier.

He had to protect her. His soul required it.

Dramatic much? Vaughn, of all people, should know that emotions needed to stay out of this interaction. If he were smart, he'd keep any feelings tamped deep down. He had another life to return to back in New York. Entanglements in Copper River weren't part of his plan.

Also, his track record with women? Poor. Which was yet another reason...

He rubbed his cheek on her silky hair. Lots of stuff didn't fit into the plan.

According to the digital clock on the dash, another fifteen minutes passed in total silence. He let go of her long enough to turn the heat up in the idling vehicle. Then he cradled the side of her head with that same hand, easing her deeper into his chest. He stared at the falling snow the truck headlights illuminated.

Finally, her muscles went limp. He held still. After another few minutes, the shaking subsided.

He felt her deep, shuddering breath echo in his own lungs.

"Sorry." Did he mistake her whisper of sound?

"You're fine." His voice came out like sandpaper. "Take your time. We're in no hurry. Are you okay sitting here?"

A nod of her head against his chin.

When she turned so that her cold lips brushed over his neck, that tiny movement took him as close to heaven as a bastard like him could ever get.

He'd stay like this forever, if that was what she wanted. Sit in the sauna of the truck cab and sweat to death, if it meant she'd be warm enough. And safe enough.

Another ten minutes elapsed. The snow continued to fall in front of the truck's beams. Peaceful. Calm.

Everything Vaughn was not.

After another sigh, she rested a small hand on his forearm. "Thank you."

"Any time." What would a real man do right now? Hell if he knew. "Uh, want to talk about what happened? Did Linc do something in there?" It took concentration not to tighten his muscles.

"I guess. Um, those guys with the guns and being inside that dark house triggered a flashback."

"From what?"

She squeezed his arm. "From when I was a kid. Men with guns trapped me in a room while other people beat my brother."

Holy fuck.

CHAPTER 16

O h, no.
　　Had she said those words out loud? To a guy she'd only met a few days ago, no less.

Damn it, Mariah was too exhausted to care about anyone's opinion tonight.

God, it felt so good in the toasty circle of his hard chest and thick arms. Like somehow those demons couldn't haunt her here, with Vaughn. He held her firmly, but it was different. Maybe because she knew he wouldn't stop her if she needed to get away. Maybe it was just…him.

Every inch of her body pressed against him registered his tense muscles. The guy was like a hard, warm radiator.

"What happened?" he asked. How long had it been since someone cared about her on a deeper level than as a professional? Besides Kevin, of course.

Poor Vaughn. He'd spent his evening getting threatened by the Brands and then letting her use him as a landing pad for a meltdown. The least she could do was explain why she had freaked out.

The act of taking a deep breath hurt. "When I was about eight, my parents got wrapped up in a fundamentalist religious group. The leaders brainwashed my parents into believing that all the kids belonged to the group collective."

"Okay. That's bizarre."

Flashes of sleeping in bedrooms with eight, sometimes twelve, children zipped in front of her mind's eye. Hot, stuffy rooms, packed full of members' kids. "Seemed normal to most folks there. But, yeah, my parents didn't have a lot to do with us."

"So not very supportive?" The rolling rumble of his voice from his chest into hers gave her even more courage.

"More like not very involved. My brother and I were raised along with the other kids. On the rare occasions when we saw our parents, they treated us exactly like the other children. Cold. Businesslike. As I got older, though, I saw what happened to other girls. It was obvious the next step would be to marry me off to one of the group members."

His arms tightened around her. "How old?"

"Me? Fourteen. The selected member was fifty or so."

"That's sick."

"No argument here. The story gets even better. The last several 'wives' had come back from their honeymoons beaten to a pulp or sexually abused. Because they weren't obedient or pleasing enough or some other bull."

"Damn."

She had that strange sensation of being in a cocoon again. Comfortable and secure but not confined. A headache came and went across her forehead. Probably due to stress. "At the same time my marriage was being arranged, my brother, Kevin, who's younger by two years, was getting systematically beaten. The older men did this to most of the adolescent boys to keep them in line. Then, as they approached their mid-teen years, many of the boys disappeared. The leaders always said that the boys 'ran away,' but I had my suspicions."

"No way."

"Yes. So, when our future plans looked like pain for him and lecherous love for me, Kevin and I snuck out one night, escaped."

"And?" It sounded like the word was ripped from his throat.

A pinch formed in her chest. For a second, she was back in those terra cotta hills—dusty, sweaty, and exhausted, running for her life. "We were caught."

"Shit. What happened?"

"We both got a beating, but Kevin's was way worse. For several days, I was trapped in a small plywood room while armed men kept me from escaping. During that time, they were systematically tearing Kevin down, mentally and physically. I didn't dare try to open the door because I didn't know what they'd do to me, or Kevin, if I broke any more rules." She sighed. "Actually, no. I had a good idea what they'd do to me because another girl had gotten caught escaping a second time. Those people hurt her in every way a human can hurt another human."

"My God. I can't believe you went through that." He ran his fingers through her hair. Not sexual. But safe. Something she could get used to, damn it.

"So I was trapped for days. The worst part? I didn't know if my brother would be alive when I left that room." The texture of Vaughn's thermal shirt under her fingertips grounded her to the present, but her memories took her right back to the compound and that damned room with the moldy floor. "After they let me out, I did my chores and obeyed like a good member. I even helped plan my upcoming wedding."

The motion of his fingers paused. "What happened to Kevin?"

"He survived, but he was severely injured. He should have gone to the hospital. They beat him and left him to crawl back to one of the houses and sleep on the floor like a dog. I felt so helpless. I should have been able to help my little brother."

He squeezed her arm. "I know how you feel, wanting to protect him."

"Yeah, I bet you do, being the oldest."

"But go on, please. It's your story."

"Kevin managed to get messages to me, begging to try again to escape. He—" She gulped. "He was going to end his own life if he couldn't get out."

"No," he whispered.

"So I couldn't fail. We planned. We waited. He endured more beatings. I had to meet with my future 'husband' and sit there while he touched me. Inspecting. Even with clothes on, it was disgusting."

Vaughn's hands tightened on her upper arms as a growl came from his throat. The cocoon sensation intensified, along with her headache. Her shiver certainly had nothing to do with the cold.

"A few nights before my so-called blessed union, I picked a lock on the window and escaped. Kevin and I crawled out again and got through the fenced perimeter. This time, we made it to Salt Lake City and found an aunt and uncle who took us in."

"And then you became a doctor?"

"Eventually. And Kevin made sure no one could ever beat him up again. He's into MMA. The guy is terrifying in the ring."

"What weight class?"

"Bantamweight. Why, are you a fan?"

"Well, yes. Again, not my story. Please continue."

"The rest is history. Here I am in Copper River, paying off my loans by working in an underserved area. Kevin's in Salt Lake City working at Starbucks to support his MMA habit." She smiled into his chest and inhaled his warm scent, as heady as mulled cider, and served with a hug. "And I help him out with the finances a little bit, too. He needs something in his life to be proud of."

"He's proud of you."

"Sure." She shook her head. "But I meant personally proud. Something he can call his own. Something he's created. I'm just the nagging older sister."

"Never." He rubbed his thumb over her upper arm, sending a welcome tingle down to her fingertips. "Are you two close?"

"Talk at least every week, usually much more." The remainder of her tight fear uncoiled and released, like a terrified animal finally brave enough to walk out of its hiding spot.

"He sounds like a good guy."

"He's great. For a little brother, that is."

"I know how about that sentiment." His rolling chuckle rumbled into her chest. "You still want to keep him safe? Even now?"

She rested her cheek against his torso. "Of course. Who wouldn't, after all of the junk we dealt with?"

"Good point."

Another few minutes went by until she leaned away. "So, I should probably do something about what happened back there."

"What do you mean?"

"The part where we were threatened with guys with guns."

He snorted.

She studied the shadows of his hard face. "What?"

"I'm not laughing at you. It's just…yes. You are correct, we should at least fill out a police report."

"But?"

"But it's not going to help. They'll just say they were defending their property against trespassers. And once they learned who we were, those guys did put down the rifles. Besides, Tommy Brand, who was the guy with the messed-up eyebrow standing in front of the truck with a gun? Yeah, he's the sheriff."

"How is that possible?"

"Bad luck, I guess." He whistled low. "That family is seriously nuts." He readjusted his grip but continued to hold her. "And I don't mean to get into your business, but please don't go back over there."

"You don't need to tell me twice." She sniffed. "So I shouldn't press charges?"

"If you want to, I'll go with you. Just don't expect any results."

"Wow. Okay. But I feel like there needs to be some documentation, in case…"

"In case something else happens?"

A shudder rattled her spine. "Yeah."

His arms cranked down around her, but stopped short of pain. "Excellent point. Then let's go fill out the report now. I'll help you."

"Really? Um, thanks. And, again, sorry for ruining your evening. I'm sure you didn't plan to be gone this long. You must have better things to do."

"This is exactly where I needed to be."

"Thanks." In the illumination from the dash, she craned her neck to meet his eyes, praying to heaven she wouldn't find pity there.

Instead, a burning intensity lit his face. Not desire, exactly, and of course not, what with her meltdown this evening. More like a guy who wanted to slay someone's demons.

Well, he could have all of her demons. He was welcome to them.

Although he loosened his grip, his firm, secure presence remained. If she needed his strength, she knew it would be right there, ready to go.

She scooted off his lap and buckled up. The lack of his heat, his touch, left her cold, and not only in temperature.

"Let's go file a report, shall we?" His teeth gleamed in the darkness.

CHAPTER 17

After an exhausting hour at the police station, giving her statement to the officer on duty, Mariah stood and stretched her back. Vaughn signed the paper in front of him as well and pushed to his feet. The grim set of his mouth confirmed her guess as to how successful their efforts would be.

Only another three years for loan repayment and then she could leave this town. Hopefully, nothing else bad would happen before then.

It was well after nine o'clock when they returned to his truck. She sighed. "So, I should get back to my car and head home. Work day tomorrow, and all."

"Why don't I take you home? The hospital is on the other side of town. I can arrange to have your car brought to your house."

"No way. I couldn't ask you to do that."

"You're not asking. I'm offering."

"Well." She paused, more to get the sudden flutters under control. When had someone truly tried to stop and help her? "I hate to impose. Only if it's no hardship for you."

He shook his head. "Absolutely not. Keys on the floorboard?"

"Under the mat. How did you know?"

"No one around here locks vehicles. Most freezing mornings, you'll see trucks and cars lined up in front of the diners, keys in ignition, running. No one around here would steal anything. Besides, with your unique…car, it would be pretty obvious who stole it." A quirk flashed across his normally hard-set mouth.

"You're not picking on my used Cooper are you? I got a great deal for it in my third year of medical school."

"Let's just say it's well suited to you." He punched in a text message on his phone. "Yep. Won't be a problem to get it back to your place." He stowed the phone in a pocket and shrugged. "Small town. Everyone knows about where everyone else lives." Buckling up, he put the truck into drive.

Fifteen minutes later, he pulled into her driveway. Then he hurried around to her door before she could open it. His warm hand supported her arm as she stepped down from the truck, the firm strength warming her through the coat fabric. With a flick of his wrist, he snagged her bag and then followed her through the garage door and into the kitchen.

It didn't escape her notice that he scanned the kitchen slowly, dark eyes observing everything in sight. Then he pinned her with a quiet gaze.

"Want to check the rest of the house?" she offered.

"You mind?"

"After tonight? No. Be my guest."

As he moved quickly through the two bedrooms and bathroom, she opened and closed the kitchen drawers. She turned to the fridge and rested her forehead on the freezer door.

"Are you okay?"

She jumped. How could someone that big move so silently? Willing her pulse to slow down, she turned to him. "I should offer you food."

"But you're exhausted."

"Yeah, but no way will I sleep with everything that happened tonight." She scrubbed at her face, as if she could wipe away the bad memories.

A minute of silence stretched to two.

Denim rustled as he shifted from one foot to the other. "Do you feel comfortable with me?" he finally said.

She frowned. "Um, sure, I guess."

"A resounding vote of confidence. Hey," he lifted his hand, "I get it. Strange dude in the house. I understand."

Her heart skidded as her past battered at her, superimposing images from Utah on the man standing in front of her.

Stop it. This was Vaughn. Different man. Different situation.

Not dangerous, at least not to Mariah. She knew it deep down inside.

"You haven't done anything wrong," she said.

He pointed a thumb at his broad chest and flashed a grin. "I'm a guy. We're always messing up. As my sister likes to say, give me time." Easing onto a kitchen stool across the island, he said, "Were you okay with me a while ago, close to you, in the truck?"

Her face warmed. "Yes." Very okay, not that she'd admit that fact aloud.

"Good. Then go get ready for bed. I'll stay here."

A flicker of panic caught her off guard, and she rubbed her neck.

"If you want me to." He lifted a hand. "No funny business, I swear. You can hold onto a hammer and bash me with it if you don't feel safe. You just seem...like someone who might rest better if another person is around."

He wasn't incorrect. "But—"

"And I feel partially responsible for the Brands' treatment of you. They hate my family. If I hadn't been with you, they might not have hassled you like that."

She worried at her lower lip as her head swam. "Could have been worse."

"You got that right." He rested his hands, palms up, on the countertop. "Seriously, though. Would you be okay with me hanging out tonight? It'll make me feel a lot better, knowing you're safe."

"Really?"

"You have no idea." Why did that statement seem deeper than the mere words?

A final knot of tension unwound in her chest. One thing she knew for certain: her gut told her Vaughn Taggart was all right. Maybe his emotions were helter-skelter, but his character was solid. "Okay, then." The smile felt good after the past few hours of reliving her past hell.

Given how reassuring he was, back in the truck, his presence now might chase away some of her personal demons. And he was correct. For some odd reason, just being around him created a sensation of safety. Besides, if Vaughn misbehaved, Mariah had only to call any one of his siblings and they would knock him into line.

And bonus: she didn't have to worry about being ashamed to appear vulnerable or weak in front of him. She groaned to herself. They had passed that milestone a few hours ago.

With a tired smile, he pushed to his feet. "Still want a hammer for self-defense?"

She studied his earnest face. "No."

Once she had brushed her teeth and changed into a tank top and pajama pants, she stood in the middle of her empty bedroom, arms crossed over her chest. Shadows played on the walls, turning painted walls into plywood. Her lungs burned as she forced air in and out.

She wiggled her toes. Plush carpet. Not a rotting subfloor. Everything would be all right.

She checked the windows. No keyed locks. She could escape if need be.

Sweat formed between her breasts.

This was not a Damned. Plywood. Room.

Vaughn knocked, making her jump again. "Is it safe to open the door?"

She turned around as he eased open the door. "You're a guest here. I should get you some food. A snack."

"Watching my figure. No worries." For a guy so big, he stepped lightly as he brought in a kitchen chair and set it next to the wall, the spot farthest from her bed. He sat down, facing the bedroom door.

"You can't stay there all night."

"I will if that's what you need. Get into bed." His growl filled the small room. "You need to rest. I need to make sure you are able to rest."

"Why?"

"It's a...quirk...of mine, looking after people."

"I don't understand."

"You don't have to. Go on." He motioned.

She slipped in beneath the duvet and sheets. The space between her and Vaughn felt wrong, like the worst kind of disconnect. And it unsettled her that he sat on the other side of the room. "It's okay. You can have some of the bed."

"No, that wouldn't be right."

"We're modern-world people. Pretty sure your reputation will be intact in the morning."

"That's funny."

"Good." She patted the bed. "It's okay."

He studied her as he stood and took a few steps to her. He rested one knee on the bed. "You sure?"

"You're not what scares me." And it surprised her how that statement was true.

He took off his boots with twin thumps and sat on the edge of the bed, making the mattress dip. Sitting on top of the blankets, back propped against the headboard, positioned as close to the edge of the bed as someone could be without falling off, he then rested a big, warm hand on her upper arm.

Connection. Warmth. Safety.

Mariah did the impossible and drifted off to sleep.

CHAPTER 18

Vaughn remained wide awake, fully clothed, and firmly on top of the blankets. This whole evening, from offering to accompany Mariah to the Brand ranch to helping her deal with the memories of her past to sitting mere inches away from her as she slept, had *bad decision* written all over it. He couldn't sleep if he wanted to. His stomach rumbled, and his power rumbled right along with it, needing to continuously seek out and destroy any danger to Mariah.

The glow from other homes nearby filtered through the window shades, stippling her skin in shadow and light. A cold wind picked up, at times creating both a light whisper and a menacing growl outside.

Her light breathing trailed like nails skimming over his soul. The tiny noises she made in her sleep airmailed inappropriate ideas to his groin. Damn it, he needed to think about something else. Anything else.

Then, with all this time on his hands, he did the singular worst thing possible.

He took stock of his life.

The grand plan to swoop into Copper River, bail his family out of their troubles, and then blast back out of town, never to be seen again? That simple strategy was crumbling under his feet.

What about the training for his upcoming bout in two—he squinted at the glowing clock digits; make that one—day? The hollowness in his gut ached. He had no idea how close he was to making weight this evening. He might lose this fight before it started.

What about his life in New York? He had the beginnings of a plum job picking stocks, and he had every intention of riding that gravy train as far as it would go. But the job would only wait so long for him.

Man, he had everything he wanted back there. Money, MMA training, fight opportunities, and freedom. No one judged him for his black past. He didn't have to deal with family responsibilities in New York. And best of all, no freakin' monster or whatever the hell that thing was.

What about his so-called noble gesture to provide comfort and security to Mariah after the visit to the Brands unearthed all her demons? He focused on the breaths of the woman on the bed next to him, and a new hunger grew inside of him. Inappropriate. Way beyond "just friends," too. How noble was he now?

Judging by a hard-on that could hammer nails, yeah, he had failed to keep his intentions chaste. He shifted in a feeble attempt to relieve pressure. When she sighed again in her sleep, his balls tightened even more, ready for action.

He ran a finger over the silk of her hair, spread out over the pillow, exactly as he'd imagined.

He was screwed.

That was the problem, wasn't it? For a guy with the ability to dodge danger, he sure kept walking into emotional minefields. Good intentions followed by bad decisions, and in the end, he still hurt everyone.

Vaughn Taggart. Like the Great Wall of China, he was such a big fuckup that he was probably visible from outer space.

He had gotten way too close to Mariah, a woman who deserved more than he could ever provide. Not with his past and not with his plans.

A future with her had *not gonna happen* written all over that idea.

He let his head roll back against the backboard. Studying the ceiling didn't help. When he closed his eyes, he could still see her terrified face and feel her slight weight nestled perfectly against his chest as they sat in the truck. Shit.

He stroked her arm. It wasn't enough to watch her; he needed the physical connection as a tether for his own sanity.

How had this happened? They had met—if you could call it that—only six days ago when she saved Shelby and Eric's lives.

His own personal interest included a tangible need to lay her out naked on a bed and work her over until every part of her body glistened with sweat and desire and every inch of her skin quivered at his touch. Of course that sounded swell. But his desire went way past the physical. He didn't want purely sexual. He wanted to surround and protect her both physically and with his power.

Did he care to explore that complex set of emotions further?

Fuck, no.

She made a tiny whimper, and he cursed to himself, loosening the grip that had tightened on her arm. Rolling halfway from him, she grabbed his big hand in her smaller ones and tugged his arm over her chest.

He moved with her, not willing to wake her up, scooting down the bed until her body tucked in to his—butt to groin, back to chest. With the blankets between them, of course. The two small hands now locked around his wrist felt like the best shackles in the universe.

Only because it was convenient and more comfortable, he bent his head forward, burying his nose and mouth in her hair. He inhaled mint and a vibrant feminine scent uniquely Mariah and relaxed. Being near her calmed him as if he were some pacing lion and she the tamer.

He fought the urge, but after a few minutes, he drifted into a blessed, dreamless sleep.

A large, heavy mass prevented her from moving.

For a split second, panic darted through her, fast and sharp. Trapped. She couldn't breathe. Where was Kevin?

After a deep draw of air, she evaluated the situation.

The solid mass of Vaughn behind her provided warmth, as did the large arm clamped around her chest. To be fair, she did some clamping herself. She loosened the death grip she had on him, frowning at the imprints her fingertips had made on his thick wrist, visible even in the early morning light.

She startled as he cleared his throat next to her ear, then she rolled over, rotating within the cradle of his arm over her chest and another arm resting on the pillow above her head. His morning stubble and half-lidded expression made her heart rhythm flip into brief v-tach.

"Morning." He smiled.

That sounded like a morning-after *morning*.

Oh no. Had she slept with him, like slept-slept? Because she remembered nothing, and damn, if they had made love, at least she should have remembered it. She looked around the room. Was she any good? Was he any good? Hell, look at him. Of course he was good. Why couldn't she remember anything more than drifting off to sleep in his embrace?

She moved her legs under the sheets. Fully clothed.

Same with a jeans-clad Vaughn. And he lay on top of the blankets.

"You're funny when you get tense." The low rumble of his voice relaxed muscles deep in her pelvis.

"We didn't…?"

"No. Not that I didn't think about it a million times last night."

"Oh."

"Yeah, *oh* is right." His grin was feral and focused. The direct stare made her shiver. "You want to change that situation?"

Of course she did.

They were two consenting adults. He was rugged, strong, and cared about his family. And dollars to donuts, he would be fabulous as they engaged in luscious, muscle-bound, hot rancher sex. If the current pre-coital happiness in his arms reflected even a fraction of the during-sex awesomeness, being with Vaughn would shoot off proverbial fireworks.

So, basically, there was nothing not to like about this scenario.

Except for a future. And, okay, her own lack of self-trust.

Her wild fantasies screeched to a halt.

Mariah needed stability in a relationship. She needed security and assurances in her own decisions where a partner was concerned. Vaughn had a life elsewhere. He was only in town for a short time.

She didn't do flings. She didn't do *risk of failure*.

So, did she do Vaughn?

Not today. Maybe not ever.

"Well. Um," she said, not meeting his gaze.

That sensual mouth locked into a hard slash, and in the early morning light, his irises turned coal cold. "Never mind. I got it." He slid his arms out from under her, stood, and cracked his back and neck.

"But—"

"I can tell when a woman isn't interested."

"Of course I was interested. It's just—"

The scratch of his short nails on his stubble sent her vagina into a fit of ecstasy, and she pressed her legs together.

"What do you want, Mariah?" The sexual weight of his words was unmistakable.

Sitting up, she rested her arms on the blanket covering her legs. "I want more. Something long term. Something solid."

"You don't think I'm solid?"

Well of course she did, given the hard muscles in the arm that had held her safely all night long. "That came out wrong."

"You bet it did," he snapped.

"Why are you being so mean this morning?" Blinking hard, she forced herself to focus on the situation. No way would he get to see her cry. She grimaced. Again.

"Shit, I'm sorry. I'm all over the place. And it's not your fault." He rolled his lips. "My fucked up life and everything…"

"You keep mentioning that."

"Because it's true. But it's also not fair that the roller coaster gets taken out on you. However, that's the reality of my messy situation right now." His eyes were dark, piercing, shuttered. His arms crossed in front of his chest. "And when the Brands pointed guns at you…when Linc was right behind you…Damn it all, but that triggered something inside of me that wanted to keep you safe. I don't know what to do with that feeling."

"I should say thank you, but it feels weird in this situation."

"Mostly because we were sleeping together."

Her face burned. "Not exactly."

"You didn't come onto me? Pulling me closer?"

"You can't be serious."

"Think about how amazing we would be together." Damn his forearms with those pushed-up sleeves. She licked her lips. Cords of muscle on display like that should be illegal.

"That's not what I was–"

"Your nipples say otherwise."

"My nipples aren't talking to you." She pulled the blanket up to cover her tight, aching breasts. And since he'd drawn attention, she did want to know what his mouth would feel like on the hard tips. Damn it.

A crazy past, the weird present, and a dash of her relationship history created a toxic, sour brew. *No, thank you.*

Time to fake some confidence. "Why? You want more?" she countered.

"Hell yeah I do." He bit the tip of his thumb. "You want some details about what I'd like to do to you?" His voice dropped to one note above pure gravel. "Guarantee you'll enjoy it."

She reared back. That level of honesty made her hotter than a 105-degree fever and also made her shake in her boots. She didn't play games, but neither did Vaughn. When he turned into an open book, it wasn't by degrees.

"Well? What's it going to be? No strings attached. Give me an hour, and I can make you scream in the best possible way." Even though she had the blanket in front of her, the way his eyes raked over her made her feel utterly naked.

"I'm not doing this teasing thing."

"Won't or can't?"

Enough. This journey had no good destination. "Both." Sniffing, she raised her chin. "At the risk of sounding rude, thank you for the help on my house call and standing up to those jerks. And thank you for helping with…the rest of it last night." Too honest. Too much. She couldn't be this open. Not without trusting herself more. Not without trusting that there was a future. She was too raw right now. "But I need to get ready for work, so…" She made a point of staring at the bathroom door. "We should stay friends, Vaughn."

His expression could have formed ice crystals. "Got the message, loud and clear. Have a good day at work, then." Picking up his boots, he retreated out of the bedroom. A minute later, she cringed as he slammed her front door.

That sexual relationship with him would be fabulous but short-lived. She wanted the chance for a long-term relationship, and Vaughn Taggart wasn't it. She needed to trust herself to make a good decision.

So she got exactly what she wanted.

Absolutely nothing.

CHAPTER 19

Vaughn could turn five hours of ranch chores into a last-ditch weight-cutting effort. Sure. No problem.

Maybe at the same time, he could sweat out the memories of a certain woman who woke up in his arms a few hours ago.

While he was at it, maybe he could go backward in time to the point *before* he had flipped a switch this morning and turned into an ass. For all the help his power gave him in detecting danger, it had a massive blind spot when Vaughn was personally about to create an epic disaster.

Like how he covered for his insecurities by insulting a nice woman. Real smooth move, there. Some days, his life truly emulated a slow-moving train wreck.

He cursed as he slung more bales of hay. His mouth had gone dry, but no way could he drink anything. Not yet.

The electronic scale in the house was a tough taskmaster.

If he hadn't slept at Mariah's house, he could have started earlier on his final weight cut. But he couldn't leave her all alone last night. Hell, if he hadn't stayed in the house, he would have sat outside in his truck all night, so insistent was his ability to protect her.

He stood and wiped his sweaty forehead with his forearm.

Now he was distracted right before his bout.

Actually, seeing his competitor at the Brand family ranch had distracted him already. Linc was a nasty bastard. That guy hit hard and fought dirty. It would take all of Vaughn's skills, both physical and mental, to beat the guy tomorrow. He needed all of his focus if he had any chance to not just win but also survive the fight. He spun in a slow circle in the barn, breathing hard.

At least Vaughn's family had given him some space.

Kerr hadn't questioned the request to move Mariah's car to her house. He must have done it way late last night, because sure enough, when Vaughn exited her house at 6:00 a.m., the keys hung from the ignition of her car parked in her driveway. Moving the car was a two-person job, so another friend or family member must have participated. Vaughn needed to thank them later.

But he'd be damned if he would explain to anyone what he was doing at Mariah's house last night. Or not doing.

How exactly would he label last night's spoon-fest disaster?

That moment when she woke up and gazed at him with that vulnerable expression would stay etched in his mind forever.

After all these years, he had experienced the perfect night with a woman, and they had both remained clothed. Hell, he had volunteered to freeze his ass off by remaining on top of the covers.

At what prior point in his life, ever, had he resisted a beautiful woman?

Maybe he had finally learned something from that fuckup with Garrison's ex-wife and after being used by that social climber back in New York.

"Want to take a break?" Garrison's even voice startled him.

Vaughn tugged the hoodie tighter around his head and kept on heaving seventy pound bales of hay from one location to another. "Can't. Two more pounds to go."

"Yeah, thought you'd gotten pudgy."

He snorted. "As if."

Garrison jutted out his chin, begging Vaughn to take a swing at it. "Trying to impress someone?"

"Yep. The fight official at the weigh-in tonight."

"Right." His brother didn't say anything for a solid minute. "Why do you keep fighting?"

Wiping sweat, Vaughn said, "One. I'm good at it. Two. I like the sport itself. Three. I like the discipline of staying in shape and improving my sorry self. Four. It keeps me sober."

"Don't you think there's an unfair advantage?"

"With my power? Maybe. It's got me out of a lot of bad situations over the years, but not all of them." Obviously. "There's something satisfying about beating the crap out of someone who very much wants to beat the crap out of me. What's even better is turning the fight into art. Using the fancy techniques to put someone on their ass or submit them. If I can get an ankle bar submission, that's cooler than a plain KO. The submission takes more planning, more strategy and leverage. More subtle proficiency."

"Okay, okay, I get it, Mr. *Artiste*. You're the Rembrandt of MMA. But you and I both know you're perfectly happy knocking someone out cold with bare knuckles."

"Well, sure."

Garrison shook his head. "I still say you're dragging your demons out into the ring and beating them up in the name of tortured redemption, but that's one man's opinion." He leaned against a beam. "What would you do if your power cut out while you were in a fight?"

"Not sure why that would happen, but if it did, I'd keep fighting."

"Wouldn't you be kind of…blind?"

"Maybe. But if my training is solid, it shouldn't matter. I don't use my danger-detecting ability in every fight, you know."

"Interesting."

"Are you out here to talk MMA? Or something else? Because I have to keep moving."

"No. I'm worried about what we're up against. What's going on here at home." Garrison paused. "Where your skills are most needed."

Ah, the real agenda. "Don't lay that guilt trip on me."

"Wouldn't dream of it."

"Yeah, right." He walked to the punching bag and started pounding the hell out of it. Anything to keep the sweat going. He paused. "You got new ideas about that creature since we last encountered it? Because that thing is scary as hell. Any connection as to how it relates to the Brands?"

"Nothing about the Brands makes sense. But, no, I can't figure out a connection."

"Their place is weird."

"Kerr said you went to the Brands' place." Garrison rubbed his jaw.

"Long story. Took Dr. West on a house call. The Brands really rolled out the red carpet, loaded guns, insults, and nasty behavior. Even cousin Linc was there to help."

"Linc?"

"Lincoln McDowell. The bastard I'm fighting tomorrow. Man, he's a big fucker."

"That's oddly convenient to have him hanging around, isn't it?"

Bambambambam. "That's what I thought. But, apparently, he's somehow related to those nut jobs over there. Anyway, the visit was downright terrifying, what with the creepy people and veiled threats."

"What did you do?"

"Got her the hell out of there as soon as humanly possible and took her to file a police report." And no, Vaughn wasn't about to share his part in the sappy episode where she poured out her deepest, most horrible secret and he comforted her in the truck. Or the not-sex later that night.

His brother snorted. "Good luck with the police helping."

"We had to do something."

"I agree." He stared up at the rafters. "You're at least in good company. Kerr and I got a similar warm weapon reception when the Brands kicked us off National Forest land near their property three weeks back."

"Now they own public land?" Memories of the fear written on Mariah's face made him slam his fist into the bag harder with each blow. That bag had become the face of any number of people over at that ranch.

"No telling how those guys think. All we know for certain is that Hank did bad things, then disappeared. And it's obvious that Wyatt's gotten weirder over the past several weeks. Best we can tell, the Brands are likely still cooking up some scheme to get our ranch. They're into mining or something. Maybe they want to strike it rich." Garrison scuffed his work boot on the dirt floor. "Oh, and they burned down the barn and probably stole a bunch of our cattle. You know, that, too."

"Yeah. Details." Vaughn wiped sweat. "So what the fuck was that black thing then?" He sniffed. "Hell, I'm just glad that Ruth and Odie bought the song and dance about a bear coming in the yard and how we needed to yell and shoot a gun to shoo it away. If Ruth leaves now, I'm not sure what will happen to Dad…" Not a thought he wanted to follow to a conclusion. "But about that black cloud thing. You really think the creature has something to do with the Brands?"

"Kind of feels that way, but I can't figure out how. I don't have your gift of detecting danger, but I sure as hell can see that we all need to be careful and stick together."

Vaughn pulled a punch and slowed the swing of the bag. "What *are* you saying?"

His brother shook his head. "Just saying it's good you're here right now. And I'm glad you're doing...better." Meaning not drinking and not "adultering." Reasonable enough.

Could he stay here? Another twinge nailed him in the chest. No way. Too much history, too many ghosts. Too much responsibility. Too many expectations. Garrison should have been the oldest. He had done a great job of keeping the family and the ranch going.

Except for Dad.

And the barn.

And Shelby and Eric.

But whose fault were those incidents, anyway?

CHAPTER 20

Despite being flattened by Hurricane Vaughn, Mariah felt super duper fabulous as she trudged through a never-ending day of work on Friday.

Truthfully, a lot of the collapse of the Very Good Night had to do with her hang-ups, where her past and her past relationships were concerned. Poor guy had no idea about the minefield he'd wandered into and pretty much got caught in the blast zone.

But his mixed messages didn't help, either. He was right: he needed to get a grip on his seesawing emotions. And he needed to get a grip on his past and stop it from affecting the future. Or the present.

They were a hot mess separately, but together?

She had an inkling about his past mistakes, so that was exhibit A. Then last night's sexy not-sex served as exhibit B. Guy went out of his way to help out, protected her from moron ranchers with guns, provided light counseling duties, and then spent the night letting her use him as a security blanket.

What woman wouldn't be all goo-goo eyed over that tender scenario?

A woman with massive abandonment and confinement issues, that's who.

Granted, she had good reason for her personal issues. But her history wasn't anything she'd project on her worst enemy, much less a warm, delicious-smelling, hard-muscled rancher. Who fit perfectly into worn jeans.

Mariah sighed as her ovaries squirmed. *Down, girls.* She had strict parameters for what she did and did not require from an acceptable partner, and not sticking around town removed Vaughn from the checklist early.

She turned back to the computer and clicked on her patient list. A few more people to see and then she could take her coworkers up on the offer to get drinks after office hours. Working tomorrow's local MMA bout would bring a nice change of pace to this bizarre week.

Pushing open the exam room door, she brightened at the sight of her next two patients.

"Hi, Shelby. Eric. How are you two doing?"

"Feeling great. When can I drive again?" The bruises on half of Eric's face moved as he talked, making an interesting light purple, green, and yellow rainbow.

Shelby elbowed him and squinted. "If you can drive, then I can drive."

"You have bolts of metal attached to your leg. Besides, you still can't see," he protested.

"Hey, I can see a lot better than a few days ago. Besides, you're not a doctor." She shot him an impish smile with a lift to her chin.

"You know, I can be. If you're lucky." He winked at her.

"Dude. Here? Seriously?" A corner of Shelby's mouth quirked as she raised a shoulder. "Sorry," she said to Mariah. "Head injury and all. He doesn't know what he's saying." She shifted in her seat, readjusting the leg with the external fixator, and groaned.

The sound flipped Eric's flirty grin into a tight grimace, and he wrapped a hand around her shoulder.

Mariah's chest twisted in on itself. She cleared her throat. "So, tell me how things have been going since you both left the hospital."

Shelby's vision had improved to the point where she could see blurry faces. Mariah unwound the bandage from the metal and pins around Shelby's lower leg, checking the wound edges and the stability of the external fixator frame. The ex-fix would stay on for another week or so until orthopedics removed it and readjusted the internal hardware. For now, there was no evidence of infection, thank goodness.

Eric passed his neurologic tests with flying colors. Per the specialist's recommendations, he had to stay on light duty, with no driving for another week until Mariah could retest him. One look at Shelby's fierce scowl, and he closed his mouth on whatever he was about to say.

"Need help getting out to the car?" Mariah asked.

"No, my brother's in the waiting room."

"Vaughn?" Heat climbed her neck as the word escaped before she could stop it.

Shelby smiled like a Cheshire cat. Mariah groaned to herself.

"No. Kerr's doing the driving today." An eyebrow rose. "Vaughn's at the fight weigh-in tonight."

"Weigh-in?" A weird prickle walked down her spine. No.

"The MMA bout in Lander tomorrow. Poor guy turned himself inside out this morning trying to make the last bit of weight."

One: How did Mariah not pick up the clues that he was an MMA fighter going to *that* fight?

Because he had focused on Mariah during their conversations.

Two: Why did he have to make weight at the last minute?

Because he had been helping Mariah with the house call and ministering to her neuroses. Great. The guy had spent time he didn't have helping her out.

Tucking her tail between her legs and slinking into the corner sounded really good right about now.

Oh no. She would have to see him tomorrow night. It had to be the same event. Her pulse skipped a beat. Hey, it wasn't her fault that she didn't know he was a local fighter. She had only been working the Wyoming fights for the past few months. Still learning the various local characters. Like Linc McDowell.

Who she would also have to see. She shuddered.

Time to don the professional armor.

The beats in her chest finally slowed down. She pasted a bland smile on her face. "That sounds interesting." Interesting? Who the hell said *interesting*? Like a bug collection interesting? Or maybe a car accident on the side of the road where the EMS crew had to use the freakin' Jaws of Life interesting?

Shelby flicked her gaze toward Mariah as a ghost of a smirk lit her face. "So are we okay to get on out of here?" She balanced on one leg and fitted the crutches under her arms.

Eric hovered until Shelby glared at him and he backed off. Then she flashed a big grin at Mariah. "Have to keep the men off-balance." She tilted her head toward him. "Don't let them know you're into them or they'll want to get all squishy and caveman on you."

Mariah's mouth gaped. "What?"

"Squishy?" Eric crossed his arms. "I'm head injured. I have zero memory of anything I might or might not have said to you in the past."

"Don't worry. I'll remind you of all the sappy stuff you said, dude." She shook her head, moving the wild orange curls. "See you later, Dr. West." She slowly made her way out of the exam room.

Behind her back, Eric circled his temple with a finger and mouthed *sorry*. Then he shrugged and followed her out the room.

Mariah might as well have given Shelby her journal. Was nothing private in this town?

Had Shelby been talking to Vaughn? Unlikely. That guy didn't strike her as the sharing type, even with his family.

She shook her head as she went into the next exam room.

Tomorrow night she'd see Vaughn again. Chances were, he wouldn't be thrilled by her presence.

Yay. Something to look forward to.

The drinks after work tonight with friends had ceased to be optional. Mariah was going to need them.

CHAPTER 21

The faint scent of sweat, male body spray, and a sharp undertone of adrenaline mixed with testosterone assailed Mariah as she entered the back door of Owl Creek Casino on Saturday afternoon.

"Hi, Doc," Angelo, the bear of a fight promoter for Out West MMA, glanced up from his desk as she passed it. "Thanks for helping us out again."

"For you? Anytime." She laughed as his half hug enveloped her. Once Angelo learned she was Kevin West's big sister, she had become Angelo's family by default. Didn't hurt that her brother had headlined an outstanding bantamweight fight for Out West last summer.

He tugged his suit back into place and handed her a paper. "Here's the final list. Fights start in two hours, if you can get the fighters ready."

"Of course. Hey, who's working with me today?"

"Dr. John Brandeis. He's running late and asked for you to do the pre-fight physicals; he'll stay late to finish the post-fights."

She gulped. "Sounds fair. Everything in the locker rooms?"

"As always, it's all ready." His smile pushed his cheeks up until his eyes disappeared.

"Anything else for me?"

With a wink, he reached around to a short file cabinet behind him and produced a disposable cup of steaming, aromatic coffee. She sipped and sighed.

Then, glancing down the list, she felt her heart sank when she reached the second-to-last fight. As she had feared, Vaughn was fighting in the light heavyweight division against Linc.

A shiver worked its way up her back to settle on her neck. Linc. She had worked a fight where he had competed before. Everyone knew Linc's reputation. That jerk had been around for years, sprinkling bad attitude and dirty tricks around many regional matches.

As for women being anywhere near the octagon? His opinions were clear: ring girls were the only females allowed near the ring. Not as fighters or officials and certainly not as a ringside doctor. The last time Mariah had done his pre-fight, he figured out who her brother was, and from there she rode a downhill spiral of his veiled, disrespectful comments. God help her if she ever disqualified him from a fight.

With a deep breath, she pushed her shoulders back. Passing the arena, busy with workers setting up chairs and testing the light and PA systems, she entered the backstage area where makeshift locker rooms had been set up.

Nodding to the suit-clad inspector as she entered the makeshift exam room, she checked her equipment. Blood pressure cuff, pulse ox, a box of vinyl gloves, a penlight, and fight forms on a clipboard, all ready. She shrugged off her blazer, draped her stethoscope over her neck, and indicated to the inspector to send in the first fighter.

Twelve fighters later, the door opened and Linc stalked in, took one look at her, and snorted. Good lord, he was a big guy when she'd seen him at the ranch. But up close and this pumped up, the man was more than a little scary. If he wasn't on steroids, then he had the best training regimen she'd ever seen. Sure enough, she turned the key on the urine cup he presented for his drug screen and it came up as clean. The guy radiated strength and killer instinct, and judging by his snarl, knew it all too well. He stopped bare inches from her, invading her personal space and hovering over her, like he'd done at the Brand ranch.

Trapped.

Didn't matter that the nice fight inspector stood ten feet away from her. Stomach acid bubbled up. She shoved it back down and faced Linc as she disposed of her gloves. No way would she let him get the satisfaction of scaring her. Again.

"Have a seat." She motioned to the chair as she fought an urge to cover her chest.

The inspector wouldn't notice Linc's tiny delay, but Mariah read the disrespect, loud and clear. Her skin twitched. It wasn't that the guy towered over her and could tear her arm off without breaking a sweat. Lots of fighters—men and women—were strong. This guy was different. Personally intimidating.

Threatening.

She needed to get through the exam and move on.

"Arm, please."

Another pause and he lifted his arm for the blood pressure cuff. Only he didn't bring it all the way up, so she had to bend down.

While the cuff inflated, he sneered at her. "Nice seeing you again, Doc. Your brother still training at that loser gym in Salt Lake?"

Ripping the Velcro cuff off, she then punched a button on the pulse ox machine. "Finger, please."

Damn him if he didn't give his middle one.

Again, nothing overt, but his leer made her want to hide. She recorded results and removed the devices. Ignoring the sweat irritating her upper lip, she settled the stethoscope earpieces in place. "Deep breath."

He complied, staring at her chest the entire time.

"Any head injuries lately?"

"For me or the guys I've fought?" He grinned. "Naw. I'm solid."

"Any skin infections?"

"Nope."

"Been ill recently?"

"Touch of the clap, but penicillin took care of that."

She tapped the clipboard with a pen. "You want me to write that down?"

"Hey, take a joke, babe."

She met his glare with one of her own. "Push me and I'll document everything you say. Communicable diseases, real or suspected, are cause to pull fighters from the bout."

"You pull me and that would be the last thing on Earth that you ever did, babe."

A weird sensation, like a flutter of a gauze curtain, formed between her and Linc. Then, with a stab of a headache into her temple, the feeling was gone. Stress reaction, maybe?

"Everything okay?" the inspector spoke up. He looked at Mariah.

"Hey, just two old friends joking, man." Linc snorted. "Carry on, Doc."

She held out her hands. Damned things were trembling. "Show me your hands."

He offered his giant paws and she flipped them over, checking each side for tender spots or broken bones.

Extending two fingers from both her hands, she said, "Squeeze." Most normal fighters gave a gentle pressure. Not this jerk. Damned if he didn't crank down on her like a sadistic vice grip. She bit back a cry. "Okay."

After signing the bottom of the page, she set down the clipboard. "You're cleared."

"Good." He turned back. "Hey, what's the deal with you and that pansy-ass, Vaughn Taggart?"

Stifling the urge to roll her eyes, she said, "There's no deal."

"Good, because you should know that Wyatt is here tonight."

"The same jerk who pointed a gun at me when I tried to care for his sick mother?"

"He was only showing affection and concern for your safety. He really has the hots for you." Linc grinned. "It's mutual, right?"

"In what alternate universe is that *affection*?"

"Oh." Linc's thinking face almost made her laugh. "He said you two have a thing going."

"Uh, no. Maybe in his dreams." The thought of being in the same space as Wyatt turned her stomach almost as much as hanging around Linc. Worse yet, the thought of Wyatt coming here as a ploy to see her again made her grind molars.

He rubbed his thick jaw. "Funny, when he found out you were working this event, he begged to be my corner guy." Dusting off his hands, he smirked. "Well, this evening is going to be awkward for everyone, isn't it?" Linc grinned, and a weird red flare in his irises came and went. Then another flash of a headache shot across her forehead. Before she could examine a connection between the two things, he snipped, "See you in the ring, babe."

Hopefully not. Thank goodness there was another doctor working with her tonight.

"Next," she managed to say, rubbing her temples.

The air shifted as the door opened and closed, and the spicy scent of shaving cream wafted past her. She suppressed the flutter beneath her ribs. No way could she show Vaughn how much his presence affected her.

But for the love of God, could he put a shirt on already? One glance at his smooth, tattooed chest made her face tingle. Not to mention how she quivered as the ridges of muscle rippled when he walked toward her. His right bicep had spirals of tattooed thorns done so well, it looked like the barbs pierced his skin.

"Have a seat, please."

He froze a few feet into the room. "What are you doing here?"

With a grin, she said, "I sometimes work as a fight physician for local events. Surprised?"

A corner of his serious mouth rose. "Not surprised that you can do the job. More surprised that you're here in this, uh, rough environment. It's just…out of context."

As in, his last memory of her involved a freak-out, fully clothed therapy session where she was a delicate flower? Understandable.

"I got into ringside doctor gigs in Salt Lake City when Kevin started fighting. It was a nice way to pick up a few extra bucks in residency. Now? It's something he and I have in common: love of MMA. Maybe I don't fight, but we're both participating."

"We're lucky to have you." Why did that sound like a promise? Wishful thinking, probably.

He eased into the chair, knees apart, and the band of his blue fight shorts peeked out from beneath the baggier shorts he wore over them. The cords in his thick legs tightened under the hair-dusted skin, and her mouth went dry.

A brain short circuit ruined her for a solid five seconds as she imagined him wrapping those legs around her while he held her tight to that chest and rolled her under him with a sexy judo move.

No. Don't go there.

She rubbed her neck. Why hadn't she pulled the blazer on over her gray button-down shirt?

As Vaughn followed her every move with his dark eyes, she shivered but for a very different reason than with Linc. Vaughn didn't look like a killer stalking small prey. Oh, no. He looked like a starving man watching steak sizzle on the grill.

Dinner analogies aside, did he have any idea how badly Linc could hurt him?

Oh, man.

His thick brows drew together as she smoothed the Velcro of the blood pressure cuff on his arm. "Are you okay?" he asked.

She paused. "Why wouldn't I be?"

"Nothing. Just a…feeling I had a few minutes ago waiting in the hall while Linc was in here with you."

Linc intimidated the hell out of her, but that wasn't Vaughn's problem. "It was fine."

"Did he do anything mean?"

"Nothing," she snapped. Cutting her eyes to the inspector and back, she said, too brightly, "Now, let's get your exam finished up, okay?" She removed the blood pressure cuff and pulse ox device.

He jammed his mouth into a tight line.

"Deep breath." She listened to his heart and lungs. Wow, ink on his back, too. Latin and more thorns. Very nice. "Good. Hands, please."

His were sturdy as two rocks. When he squeezed her fingers, warmth flowed through the solid but not painful grip. His touch seeped like melted caramel up her arms and into her chest and belly. What would that firm grip feel like on her arms? Her breasts? Oh, God, what about on her...

Stopping herself before she licked her lips, she stepped back. Anything to get hold of her overreacting libido. "Any injuries lately?"

He paused. The corners of his sensual mouth crept upward, triggering a wash of warmth over her neck. "Nothing physical."

Good one. "All right, you're cleared. Good luck."

"Maybe we can talk after the fight?"

"Sure thing."

As in *no*.

No way would she stick around and wait for him. No matter how much their chemistry intrigued her, she had made her feelings clear.

She would leave as soon as her fight duties were completed and stay far away from the temptation that was Vaughn Taggart. The guy possessed everything her body wanted and nothing her heart could handle.

CHAPTER 22

Fuck it all. Mariah. Here.

The black slacks that hugged her curves and a gray shirt that skimmed her chest down to a trim waist were business casual clothes designed to drive him insane.

Despite his appreciation for her attire, all he wanted to do was peel every last garment off. Damn it. He was in trouble.

Hell, his hands ached with his need to see if they would truly fit around that waist. Her rich brown hair was pulled back in a low ponytail, showing off the soft skin of her neck that begged to be kissed, licked, and tasted.

Not going to happen. Ever. She'd made her decision clear.

Even worse, when Linc was in there with Mariah, Vaughn's power had gone all Geiger counter, crackling and buzzing through his brain like a cloud of deranged hornets.

Now, outside of the changing room, he leaned on the cement wall and did whatever mental tricks he could muster to pull himself together for this fight and prepare to deal with that stupid Neanderthal. The last thing Vaughn needed was a distraction.

Mariah West was a massive distraction. More specifically, how his power responded to her was a massive distraction.

Shit.

Even now, his power wanted to ping back to her location, find her, wrap that invisible bubble of protection around her. Even worse, with his stress level so high, he could use a stiff drink or four. He licked his lips, shook his head. No.

What about Mariah? What the hell was she doing here? When he had a chance to talk with her later, he'd tell her to...to what? He had no right to dictate her activities. His opinion meant nothing. He wasn't anything to her. And she was...what? Someone he'd like to get to know more, sure, but for all the reasons they had parsed, getting to know her wasn't going to happen. Therefore, he was nothing to her and vice versa.

Or at least, nothing he'd admit to. And that was the crux of the entire problem. Christ, could this evening get any worse?

"Hey, asshole."

His gut clenched. A whiff of burnt matches irritated his nose.

Wyatt Brand.

"What the fuck are you doing here, Brand?"

Wyatt's eye twitched. "Hanging with my cousin. I'm his corner man."

"Since when did you become a corner guy?"

"It's a free country. People can do what they like. Besides, I'm a fan." He adjusted his black jeans. "A fan of that tasty doctor. She digs me, you know. It's nice being here with her."

It took every ounce of willpower not to drive Brand's face through the back of his skull. "You came here to make a pass at Mariah? After threatening her at the ranch?"

"She got to see me as I defended my property. Probably turned her on."

"You're one messed up dude." Vaughn leaned forward. "Friendly warning: stay the hell away from her."

"You can't touch me or you get the big DQ tonight." He swiped a knuckle past his nose. "Hey, good luck out there tonight. You're gonna need it."

"What are you talking about?"

An insincere grin contorted his features. "Let's just say Linc has a secret weapon in his corner."

"What?" Maybe Linc was juiced. Wouldn't put it past the dirty fighter.

"Can't tell you." A strange, red glow flashed across the guy's eyes. Had Vaughn imagined it? Possibly. His nerves were stretched like a thin wire. But something about those red eyes reminded Vaughn of the creature on the ranch. Shit.

Wyatt snickered. "That's for you to find out. If you're lucky, they'll call the fight before he kills you."

"Whatever. I don't have time for empty threats." Or head games right before a bout.

He nodded to the inspector approaching. "Sooner or later, it'll be your funeral."

Unable to do anything without disqualifying himself from the fight, Vaughn knocked shoulders against Wyatt as he pushed into the locker room. Holy fuck, he wanted to destroy that man.

Why? Because the guy was a dick? No law against that.

Because Brand had the stones to come out here and make a pass at Mariah, when Vaughn's feeble attempt had crashed and burned?

Slumping on a bench, he scrubbed his hands over his face. Damn it. He needed to get a grip on his brain, his emotions, his ability to fight...or he wouldn't end up losing. He could end up dead.

Mariah's colleague, John Brandeis, was stitching up a fighter in the locker room. The woman who had lost the bout before Vaughn's fight had sustained an impressive cut above the eyebrow, and John was up for suture duty.

Which left Mariah to monitor the fight between Vaughn and Linc.

The shouts of the spectators swelled around her, anticipation driving them into a frenzy. Linc had a reputation for devastating his opponents, and, according to Angelo, Vaughn hadn't fought locally in a few years. The crowd welcomed Vaughn home.

But the crowd also wanted blood.

Vaughn's blood.

Her job placed Mariah firmly in a lose-lose situation. If she stopped the fight to protect Vaughn, he would never speak to her again. Fighters despised anyone who ended the fights. But if she didn't intervene, Linc could inflict serious damage. Or kill Vaughn. This fight was no joke.

The lights dimmed. Zips of adrenaline shot ice and heat through her veins.

Linc walked out from backstage, hoodie pulled over his head, AC/DC's "Dirty Deeds Done Dirt Cheap" blaring over the PA system, and he swaggered like the champion of the entire world. The crowd roared as he ripped off the hoodie. Linc sneered over her while the cutman smeared Vaseline on his brows and cheekbones.

One of his entourage grinned and licked his meaty mouth. She groaned. Wyatt Brand.

She'd rather eat mud than be around that guy. After the incident at the hospital and then again at the ranch...God, he was so creepy, especially how he scanned her up and down. Didn't matter that she had the blazer on. She crossed her arms.

After Linc entered the octagon and his crew went to the other side of the ring, the music changed to the screaming angst-filled chorus of Linkin Park's "Numb." The shouted vocals and streaking guitar chords fit with the thick, angry mood.

Vaughn came out shirtless, letting the crowd see all of him. Raw. Sweaty. Powerful.

When he stopped a few feet away from her, she gulped. His dark blue Spandex fight shorts covered him from his narrow waist to the top of his solid thighs. As for the front of the shorts? *Give that man a standing ovulation, ladies.*

As if sensing her perusal, he turned his head and winked. Like today was no different than any other day.

What if every day held a view like this? *Quit it.* She needed to concentrate on the fight and do her job.

He entered the octagon, the announcer bellowed the introductions and rules, and the ref lowered his hand.

Instead of touching Vaughn's outstretched glove, Linc feinted and kicked his leg. Pain turned to brutal focus as gold glinted in the furious depths of Vaughn's dark eyes.

He withstood a flurry of jabs from Linc and sidestepped when the guy shot to his knees in a takedown attempt. A well-placed kick to the ribs knocked Linc on his ass, but the guy jumped up like he felt nothing.

Mariah held her breath and wiped her sweaty palms on her pants.

During the next furious exchange, Linc missed a bunch of shots, almost like Vaughn fought a half step ahead of the guy. Must be great reflexes.

Then, Linc's fist connected with Vaughn's cheekbone, and Vaughn staggered and hit the cage wall.

Linc laughed.

Vaughn raised his gloves to defend himself.

Mariah's heart pounded, each thud a miniature of the blows the men exchanged. Her head ached.

Linc's fist shot out and caught Vaughn again on the left cheek, knocking him to the mat. In a flash, Linc had top mount position, pounding away until Vaughn flexed his torso, rolled, brought his legs up, and clamped them onto Linc. The individual cords of muscles in Vaughn's taut calves and thighs shook with effort to pull Linc down and away from his face.

Mariah's own legs burned, locked as they were while she watched.

The crowd screamed. Her ears rang. Linc drew back a massive fist and dropped it down on Vaughn, who deflected the brutal face blow at the last minute.

As Linc leaned forward, his forearm forced Vaughn's trachea inward, pushing harder and harder. Vaughn's face turned beet red. Sweat and blood from a cut on his forehead rolled down his temple. He couldn't breathe. If the brutal pressure continued, the cartilage would be crushed.

She didn't move.

Thank God the bell rang and the ref stepped in.

The men separated, but not before Linc spun and caught Vaughn in the upper arm, Vaughn's grunt of pain audible over the gasps of the crowd.

She studied the men in their corners and then checked over to the ref. The official shook his head. No need for Mariah to enter the cage; both men would fight another round.

Oh, God. Could Vaughn survive five rounds?

The Latin script on his chest rose and fell rapidly as he sucked in lungfuls of air.

The bell rang. She held her breath as Linc drove Vaughn back with hands that fell like deadly bricks. Even worse, for some reason, Vaughn kept glancing over at her, opening himself up to even more brutal blows to the face and kicks to the legs.

Why the hell wasn't he paying attention to the fight? He needed to defend himself or Linc would kill him.

"Hi, Mariah."

She jumped.

Hot, foul breath blew by her.

"Wyatt, move away. You can't be here. I'm working." She continued to monitor the fight. When his hand drifted over her lower back and below, she flinched away. Damn this guy. Another brief headache stabbed her in the temple.

"How about breakfast in bed tomorrow?" He chuckled.

Seriously? She hazarded a quick check. Yeah, he was about to put his other slimy hand on her. Although she wanted to yell at him, she had to concentrate on keeping the fighters safe. Make that one particular fighter. When Vaughn's focus drifted over to her again, Linc tagged him in the ear. Vaughn stumbled back into the cage, shaking his head like he needed to clear it.

A lump formed in her throat. Oh, God. She'd never gotten this emotional over a fight.

Wyatt's hand closed on her shoulder. Gross. Mariah leaned away. "Get away from me now or I'll have security called."

"After you witness Taggart get beat to death, maybe you'll be more interested in me." Wyatt's voice grated along her nerves.

"Get out of my space. Now." She put as much force into her words as possible.

She waved to get Angelo's attention, ten seats over. The promoter's brows shot up as he shoved out of his seat and motioned for nearby security personnel to join him. With a determined scowl, he waded through the crowd toward her.

A tingle of warmth seeped over her. Like fine chain mail. Light but secure. Followed by that headache. A compulsion forced her gaze back to Vaughn. He squinted at her and shuffled his feet to move sideways and avoid a lethal roundhouse kick.

Wyatt tightened a hand on her waist. "You'll be crawling back to me soon. Very soon."

Having his breath on her neck made her want to scour her skin with bleach. "Leave me alone or you're going to be in big trouble."

His laugh, like a sack of rocks tumbling, made her grit her teeth.

"No. You'll be in trouble." He snickered. "And pretty boy is getting his ass handed to him up there. Hope you're ready to do some CPR." He pointed as Linc unleashed another hammer of a fist into Vaughn.

Angelo slid between her and Wyatt, pulling her away from the jerk and setting her behind the considerable bulk of his body. Security grabbed Wyatt and removed him from the arena.

She patted Angelo's arm and stepped away to refocus her attention on the fight.

Just in time for her to watch Vaughn eat a knee to the face and crumple to the mat, courtesy of a snarling Linc.

CHAPTER 23

What a goddamned nightmare.

Vaughn needed to end this fight, pronto, or it would end him. Those punches were harder than any he'd felt in his life. Like, even the knuckles didn't feel right. Vaughn would bet his left nut that the cheater had illegal fiberglass layered under the gauze beneath the gloves.

Another concrete fist glanced off Vaughn's cheekbone, making him see Tweety Birds for a second. He had to stay on his feet. Couldn't go down.

Holy fucking mother of God, this was bad.

Didn't help that his mental power kept shorting out, demanding that his attention focus on Mariah. Every time that damned ability flowed to her, he lost the beat that kept him ahead of Linc's rapid strikes. Another bad blow like that roundhouse a few seconds ago, and that bastard would drop kick Vaughn's head into next week.

When Wyatt snuck up behind Mariah, Vaughn almost climbed out of the octagon, so badly did his power beg him to get over there and protect her. And when that slime wad dared to touch her? Screw the fight. He'd kill Wyatt and then take out anyone who got near her.

What the actual hell was wrong with him? He ate another fist. Damn it. He swiped his glove over his mouth. It was a miracle he didn't spit out teeth.

One more scan outside the cage; Angelo now stood behind Mariah like an oversized guard dog, and two inspectors were positioned on either side of her. She was safe. Good.

One problem solved.

Next problem? Staying conscious so that the referee or the good doctor had no excuse to stop the fight.

And staying alive. That was important, too.

He sucked wind as Linc nailed him in the solar plexus with his foot. Good shot. Had nothing to do with rigged gloves, either. But the uppercut that followed? Yeah, that *thunk* was all counterfeit goods.

Shit. As the bell rang to end another round, Vaughn stumbled to his corner. His friends from Bar None MMA rubbed his muscles and shoved freezing, wet sponges on his head and neck, waking him the hell up. The cutman nailed a bleeding spot with the epinephrine swab. Stung like the devil.

Damn it. No way could he last five rounds with Linc. Not with Vaughn's ability on the fritz. Not with those illegal fists.

Those first two rounds went to Linc, no question. Vaughn had to finish this ass wipe once and for all or Linc would finish him instead.

As the seconds ticked down, he did a mental shakedown on his ability, pulling it around him like a blanket. Mariah was safe.

Now. Time for Vaughn to end this joke of a fight. Time to feed his demons. Time to destroy Linc. Did he have enough left in the tank?

He glanced over at Mariah, her wide eyes swimming in that pale face.

Her fear was unacceptable.

As he met Linc's icy glare across the cage, Vaughn's rage grew like a magma chamber under the earth, pushing his world into a new shape. The heat inside of him turned him into a crucible, fired to the point of shattering.

Vaughn wanted her safe and protected? To meet that goal, he'd have to go through Linc.

Suited Vaughn just fine.

Vaughn pushed to his feet as the bell rang.

Mariah held her breath.

After the first two rounds, normal fighters would come out of their corner tired or in pain. Not him. With a glare locked onto Linc, Vaughn strode out to the center of the ring, refused to touch gloves—and unleashed a blurry barrage of punches, kicks, sweeps, and combinations. Every time Linc pressed him, Vaughn dodged, like Neo in *The Matrix* watching the bullets pass slowly by him.

Linc still got some blows through the offensive onslaught, but if Vaughn noticed the crunches and thuds of fist on flesh, he gave zero indication.

One hit.

It would take only one blow to the head or body to end the fight, for either man. It would take one blow to end the fighter's life, too. Unable to look away, she leaned forward, taking a step away from Angelo.

The two fighters circled each other, jabbing as they moved forward and then feinting back several steps. Sweat and blood dripped down both of their battered faces.

Around her, the crowd screamed its approval.

Vaughn's left cheek had already turned purple and sported an oozing cut, but his left eye was open. Linc, on the other hand, had one eye that threatened to swell completely shut. The cut on his brow dripped blood but didn't appear to impair his vision. He'd need stitches afterward, of course. By the way Linc was fighting, nothing would stop him from killing Vaughn.

If the serious scowl of concentration on Vaughn's face was any indication, the feeling was mutual.

Ten seconds remaining in the round.

Vaughn's fists blurred in muscle-driven hisses of air as he pummeled Linc to the ground and kept pounding on the man. Mariah winced at the thuds of fist impacting flesh and bone. Linc's eyes glazed over. He stopped defending himself.

Ref, call the fight. Dear God. Call it.

As the ref lifted a hand, about to reach in, the bell rang. Vaughn jumped off Linc and strolled to his corner. Like he wasn't exhausted. Like he didn't have burning arms.

Just another day at work for the guy.

His massive chest heaved, and then slowed to a normal breathing pattern over about thirty seconds. Amazing.

Linc still laid on the floor of the octagon, the ref talking to him.

When the ref motioned to Mariah, her heart dropped—like off a cliff.

The crowd booed.

Linc sat up and waved off the ref, even as Mariah entered the cage. Her steps faltered at the sharp scents of adrenaline, sweat, and blood.

"Check him out, Doc," the ref called to her. "I need an opinion."

Sweat beaded her upper lip as she knelt next to Linc. "Tell me your name."

He pulled out his spit-and blood-covered mouthpiece. "Lincoln fucking McDowell, dammit."

"The month and year?"

"October. 2014."

Wrong answer.

"Where are you?" She projected her voice above the shouts of the crowd.

"In the octagon, about to fight again. So you'd better get out of my way, babe." His words slurred together, the consonants running over each other. His unswollen eyelid drifted shut, like he couldn't stay awake. He swayed back and forth where he sat.

She fished for her penlight. "Look up here at me, please." Checking his pupils, she shook her head. "He's got a brain injury. Not oriented. Pupils sluggish to react. Not tracking."

"Stop?" the ref asked.

Visions of litigation if she failed to protect a fighter from permanent brain damage danced in her imagination. "Yes. Stop. Concussion."

The ref jumped to his feet and waved his hands. "Fight's over. Medical stoppage."

The boos and jeers escalated.

Linc got up and staggered, off-balance, grabbing the ref's arm. "No," he screamed. "I'm fine. I can fight."

The ref shook his head. "It's done. Medical stoppage. That's final."

Linc spun around to her and threw the mouthpiece to the mat. "You did this!" His one open eye glowed red, and she recoiled from the acrid sulfur wave that blew past her.

She froze.

Time slowed. Light and motion and sound blurred.

From the opposite side of the cage, Vaughn whipped his head up and lurched toward her as if pulled by a magnet, arms outstretched, mouth open in a yell.

Before she could react, Linc grabbed the lapels of her blazer, lifted her off the ground and tossed her hard enough to crash into a padded cage corner. Her head banged off the cage beam, and all the air left her with burning, starving lungs. The roar of the crowd faded and stars sparkled on the edges of her vision.

As a furious Linc closed the short distance with his fist raised, Mariah ducked her head behind her arms, shielding herself against a blow...

That never came.

Vaughn's massive frame slid in front of hers, and he grunted with the impact of the blow meant for Mariah. But he remained standing, vulnerable to attack, legs spread, arms extended, fingers looped into the sides of the octagon corner, so that he caged her behind his body. She peeked around his massive back.

A thousand people took a collective breath.

Heat radiated from Vaughn's sweat-covered torso. Funny, even though he didn't fold her into his arms, she still felt enveloped by him. This new stupid headache had to be from hitting her head.

The ref, both corners, Angelo, and the inspectors poured into the octagon, yelling at Linc and pushing the raging man back to the opposite side of the ring. Police followed, and soon they had Linc hustled away, much to the glee of the fickle crowd. The audience who had hated her for stopping the fight thirty seconds ago had some sense of ethics and apparently drew the line when the fighter knocked down the medical personnel.

The announcer, trying to regain control of the event, windmilled his hand in a frantic bid to get Vaughn to join him in the middle of the ring for the announcement.

Instead, Vaughn whipped around, relocking his fingers into the metal mesh on either side of Mariah's head. The gold glinted in his eyes as his face contorted. He was ungodly fury on the edge of losing all control. She'd never seen anything like it.

She suppressed a shiver for anyone else who got close to him right about now. That included herself.

He sucked in a lungful of air. "Fuck," he exhaled, all heat and male sweat and wild adrenaline. Thousands of people surrounding them, and he ignored them all. After a few seconds of staring at her, he said, "Are you okay?"

His sheer intensity made her weak in the knees. "I'm fine. Thanks for helping." She swallowed. "You should, um, go get your winnings. Get your hand raised. That was a great fight."

"Not until you get checked out by another doctor."

"I'm not hurt." On what level was this statement true?

Like he clawed the words out of his throat, he growled, "I don't fucking care what you think. My mind will not function until I know you're okay." His Adam's apple bobbed. Cords of neck muscle flexed. Being the pinpoint focus of this much-concentrated power? Thrilling. Edgy. Sexy. Terrifying.

Sometimes fighters got so buzzed on adrenaline they couldn't concentrate. Maybe he was dealing with something along those lines. "Not a problem. I'll have Dr. Brandeis do a quick check. See? All taken care of," she tried to soothe him. She licked her lips. God, Vaughn was only inches away. Heat poured off of him. "Now. We're making a scene, and I'm getting embarrassed."

"Tough." He turned to the announcer and his corner guys. "Be right back," he barked. Then he held out a hand. "Allow me."

"I don't need help."

"Or I can carry you, which will be way more enjoyable for me, and I guarantee will make a hell of a bigger scene."

Her belly quivered. She reached out, and he snugged his hand under her arm and drew her close to him as they stepped down the stairs out of the octagon to the audience's clapping. Her face burned. Great.

Dr. Brandeis ran up to her.

"Can you check on her?" Vaughn said.

She mostly ignored the exam as Vaughn retreated, his posture rigid, muscles twitching. The announcer called the fight result, much to the wild enthusiasm of the crowd. As Vaughn exited once more, he paused in front of her.

"I want to see you before you leave."

The cold blast shooting down her spine had nothing to do with it being winter in Wyoming.

CHAPTER 24

After stitching up one of the guys from the last fight of the night, Mariah washed her hands and snagged her coat and bag. Angelo waited outside the medical room, a tormented expression plastered on his round face.

Lifting a hand, she said, "These things happen. Not to worry."

The corners of his mouth dipped. "But I do worry. That's my job. And you're like family here."

He wrapped her in a bear hug, making her voice come out muffled and squished. "Aw, thanks."

"Will you ever work for me again?"

"Of course."

"Maybe not," a low voice filled the hall, skimming over her nerves. Vaughn, freshly showered with his damp hair brushed back from his forehead, strode toward them. A whiff of spicy soap came with him, making her inhale deeply. "What'll happen to Linc for that violation?" He lifted his chin toward Mariah.

The fight promoter swallowed. "At least a year-long suspension. And I'll report this to all state athletic commissions. Even if he comes back after a year, I'm not sure who would let that loose cannon fight again. I sure won't." Angelo gave her one last squeeze and stepped back. "You did your job perfectly, Doc. I feel terrible about what happened. If you need any treatment or anything, I will cover the expenses."

"No harm done. I'll see you in two months for the next event, right?"

"No one I'd rather have working ringside." The promoter strolled away.

In the empty hallway, she studied Vaughn. The skin under his left eye over his left cheek had swelled and turned a reddish purple color. Abrasions dotted his forehead, nose, and chin, and a few butterfly bandages closed the cut on his brow. But take away all that facial trauma and the man in the navy slacks and striped Oxford button-down shirt fit the part of a businessman on Wall Street. Except that the average financial analyst probably didn't have pecs that shifted when he moved.

Good Lord, Vaughn looked good enough to eat.

Jolting her out of her daydream, he blurted, "Why was Wyatt Brand here tonight? Near you?"

Rocking back on her heels at his pissy tone, she said, "Why ask me? He's a creep. But beyond that, I have no idea why he showed up. It's a free country, I guess."

"Bizarre, if you ask me."

"How so?" She leaned a hip against the concrete wall and set her bag down. This might take a while.

"Well, besides his family's feud with mine, he also has a weird thing for you."

Oh really? She flicked a tooth with her nail. "So, you think it's strange some guy is interested in me?"

"Damn it. That didn't come out right." He looked at the ceiling and then back down to her. "And no, it's not strange at all for a guy to be interested in you. Hell, every unmarried guy in the place tonight wanted you." Raising his hand at her sputtered protest, he said, "What I mean is, Wyatt is fixated on you. I'm guessing you being here, me being here—he couldn't stay away."

"Good point. He did get too close while I was watching your fight." She rubbed her upper arm, but goose bumps still rose.

"Wonder if he was working with Linc. Distracting you so Linc could do whatever he wanted in the cage." When Vaughn ran a hand over his bruised cheek, she flinched in sympathy. "You know Linc had illegal material in his gloves?"

"No way."

"Yeah, ran some fiberglass between layers of gauze before putting on his gloves. Hit like a brick sonovabitch, too."

"You could have been seriously injured. That's dangerous."

That grin molded his swollen face in a strangely endearing way. "Yup. Luckily, I've got a pretty hard head."

"True." Awkward silence stretched. "So." She pushed off the wall. "I need to be getting back to Copper River."

His eyes darkened. "Can I walk you to your car?"

A frisson skated over her skin. She considered the nearly empty event venue. What if Wyatt or Linc waited out there for her? "Yes, I would appreciate that."

He snagged the straps of her bag with the hand that also held his gym bag. He waited for her to put on her coat and then rested his free hand at the small of her back. Despite the layers of clothing, the warmth from his palm seeped into her skin.

Light snow blew as the arena door closed behind them. The back parking lot had only a few cars left. Pulling her coat closed, she wanted to hurry to her car but at the same time linger in Vaughn's presence.

Déjà vu hit as they stood next to her car.

Right, because of the last unfabulous encounter in a parking lot.

She turned and held her hand out for the bag, which contained her car keys. "Well, okay. Thank you."

A shadow came and went over his face. "Screw that." He dropped the bags behind him and faced her squarely, nostrils flaring. She took a step back. "Do you even know how worried I was that you might have been hurt? Do you know how much I wanted to kill Linc for touching you?"

"I—"

In a fluid move, he backed her into the side of the car and took her face in his rough hands, not a hard grip but firm, insistent. With a low moan, he ground his mouth into hers. But not painful or intrusive.

Oh hell, he could intrude like this any day of the week.

He changed angles, and liquid heat pooled down low in her abdomen. His harsh breaths shot straight into her bones, and she purred.

When he paused, she groaned in frustration and yanked him back down by his fancy shirt. A test nip to his lower lip, and his response went thermonuclear as he growled and pushed his hard groin into hers. His big arms snaked around her and pulled her even closer than she thought possible with this many clothes on. Trapped in a sensual prison, waves of throbbing need built inside.

Normally confinement terrified her, but not with Vaughn. On a basic level, her body and mind responded to the reality that he was safe. Their connection pressed them, like two poles of a magnet, together. Tight. Melded.

He separated the seam of her lips and tangled with her tongue in a rhythm to match the roll of his hips. Her knees wobbled, and he tucked her more firmly against him.

"I won't let you fall," he breathed against her lips, before using his mouth for more than talking.

Frigid temperatures weren't a problem, encased as she was in the circle of his arms. Dampness and heat bloomed between her legs as her hips went loose.

He came up for air, cupping the back of her head.

"Shit. I want you so badly," he gritted out, resting his chin on the top of her head.

Things like carpe diem and YOLO raced through her head. Could she be with Vaughn even if they had no guarantee of a long-term relationship? What about her own fears? Could she risk the same rejection she'd experienced before?

The moment he ran a hand over her jacket-covered breast, her breath caught in her throat. Logic and mapping out life didn't fit this situation. She had to make a leap of faith.

"I want you too." Licking her lips, she rose on tiptoes to kiss him. Thank God he obliged by lifting her to meet his mouth. Barely touching the ground, held in his arms, beneath the sweet onslaught of his kisses, Mariah was flying.

She didn't want to return to Earth.

He pulled away and let her slide the inches back to the asphalt; his chest pulled air in and out. For a guy with amazing aerobic capacity, he sure breathed hard. "You sure?"

"Yes. I am."

"I don't want to drive back to Copper River."

"Me neither."

"Well." A brief, boyish grin softened his hard, bruised face. "Casino hotel?"

"Sounds like a good plan to me." She kissed him again until neither of them could see straight.

CHAPTER 25

For the love of God, how long did it take to check into a hotel room?

Vaughn blindly signed the forms and handed over what he hoped was a credit card. No idea what room they got. As long as the room had a lock on the door and a bed. Or some chairs. On second thought, a room where the door locked would be dandy, and he would make any furniture work for his needs.

In almost a run, he ignored his aching muscles, grabbed the bags in one hand, and with his other hand tugged her to the elevators. He counted the seconds until the doors closed, and then dropped his mouth back down on hers, savoring, licking, nipping. Each kiss stung his bruised lips, but he didn't care. Vaughn wanted to imprint her taste in his memory forever. God help him, but he would never get enough of this woman. She was some kind of mind-altering drug and he'd become an instant addict—the second he had met her pretty green eyes in that emergency room, if he was being honest about it.

His damned power totally dug whatever she was doing to him. The ability wanted to surround her. Just like he wanted to surround her in a literal and much more biblical manner.

Exiting at whatever floor he had selected, he hurried down the hall like a desperate rodent in a maze, checking each room number to see if it lined up with the one on the electronic card in his hand. At the end of the hall, he swiped the card in a door slot and came damn near to passing out with relief when the green light blinked.

Hotel room. Big bed. Desk, chair, couch. Standard items. Check. He flipped on a lamp.

Couldn't give a fuck about the spa-level amenities in the bathroom or if the towels were spun out of gold threads from a Burmese silk spider's ass.

All he wanted was this woman naked and beneath him, pronto.

He paused. Maybe he should be using something like finesse or foreplay or some other tool besides his current drive to bury his cock as far into Mariah as humanly possible so he could lose his entire mind and sanity in this woman.

How about sweet nothings? Damn. He should be saying something nice to her instead of gaping like a land-based goldfish. *Think, damn it. Say something romantic.*

Forget it. His brain had nothing but penis-in-vagina available for preview.

Shit.

The color on her cheeks flared red as he stared at her like a drooling imbecile. She bit her lip and dropped her gaze to the floor.

"I—" he started. "Um. Food? Anything?"

She frowned. Oh, no. Bad. Why the hell did he ask a question? No distractions. *Backpedal, dammit.*

Plan B was to dive back in for a second taste of her sweet mouth, but she beat him to the next step as she shrugged out of her coat and licked her lips.

Then she slid off the blazer, leaving her in a trim, button-down shirt and those sexy business pants. Her petite, toned body made him want to throw her on the bed and pounce on top of her.

"Room service? I can order you something," he stammered.

She grabbed his shirt in two hands and pulled him toward the bed. "Oh my gosh, why are you still talking?"

"Hell if I know."

She leaned into him, and he gladly toppled backward, pulling her down on top. Her slight weight felt beyond perfect stretched out over him. As for his battered body? What bruises?

"Scoot up. We're hanging over the bed," she said with an impish wrinkle to her nose.

As he shifted up and rested his head on the pillows, with her still perched on top of him, he grinned. "Are you always this bossy?"

"Are you complaining?"

He bucked his hard erection beneath her. "What do you think?"

She tilted her head, mischievous as a wood sprite or nymph or something else fucking magical that wasn't a goddamned leprechaun with a beard or something else buzzkill unsexy.

When she popped the hair clip and those shiny strands fell forward, he reached up to let the hair slip through his fingers. Wow, she heated parts of his heart that had been ice cold for far too long.

She skimmed her hands down his shirt-covered arms to his hands and threaded her fingers through his, easing his hands away from her. Then she leaned against him and pressed his hands to the bedding next to his head. With her torso this close to his head, he wanted to tear off her clothes and bury his face in what lay beneath.

But the lady was having fun, judging by her smile, somehow both excited and shy at the same time. Let her enjoy, by all means.

"Looks like I submitted you," she exhaled.

"I'll let you win a match like this any day." With effort, he sucked in air. "Want to try a rear naked chokehold?"

A laugh bubbled up and lit her glowing face. His heart paused several beats. She was beautiful as she straddled his torso, and he wanted to remember this moment for the rest of his entire life.

She winked—fucking winked—at him. "That was my next go-to move. You've figured out my game plan."

Burying his hands in her hair again, he pulled her down to his mouth and kissed her until she melted into him.

When she rose again, he groaned with frustration, then excitement, as her nimble fingers undid each of his buttons until cold air licked over his chest. The light drift of her fingertips shot zingers of hell-yeah right down his spine. Her butt wiggling against his groin tormented him in the best way possible, and when she gave his hard nipples a light pinch, he came close to embarrassing himself right in front of her.

"Mariah," he growled.

"Ref hasn't called it yet. Patience."

"My God," he gritted as she scooted down. She stroked him through the pants fabric, making his cock jump.

Then she slid that same hand beneath his waistband and circled him. Christ.

Some men needed to be in control.

Some men needed to be on top.

As Mariah stroked his hard erection, he realized that he wasn't like some men.

All he needed was Mariah. If this woman wanted to run the show, there was no way in hell he would complain.

He groaned as she rubbed her thumb along the damp tip of his cock.

However. He wouldn't survive if she continued what she was doing. He'd let her play later. He had work to do.

With a buck and a heave, he lifted and flipped her over, reversing their positions. Better.

Like in his midnight fantasies, she lay beneath him, her hair spread out in a dark halo, her arms splayed out next to her. Perfect.

"You need to give me a chance." He took care to hold his weight with his legs and arms as he knelt over her.

"I'm okay with that." The way her eyes widened, he felt ten feet tall.

"Damn it," he cursed his thick, rough fingers. He finally managed to unbutton her blouse without ripping the garment to shreds. With the amount of patience he showed, he ought to be named a saint.

Saint Take it Slow or Saint Ladies First or some bullshit name like that.

Smoothing the fabric to the side, he sucked in more air as the sight of her took it right out of him. Her smooth skin glowed. The small lace cups hid twin points pushing against the fabric. Part of him wanted to spend quality time with those breasts, and part of him wanted her naked, like, yesterday. She was a dessert buffet and he couldn't decide where to start.

She sighed, making those hard nipples strain against the lace.

Decision made.

Each of his hands palmed a firm breast, and he rubbed the skin beneath the lace fabric, taking cues from the sexy, breathy sounds that came from her. He leaned back on his ankles and drew her to sit up. Concentrating on her face, watching for any hesitation and seeing none, he slid the shirt off and away, followed by the bra. With his hand supporting her behind the shoulders, like she was a delicate piece of crystal, he eased her back down to the bed.

Trailing his fingers over her neck, breasts, and stomach, he wanted to feel every single inch of her body. Memorize it. In case they never…no. He shook his head and paused.

"You okay?" Her voice, both soft and rough, snapped him the hell off of whatever path his mind was heading. With a featherlight stroke of his bruised cheek, she asked, "Is this bothering you?"

"With you in front of me, I feel zero pain." He shifted his position on her hips and grimaced. "Well, maybe a little pain, but it's the good kind of pain. Besides, your touch takes it away."

Reaching for the front of his slacks, she whispered, "Then I've got some more cure."

Keeping his grip gentle, he manacled her wrists and drew her hands away. "If you go there, this night will be over before it begins, and that is not my intention. Not by a long shot." He let go and skimmed up her waist until his thumbs rested on her breasts. "Besides, I want to find more ways to make you squirm first." He bent and latched his mouth onto one nipple, flicking his tongue over the tip until she gasped.

She scraped her nails over the nape of his neck and closed her hands on two fistfuls of hair. Pleasure mixed with pain sent him into low synchronous orbit.

He gave her other breast equal attention, then licked his way down her belly. Inhaling the faint, warm musk of her arousal, he grimaced as his cock jumped for joy.

After unbuttoning her pants and sliding them and the underwear off of her hips, he stood and rifled through his gym bag. He'd need that foil packet soon enough, God willing.

Mariah was a vision. All puffy, well-kissed lips, smoldering eyes, soft skin, and tight little body. The tiny patch of dark hair above her...wow.

He dropped like a fighter shooting for a takedown and positioned his face at the juncture of her thighs. Delicate, pink skin and moisture. The idea that she was wet for him had his cock straining for release. *Soon, buddy. Real soon.*

One gentle lick and she bucked against him with a cry. Yeah, that was a winning move. He stroked with his tongue up and down her soft folds and over her clit. Her panting mixed with his. Heat and wetness poured from her, and he lapped it up, loving the taste of her. Licking his finger, he slid it into the liquid heat and groaned as her inner muscles rippled. At the same time, he crooked his finger to rub the rough spot inside her and flicked his tongue over her again.

Christ, for a small woman, she was freakishly strong as she writhed beneath him. So good.

Adding another finger, he pressed inward slowly, letting her adjust to him. He'd kill himself before he hurt her in any way. But he wanted her so much. He never wanted to stop. Increasing the rhythm, he stroked her until she bowed under his touch and his mouth. She gripped the bedcovers and came apart in his hands. Her hoarse cry and gasps raked across his soul, making his heart swell and his chest tighten.

He eased away from her hips and licked the glistening sweat on her stomach before kissing her beautiful mouth.

"God, Vaughn."

"Yeah," he managed to grit out.

"Wow." Her chest rose and fell. She lolled her head to the side and, with a flop of her arm, grabbed the crinkly packet. "All right. Your turn."

"Hell yes. Round two."

CHAPTER 26

I f Mariah's main goal was to not think about the future and live for the moment, then, holy cow, had she succeeded. What a hell of a moment. Even her fingers and toes tingled. It took a minute for her heart to stop the orgasmic tachycardia.

Vaughn knelt over her, all cut with massive muscle, covered in bruised skin, and sporting a happy, overgrown schoolboy expression.

Get up, lazybones. This night isn't over yet. She rose to her knees and pressed against him, chest to chest. His arms locked around her, secure and warm. The hot kiss ramped her up even further, and his erection pushed against her belly.

With a grin, she shoved at his chest. He flopped to his back, exhaling a whoosh of air.

"Now you're the one with too many clothes on." After she undid the button and zipper, he lifted his hips and she pulled off the pants and briefs. The hardness of his buttocks and thighs made her heart jump again.

The hardness of other areas made her insides clench. His erection, thick and pulsing slightly, jutted out. As she lowered her head, she glanced up. His irises glinted with gold sparks. When she circled the tip of his penis with her tongue, his face went rigid.

"Oh, fuck," he hissed.

She licked down the length of him and cupped the weight of his testicles. Even the tiniest movement made him jump beneath her mouth. Super. She met his avid, hungry stare. He watched her like his life depended on it.

His groans increased, and his spread legs twitched with each pass of her mouth over him.

She raked her nails up his ridged belly while she tongued him and hummed. The muscles beneath her fingertips tensed. So fun, turning this big guy to putty in her hands.

"I don't want you to stop," he panted. "But you have to stop." When had his voice gotten so hoarse? "I want to be deep inside you when I come."

She lollipopped him one more time. "That's a plan I can get behind." With a smile, she opened the packet and sheathed him, stroking him through the latex.

"What you do to me. Amazing."

He surged up, turning and pinning her beneath him with an ease that took her breath away. Maybe he had injuries from the fight, but they sure as hell didn't hamper his seduction abilities. His arms snaked under her shoulder blades and met in a cup behind her head. His knees rested between her legs, and his erection nudged at her opening. She pulsed and strained upward, eager for him.

"Vaughn. Please." Was that really her desperate gasp? She grabbed onto his back.

"You bet." He pressed into her and sank in deep. Then he held still. "Man, you feel so good."

She gasped, "It's. Mutual." Every inch of her body and soul stretched to accommodate him.

He thrust gently, and she dug her nails into his back.

He hissed. "Yeah, go for it. Scratch away. Damn, you're sexy."

"Vaughn. Oh my God."

He pressed his forehead to hers and worked his hips in earnest now, each movement deeper and harder as he filled her completely. In the cocoon of his arms and his body, she floated on a cloud of bliss centered on the bone-loosening desire deep in her pelvis. Their pants and moans filled the room as he rotated his hips faster and she lifted her pelvis to meet his movements.

More. She needed more of him inside. When she hooked her heels around the bunched muscles of his buttocks, he seated himself even deeper, with a bit-off expletive. She grabbed as far around his broad back as possible, wanting every part of her to come into contact with him. His skin—she would crawl inside his skin if that were possible. A sensation of safety followed by a light headache flitted across her forehead, an almost familiar feeling.

As she met his strong thrusts with her own, the pleasure spiked. He opened her mouth with his and swirled his tongue inside, creating stars that rimmed her vision. His scent filled her nose, their combined tastes filled her mouth, and the heat from his skin warmed her inside and out.

With a groan, he pumped harder, every cord of his powerful muscles flexing. He clenched his hands in her hair and locked her underneath him, creating the best prison she could ever imagine.

Another two thrusts and she flew high, bursting into a supernova of shuddering pleasure. Her hoarse cries filled the room. A few seconds later, he raised his head and yelled. The pulses of his erection inside of her created aftershocks that let her skim along, prolonging her orgasm. When she didn't think her muscles could clench anymore, he swirled his hips, and another wave hit her.

"Good God," she gritted out, loving the sweat slicking their bodies as they moved against each other.

"I'll say." Holding some of his weight off of her, he stayed on top for a few more minutes or moments? Muttering, he withdrew, rolled off the bed and disposed of the condom.

Without his presence, her damp skin cooled. Then Vaughn scooped her up, yanked back the sheet and covers, and laid her down on the bed. Settling in next to her, he pulled the bedding up and tucked it around her. Safe. Cocooned.

Her last conscious thought was of his legs scissoring hers and his arms latching around her, like she was the luckiest life preserver in the universe.

Everything in his life had come down to this moment, Vaughn was certain of it. His power flowed around him, encasing both of them in a protective, invisible bubble. So right. So perfect and complete. He couldn't imagine a day in his life without Mariah in it.

No.

He shouldn't be thinking like that.

Shit.

If he wanted to atone for his bad decision-making a year ago, he'd picked a hell of a way to do it. He hadn't even told her everything he'd done in the past, what he had been. What he currently was. If Mariah knew, no way would she have jumped into bed with him. And what about her need for a long-term relationship? It was clear that he couldn't deliver on those goods.

But could he walk away from this woman?

Even if he stayed, no way would she want a relationship with a guy with as much baggage as Vaughn.

Damn it.

She mumbled in her sleep, and he loosened his rigid grip on her. Not an easy task, considering that every cell in his body screamed at him to surround her more. Hell, there were a few inches of her still uncovered, vulnerable—a fact that made him slide more of his body over hers. His damned ability drove him beyond paranoia. He needed to protect her in every way possible.

Was that Vaughn or his power talking?

Didn't matter. They were one and the same. Which was yet another reason he was one messed up dude. What woman wanted a guy with weird psychic powers that turned him into the biggest Cro-Magnon man in the universe. What woman wanted an adulterer? An alcoholic?

Oh, Christ. What had he done?

When her mumbles turned to soft cries, he flipped on the bedside lamp. Liquid pooled between the corner of her eye and the bridge of her nose. Shit.

"Mariah? Sweetheart?"

She struggled against him, her small body no match for his. But he let go completely.

"Mariah? You're having a dream."

Her spiked lashes fluttered. A second of brow-raising terror was swiftly followed by a droop to her pretty mouth. A fist formed in his chest.

"Okay. It's okay." Was she talking to herself or to him? "I'm good. Fine. All good. It's okay."

"Um." He wanted to roll on top of her to keep anything bad away, but that might not be the best tactic. "You want me to hold you?"

Turning to bury her face in his chest, she mumbled, "Yes, please."

He might have no future with her. He might have a bad past. But for right now, he'd hold her like his existence depended on it, for as long as she wanted. He cradled her, shifting and shifting again, restless, desperate to surround her. "You're safe."

"I know. Sorry. Just…bad memories sometimes."

"From being trapped in that room?"

Her nod made her hair tickle his nose, but he didn't move. "When I get stressed, sometimes the bad dreams come back."

"Was I that bad?"

"What?"

"So bad that you got stressed out?"

Her giggle dropped the tension in the room.

"I'm fine," she said.

"Of course you are. You're one of the toughest people I've met. Considering my side job, that's saying a lot." He made a show of bending his arm and flexing until she laughed again. Then he frowned. "Um, you never actually answered the question."

"What question?" That frown begged to be smoothed, and he indulged with his fingertip.

"If the night with me was bad enough to stress you out?"

"What do you think?" One dark eyebrow rose.

He pulled back and kissed her forehead. "I think you should give a guy another chance at redemption before you pass judgment." His cock, already anticipating the pleasure, snapped right to attention.

"Another—oh…" She wiggled against him. "Really?"

"If it's okay with you, of course."

That shy smile made the corners of his own mouth turn up. "Well, all right, if you insist," she said.

Trailing a hand down her spine until goose bumps stippled her skin, he nipped her lower lip, drawing a purr from her throat. "Oh, I insist."

His mental power and short-timer relationship issues? The issue with his entire life existing two thousand miles away? Yeah, he'd have to deal with that later.

Right now, Vaughn had a beautiful woman in his arms to satisfy.

CHAPTER 27

Mariah woke to a light knock at the door, followed by the aromas of bacon, pancakes, eggs, and coffee.

Wait.

And coffee?

She went from REM sleep to bloodhound alert in a split second and sat bolt upright. The bedside clock read 7:00 a.m. On the laminate wood desk was an impressive spread of steaming breakfast dishes. A sheepish Vaughn was pulling metal lids off the plates. He had his slacks on but nothing else. The fashion choice worked for him.

"And a good morning to you." He surveyed her and licked his lips, reminding Mariah to pull the sheet up. "Not that I am complaining about the view one bit."

"Oh wow. I need…"

He picked up a mug full of mocha heaven. "This?"

"Gimme. Please."

"It will cost you a kiss."

"I'll pay. Anything."

He sat next to her and did some magic trick with his lips and mouth that set her synapses on fire faster than a double shot of espresso. "Yes, it is a good morning."

A few sips of bliss later, she leaned back on the pillows. "That's a lot of food."

With a shrug, he said, "Didn't know what kind of breakfast you liked, so I ordered one of everything on the room service menu." He closed one eye. "Minus the mimosas." He opened that eye, then cringed. "But I'll order some if you really want."

"No thanks." She clutched the mug to her sternum, prepared to die before letting go of the beverage. "This is perfect."

"Obviously. I'm kind of jealous of the mug."

"Give me another few sips and I will be able to respond."

His laugh filled the room as he hovered over the spread of food. "Do you mind if I dig in? I'm kind of hungry."

"Save me a few pancakes and eggs. Everything else is fair game. You earned it."

"From the fight or from last night?"

How many rounds did they go? She'd lost track after her fourth orgasm. Her cheeks warmed. "Both," she mumbled.

Swaggering like a fighter who won the championship belt, he piled a plate and sat in the office chair, facing her.

After a few minutes, she set the mug down. It was almost like letting a family member go.

"Want some food?" he asked before starting into his second plate.

"Sure."

He handed her the plate and fork and resettled in the chair. The dark ink shifted as he adjusted his position in the seat.

"What's that mean?" She pointed.

Setting the fork down, he glanced at his chest. "Which one?"

"All of it." At a flash of his pain, she blurted, "Unless you don't want to tell me, and that's okay."

"Um, no. It's not like anything on my body is a secret anymore."

Her heart skipped a beat.

Clearing his throat, he said, "What I meant was that people can see this any time I fight or train." A grin. Then he pointed. "*Vincit qui se vincit.* Means 'He conquers who conquers himself.'"

"Sounds deep. Wrestle with demons much?" She leaned against the headboard and took another sip of coffee.

"Probably, yes."

Sounded like he had even more history there.

"And on the back," he said. "*per avesitatem redemptio.* Um, 'through adversity, redemption.'"

"So that would be a definite *yes* on demons?"

"Yes." He rested his elbows on the arms of the chair and hung his head for a moment. "I don't talk about it much. And…I'm not ready to go into details right now."

The drowning weight of his words stopped her from asking anything more. "That's okay."

"Yeah?"

"It's your story to tell. Do so when you want to."

They ate in silence. Once they'd finished the meal, she sighed again and scooted down into the blankets while watching him.

He set down his plate. Opened his mouth and closed it. Twice. Tight lines bracketed his lips.

Uh oh. That look had bad news written all over it.

She needed another coffee before having the Post-Sex Relationship Talk, and by the deepening frown, the Talk was gearing up to be a doozy. True, she had questions about long-term plans, but for now, she wanted to bask in the glow of good lovin' and good breakfast a little longer.

"Shower?" she yelped.

He did an agonal breathing move with his mouth and finally said, "What? Uh, yeah, sure. In there."

That's not what she meant. Another wave of heat poured through her and she pressed her legs together. Her mouth watered, and not for breakfast.

Could she do it? Could she let a man know exactly what she wanted? And get it—that was the real question.

If not with Vaughn, then with whom?

No one else, dammit. The guy had ruined her for any other man. Maybe he didn't have *forever* stamped on his forehead, but she would make the best of the time they did have and be proud of going for what she wanted.

To meet that goal, she would have to walk in front of a sculpted MMA fighter, naked.

With a gulp, she slipped out from under the sheets. His eyes darkened as he watched her every move.

She stepped in front of him and stood between his legs. She laced her fingers together in front of her to fight the urge to cover herself.

"Wow." He traced her hips with his hands.

"So, um. Shower?"

"I can't believe you had to ask me twice. Christ, I'm a dumb fuck." He surged to his feet and shoved his pants off, his hard and ready erection making her belly clench in anticipation. He scooped her in his arms with a kiss that tasted like breakfast and Vaughn as he strode to the bathroom.

* * *

"So, would you be interested in seeing our ranch?" Vaughn asked, buttoning his shirt.

He didn't want this day to end, ever. He prayed that Mariah would feel the same.

And if his family didn't like him bringing a woman home for a visit, they could shove it.

All he wanted was more Mariah.

Question was: did she want more of him? Maybe he could figure out the answer to that question later today.

Like it mattered for a guy planning to blow out of town.

"Sure."

"What?"

"I'm game to check out the ranch, if it won't disrupt...anything you all have to do there." She pulled the wool coat around her and picked up her bag. "It would be good to run home and change first, though."

"Want me to follow you back to your house?"

"Sound like a plan." She didn't protest as he took her bag from her.

He opened the hotel room door and motioned for her to precede him. As they walked down the hall, he gritted his teeth and let his power flow out of him. A noise there, a flicker of light here, made him tense, sensing threats everywhere.

But not threats to Vaughn.

The power was searching for potential danger to Mariah. And the power was doing it in a hypersensitive manner. The blood drained from his head, turning sound hollow.

Not detecting danger to Vaughn. Not at all.

No way. Impossible.

As they got in separate cars, he clenched the wheel, his knuckles turning white. Shit. Too much distance between them. He'd be behind that ridiculous Mini all the way back to Copper River, a two-hour drive. He tried not to tailgate as he followed her vehicle's shallow tracks in the dusting of snow.

Thirty minutes into the drive on the empty highway, his power screamed and threw out a wave, reaching forward.

A mule deer bolted from the trees and ran in front of Mariah's car.

Before he could slam on his brakes, she had slammed hers, stopping just in time to avoid hitting the deer. He managed not to hit her car, and they carried on down the highway. No harm, no foul.

But that wasn't the point, as the pounding in his chest reminded him.

He had *felt* the danger to her before it had appeared. More to the point, his power had sensed it and tried to do something to protect her. What he'd felt last night when Linc attacked her, what he felt this morning…none of it was a fluke. In the most fundamental way, his power had changed how it functioned. Changed its purpose. Would the power continue to morph, and if so, into what?

Hell, Shelby had gone into a coma when her power shifted gears.

Maybe the effect on his mind would wear off if he spent time away from Mariah.

What a shitty existence that would be.

A flash of memory from this morning: Mariah against the tiles in the shower, water sluicing over her breasts as she bounced with the force of his thrusts. Their connection was so perfect, so right. He had to shift in the car seat to relieve pressure. What if he lost his mind but he still got to enjoy good mornings like that?

What a way to go.

When they reached her house, Vaughn stayed in the car while she ran in to change. He dialed home.

"Hello?" Shelby answered.

He groaned. His baby sister, with her radar to pick up emotion, was the last person he wanted to talk with. "You're home."

"I do live here, you know." All snark. Classic Shelby.

"Just figured you'd be at Eric's."

"We're both here. What's going on? Your text to Garrison said you stayed over at the casino. Everything okay?" She paused.

"Shit," he muttered.

"Ahh, got it," she chirped. "More than okay."

"Shut up, Shel. You're not supposed to use your ability."

"Don't hate on the psychic. You're an open book. Takes very little effort to read you." She chuckled. "You really like her, don't you?"

"Come on. That's not why I called."

"Isn't it? You might be older, but I have enough life experience to know when I'm being bullshitted. Try again. Is she right next to you?"

"No. In her house. I'm bringing her by the ranch."

"Awesome! I'll make sure we have lunch ready."

"That's also not why I called." He rubbed his face, like somehow he could scrape away the uncertainty. "My power's doing weird things around her."

"Weird, how?" The teasing tone disappeared.

"Like, changing. Not protecting me anymore. Protecting her."

He started to repeat himself when it took her too long to answer.

"What?" she whispered.

"The ability is shifting. I'm going nuts."

"Oh, wow. It's almost like you got a variation on my power to detect emotion. Now that Eric and I are…together, I'm more keyed in on him than I ever have been with anyone. So it could be the same with you and Mariah."

"What if I'm linked to her forever?"

"Is that a bad thing?"

"Damn it, I don't know." He rested a fist on the steering wheel. "What the hell do I do?"

"For starters, you be good to that woman. She's a nice person, and you will not pull a disappearing douchebag act on her." She cut through his spluttered protest. "Second, you have to tell her about your power. And about your past. All of it."

"I don't know if that's a good idea."

"Dude, are you naturally stupid, or did you audit extra classes to get that dumb? Take it from the human emotion detector: tell her the truth. Let her know what's going on with your power and what makes you tick. She needs to participate in decision-making."

"What, now you're Dr. Phil?"

"No, but Kerr likes the show. And since I'm laid up, I've been watching way more daytime TV. Kerr is right. That Phil guy is good."

"Okay. Crap, here she comes. I'll see you in a while."

"Tell the tru—"

He ended the call as Mariah scooted into the truck. She'd changed into hiking boots, jeans, sweatshirt, and a jacket suitable for the outdoors. Her hair stuck out from under a wool beanie.

Adorable and sexy.

She could wear sackcloth and roll in dirt and he'd think she was the most beautiful woman on Earth.

He was so screwed.

Like an invisible sigh of relief, his power settled down now that she sat in the truck next to him.

"All set?" he asked.

Because Vaughn wasn't certain that he was ready for what awaited them on the ranch.

CHAPTER 28

Being around people didn't make Mariah uneasy. Her day job meant she interacted with people all day long. No problem.

But this particular group of people? They intimidated the hell out of her.

The Taggarts and assorted extras weren't mean to her. Just the opposite. The minute she arrived at the ranch house, the family welcomed her as if she were part of the clan already. Yet she caught an uneasy frown on Vaughn's face; they'd never had the Relationship Talk because of the Morning Shower Sex, but at some point a painful discussion would happen. Biding her time until then was like waiting for a second shoe to drop.

So she had two choices. She could enjoy the illusion of family and fitting in and a normal relationship for as long as it lasted.

Or she could stay detached and not let herself be lured into the welcoming arms of this family.

Either option hurt like hell.

Rather than decide right now, she took the BLT Garrison offered instead.

"How do you like working at the hospital?" he asked, watching her intently.

She stared with significant longing at the sandwich, then answered, "Um, yes. Of course. It's challenging."

"But you like it? Here? At the hospital?"

Okay, fifth degree. "Yes. Some days are crazier than others, true. But at the end of the day, it's worth it. And Copper River is a nice place." She winced as a headache zipped across her forehead. Maybe she was more tired than she realized.

"Garrison. Quit it!" Shelby glared a hole into her brother.

Mariah's headache faded as soon as he stood from the table and excused himself, followed by his pretty girlfriend, Sara. The entire time, Shelby scowled at him. Weird. It was like half the conversation had occurred on a different level. It was almost like the headache had something to do with them. Which made no sense.

"So how many Taggarts do you see as patients?" Kerr asked.

"She can't answer that. HIPAA rules and all," a serene, studious woman whose auburn hair was pulled back in a bun walked into the kitchen and interjected. With a wink, the woman held out a hand. "I'm Ruth. A nurse taking care of Mr. Taggart while he recovers from his stroke." The woman studied Mariah with a bemused expression on her face.

"Nice to meet you." She released the woman's hand. "How long have you been here?"

"A few weeks. It's been pretty eventful around here."

Kerr nodded.

Shelby's and Eric's gazes locked for a second. A twinge flashed through Mariah. Fair enough, those two had gone through hell and back and had earned their unspoken connection. It was obvious by the way he rested his arm around the back of her chair and how he homed in on her as she spoke. The red color that tinted her cheeks at his touch. The tiny glances. Those two were in tune.

What would that be like on a daily basis?

"So, Mariah, you've been in town here for what, a year?" Kerr asked.

"Less than that." She chewed and washed down a bite, all too aware of Vaughn's presence next to her. "Started in August, fresh out of residency."

Shelby blurted, "How long are you staying in Copper River?"

"Shel!" Vaughn said.

"It's a legit question." She raised a negligent shoulder. "For medical care needs, of course." With her eyes crossed, she made a face at him. "There. Happy?"

He dropped his forehead into his palm.

Mariah wiped her mouth with the napkin. "Honestly, I'm not sure how long I'll be in Copper River. Part of being here is to pay off considerable debt from medical school. But I like the area and the people." Okay, maybe one person in particular, but he wouldn't be here when her loan amounts rolled to zero. "So I'm taking things as they come," she hedged.

"Sara came here to pay off school loans for her teaching degree, too. Worked out for her long-term future, it would appear." Kerr laughed when Vaughn growled.

Mariah's neck heated. Every part of this conversation hit too close to home. "So, Vaughn fought a great bout last night."

Silence. Then Eric barked out a laugh. "She catches on quickly to the nosy Taggart clan. Good job changing the subject, Mariah. I like you." He jumped. "Ow, Shel. Why'd you have to pinch me?"

Shelby talked to the ceiling. "Why me, God? Why surround me with these idiots?" She winked at Ruth and Mariah. "Female company excepted."

"So, to take the conversational bait, as it were, it's lucky that Vaughn didn't get his geriatric ass pounded in last night," Kerr sucked on a tooth and lifted a shoulder. "I got the scoop from a friend who was at the fight."

Vaughn's hands curled into fists. "I'm not that old."

"You're too old to be running around and taking a beating like that. With each bout, you're not getting prettier, either." His younger brother rocked his chair back on two legs. "Hell, we could rough you up on a regular basis right here at home, if it will make you stick around."

Silence.

Ruth spoke up. "Any injuries?" A tight smile came and went. "Sorry, Mariah, old habits. You're the doctor."

"Not today. I'm off duty. Go right ahead. Maybe he'll listen to you." She ducked her head at Vaughn's scowl.

Ruth smiled. "I'm just happy you are both all right." With a quiet step, she excused herself from the room.

"Both of you?" Shelby stared at Mariah.

She rubbed her forehead again. The headaches weren't severe, just odd and fleeting. No numbness or burning pain, so not due to trigeminal neuralgia. No aura, so not a migraine. Happened around the Taggarts, which made zero sense. Hopefully the headache wasn't due to too much coffee. The cure would be unbearable.

"Shelby, quit it," Vaughn growled. Almost like she really did have something to do with Mariah's headache. No way.

His sister raised her orange brows. "Then spill. What really happened last night? At the fight."

She said it like she knew the *after the fight* part already.

Vaughn filled them in on Linc's antics, adding that Wyatt Brand showed up for the opponent's corner.

Shelby leaned forward. "Wyatt? What was that moron doing there?"

"That's a good question." Lines bracketed Vaughn's mouth. "Remember how Wyatt was fixated on you for a while?"

"I sure do," Eric spat.

Vaughn glanced at her. "Well, he's moved on. To Mariah."

Kerr made a fist. "Bastard."

"Agreed." Vaughn pressed his hand to the tabletop. "Either he's trying to make a pass at Mariah or he's doing it to retaliate against us."

"Against your family?" Mariah asked.

"As I mentioned before," Vaughn replied, "the Brands have it in for us. Wouldn't put it past them to get at one of us by using, uh…"

"Someone we care about?" Shelby grinned.

Mariah shifted in her seat, studying the last crumbs of her sandwich.

Vaughn cleared his throat. "Mariah, maybe I could give you the grand tour."

"Smooth move, Ex-Lax," Kerr quipped. "You two go on." He pointed to Shelby and Eric. "And you two invalids stay right there. I'll keep doing housework. No, no. Don't lift a finger on my behalf." He gave a dramatic sigh. "My work is never done."

Vaughn lifted his chin toward the door. "Ready?"

"Sure," Mariah answered. Anything to escape the friendly Taggart interrogation session.

What in the world possessed her to say, *Oh sure, I can ride a horse?*

Mariah had been on a horse, what, once in her life? Years ago, she and her brother had gone to a dude ranch with a group of friends, and her Old Paint tried to bite her during the entire miserable experience.

What possessed her? The need to be accepted. To be *a part of.*

Tiny flakes straggled down onto the several inches of snow already on the open fields as she and Vaughn rode toward the forest. The sky hung gray and thick. Heavy. Like it was waiting to unleash far more than a few flakes.

Earlier, they had checked out the progress of the main barn that was being rebuilt after the fire several weeks ago. She was happy to tour anything as long as it bought her freedom from the whirlwind of questions inside the house.

That familiarity they all shared? The Taggarts had grown up rough and tumble, running all over the ranch, raised by loving parents. Mariah and Kevin's childhood was the complete opposite. No play. No learning. Nothing comfortable.

Quit being morose. That's the past. Concentrate on the present.

How about the future?

Damn it.

She shifted her uncomfortable backside on the hard leather saddle. Could she fit into this family? More to the point, did she have any business considering that question? If this relationship with Vaughn continued, then, yes, she wanted to fit in.

For the first time in her life, she truly pictured herself as part of a full family with people whose lives wove together, who supported each other, loved each other, and even argued with each other.

As they reached the wooded National Forest land that bordered the ranch property, Vaughn pulled his horse to a stop with little more than a flick of his wrist. He shifted in the saddle. Damn him in his tight jeans and Stetson. How great would it be if he tipped that hat back and kissed her, right here in the wild outdoors?

Unable to stop the response, she licked her lips.

He reached over and snagged her reins. "Can I talk with you?"

No. "Sure."

Their thighs brushed against each other, but he appeared to ignore the contact as he peered into the trees. The main ranch compound was a mere dot below them in the low, flat area of the property.

"About what happened last night."

Crap. No preamble? The muscles in her stomach tightened. "The fight or the hotel stay?"

He rubbed his chin and didn't make eye contact. "Hotel."

Her heart stopped, then started again, threatening to pound its way out of her chest. "All right."

"So. I'm wondering if that was a mistake." His mouth compressed into a hard line.

The slice of his quiet words went deep, scoring her soul. All those images of fitting in, of belonging, of having a family burst like little stupid bubbles. "You went to a lot of trouble, bringing me out here, to share that conclusion. Seems like a simple text message would have been a lot less effort." Just like that, she began to pull inward. Like she did in that room when she was a teenager. Like she had done when her ex had told her to be *less*. Like she had done at the Brand house.

Shutting down.

Could she handle rejection from Vaughn? She was about to find out.

Avoidance of pain was probably not the best reason to pursue a relationship with someone. She could do this.

"I want to explain." His low voice whipped away on the wind.

Damn. This was going to hurt like hell.

CHAPTER 29

Thoughts chased each other through Vaughn's mind. He needed to have this conversation the right way, and he'd already fucked it up right from the beginning, if Mariah's frozen expression was any indication. He wanted a do-over, not just for the conversation but for a lot of crap in his life.

"You're a great woman," he began. Then he mentally face-palmed himself.

"But?" She blinked. "Hey, you can say it. I know how these talks go."

"Damn it. That's not how I meant to say it. It's just…I'm not sure we should be pursuing anything for the future. If there even is a future for us, together."

"All right." Her flat tone almost broke him. Garrison or Kerr would be so much better in this situation. The way she retreated in front of him made him want to wrap her in his arms and never let go.

Where had all of her determined energy gone? He wanted the old Mariah back. The woman who didn't sit with her hands on her lap, staring at the back of the goddamned horse. The woman who had—

His groin tightened. Apparently his cock knew exactly the woman it wanted, too.

He swallowed. "No, you don't get it. I do want us to have a future together. I really want that."

Shaking her head, she murmured, "I don't understand where you're going with this conversation. First we're done, then we have a future. You need to choose."

"You have no idea how much I'm into you, Mariah. If we wouldn't get hypothermia, I'd get us both naked and work you over until we can't tell where one of our bodies starts and the other one stops."

"Wow." The breathiness of her voice flipped his heart over and then stomped on it. "There's still a *but* in there somewhere."

"Damn." He thumbed his hat up a few inches and peered at her. "I want for you to know some stuff about me first. And my family."

"You're all axe murderers? Run a Ponzi scheme?"

His harsh laugh loosened tight muscles in his chest. "Nope. But there are some things going on."

"Besides the part where you slept with your brother's wife?"

"*Possibly* slept. And I don't think I truly did, but I can't be sure." He squirmed in the saddle. "Damn it. Anyway, I need to tell you the whole story of my past so you can decide on a future."

She scowled. "So you're already assuming I want to have a future?"

His chest deflated. "Good point. I just assumed, and you know what they say about assuming."

"Sure do. Why don't you start over by being super duper clear?"

Thank God. He collected his pride, wadded it into a virtual ball, and threw it on the snow-covered ground. "Okay, here's what I am saying: I hope that you might one day consider a long-term relationship with a worn-out MMA rancher with a somewhat checkered past."

"You make it sound so enticing." He died while she chewed her lower lip and stared up at the cloudy sky. "Your offer depends. How long are you sticking around?"

"Good question. Honestly, I don't know."

"Even better deal." Only a little twinkle in her green eyes gave away her impish jab. "Fine, I'll consider the new information." Damn, she was good.

"Fair enough. Let's say that one day you want to be in the same zip code as I am. And let's say one day you let me back in your pants." He pressed a fist to the bridge of his nose. "Shit. Forget I said that part."

"Hard to, you know, what with how much fun it is to see you squirming and all."

"Are you making fun of me?"

"It's kind of fun when the mighty Vaughn Taggart flounders."

She thought he was mighty? Well, now, that had some promise.

"Anyway, I have a little mental condition that may impact any relationship."

Her brows drew together. Damn it, with her hair all tucked into the wool beanie, her face was an open book. If he hurt her, he'd know it immediately.

If? He'd already caused her pain.

"Do tell." She pressed her lips into a line.

"Okay, bear with me. It's going to sound strange." At her curt nod, he continued. "Ever since I was a kid, I've had a weird sixth sense about things. Danger, in particular."

"I don't follow."

When the horse jostled under him, he loosened his clenched grip on the reins. "Somehow I can anticipate danger and avoid it."

"I don't understand."

"Not sure how or why, but I can detect danger. Like an odd radar. Something bad comes my way, my brain gets my attention and pushes me out of the way."

"That's kind of weird." She leaned away.

Damn it. "Uh, comes in handy in the MMA fights."

"Sounds like an unfair advantage."

He peered into the woods, searching for any danger. Was that a shadow…or something more? He forced his focus back to Mariah. "Well, yes, it does give me an edge, but that's not the point of the story. In the past week, my power has changed. Instead of protecting myself, my power kind of wants to protect…you."

She tilted her head to the side. "I don't understand."

"Me neither. None of it makes sense. But when Wyatt harassed you in the hospital last week? My power *demanded* that I go there to keep you safe. When Linc went after you in the ring last night, the power overtook my conscious decision to protect you."

"That is really strange, Vaughn." She rested her gloved hands on the pommel.

"I agree. Recently, the power has started wanting me to stay close to you. Like it has to cover you, even now. Mentally, I'm having trouble telling where danger to you stops and danger to me starts. Or if it's all just paranoia." He sat up straight, even as his body tried to lean toward her. "It's taking over my brain. I'm worried that I might be losing my mind."

"Literally?"

"Yeah."

"I'm sure there are tests, specialists to check things out." Leave it to her to jump to the medical solution.

"Pretty sure that won't help."

Her fine teeth worried her lower lip. "Should I leave you alone, then? For your own mental health?"

"I don't know the answer to that question. I think that you riding away into the sunset without me might make me go crazy."

"But if I stay, you also might lose your mind? Because of how the power is changing your thoughts?"

"Yeah. Kind of…yeah." Damn it, he wished he had good answers for her.

"Well." She straightened in the saddle. "Then it's a mixed blessing that you plan on leaving soon."

"About that." The thudding in his chest increased. *Put everything on the table.* "It's crossed my mind to change plans."

"Oh?"

"Yeah."

"Because of…us?"

"That was the major reason. But I also realized that I have been running away from mistakes I made in the past. In doing so, I left my family in the lurch."

"Mistakes?"

"I hadn't told you the whole story before. The story with Garrison's ex-wife."

Her sharp intake of breath hurt him more than getting stabbed with a knife.

"You already mentioned that. How come you don't know for sure if you cheated?" she asked.

He folded a hand into a fist on his knee. "I, uh, had some serious problems with alcohol in the past." The words burned sharper than a swig of whiskey.

"Okay."

Swallowing, he said, "The alcohol…it really messed my life up for years. Messed everything up for other people, too. Tommy Brand has booked me in jail for alcohol-related charges more times than I can remember. I've made bad mistakes. That night with Garrison's wife, I was completely shit-faced. All I know is that we woke up together and…she had pictures that she was going to use to blackmail me."

"What did you do?" Mariah's words puffed out a cloud of cold vapor, and she stared at her gloved hands.

"Turned coward and ran." Kneeing his restless horse back to Mariah, he continued, "In some ways, it was a good decision to leave. I got sober—still am. I ran away from the responsibility of the ranch, not that I was really carrying my own weight. Then the MMA took off and, well, it probably saved my life. In New York, I had no past to explain. I now have a financial career that has started to grow."

"That's a hell of a story."

"The worst part? I was so involved in building my new life, far away from the wide spot in the road that is Copper River that I wasn't here when my family needed me. When Dad had his stroke, I wasn't here. I wasn't here when Garrison's son and girlfriend got kidnapped. I wasn't here to protect Shelby when she got hurt."

"How are these things your fault?"

"I'm the oldest brother. It's always my job to protect them."

"Okay, like how I should have protected my brother back in Utah, and how I failed?"

"How could you have prevented that?"

"Exactly. Now you understand why those things are not your fault." She drew in a lungful of air. "No question, you made some mistakes."

He flinched. The neutral tone hurt more than if she called him a bastard for what he'd done.

"And you should have told me about your past before we…"

"Yeah. I know."

"But the things with your family? Not your fault. The thing with your head? You didn't cause that to happen." She glanced to the sky as a tiny flake melted on her pink nose. "So. Let's see if I have the gist of things. You have psychic powers. Okay, that's weird and I don't understand it. The powers are changing and that scares you. Somehow I'm making it worse." Pursing her lips, she said, "So far so good?"

"Yes," he said miserably.

"And you need to take ownership of the mistakes you've made in the past. And let go of the things that aren't your fault." She pinned him with a bold, emerald stare. "That about it?"

"Sort of."

"Wait. There's more?"

He groaned to himself. He had to tell the whole truth. "The Brand family has it in for the Taggarts. Despite anything we do, this damned feud isn't going to stop."

"You mentioned that before. What's that have to do with you and me?"

"I don't want you caught in the crossfire. They have threatened anyone we…care about."

"Anything else I should know?" Spoken like she had already made her decision but wanted to give him more rope to hang himself with, or throw a few more loops on the noose.

"One more." He grabbed his head and curled forward. "Holy fuck." All around him, sound splintered into pieces.

His power flared into overdrive, shoving itself into a protective bubble around Mariah. She flinched and pulled back. The power came on too fast, too strong. He needed to get her away from here. His head was splitting. Too much power. Too much fear. What the hell?

"What is—Oh my God, what's that?" she whispered.

CHAPTER 30

M ariah's temples throbbed. She didn't want to look, but curiosity drove her to peek at…whatever it was.

A black creature rose in front of them, not quite walking, not quite floating. It had mass but appeared cloudlike. Snow in its path melted in evaporating clouds of acrid sulfur, burning her nose. Even in the overcast daylight, two red dots, like cigarette butts, glowed brightly from the upper part of the thing.

"My head is going to fucking explode. Shit." Vaughn gritted out the words through his clenched teeth. "I was about to mention that my family is being stalked by whatever the hell this thing is." He fought to keep his whinnying horse under him.

Her own mare wrenched its head back and rolled the one visible eye.

Mariah couldn't stop staring at the creature approaching them. It didn't so much approach as consume more light and space as it grew.

"The time is near." The hot rumble of the voice made the ground tremble right along with Mariah's insides. "The Great One is coming on the day of darkness. The legacy will come to me. Willingly. Soon." A slither of burnt sulfur sliced the air in front of her, and she breathed into the sleeve of her jacket to escape the stench.

With her heart rat-a-tatting a frantic snare rhythm, she clutched the pommel of the saddle. The horse tensed beneath her. *Oh, no.*

"Might need to take a rain check on the day of darkness and all." Vaughn moved his horse to bump hers toward the ranch house. Her skittish mare didn't do anything except paw at the snow-covered ground and lay its ears flat.

Black, thick smoke stretched out toward them as the creature rumbled, "The legacy will end with you and your family. And I will have my final revenge. You will become the foundation for the new beginning of my reign upon the Earth. And anyone who stands in my way will be destroyed. Anyone the legacy cares for will be destroyed."

What the heck was 'the legacy?' Why was this thing targeting Vaughn's family? Nothing made sense.

And, yes, she would gladly not stand in its way, if only her panicked horse would cooperate.

A sliver of smoke lashed out, fingerlike, and Mariah flinched away. The tendril seared the back of her horse, bringing with it a sharp sizzle and the stench of burnt flesh. The animal kicked and reared.

No matter how hard she gripped the pommel, she was helpless to stop the arc as sky and ground whirled and blended. She came off the back of the horse, hitting the ground in a heap. Pain lanced through her skull. From her sideways, ground-level, head-spinning location, she watched as Vaughn faced the thing from the back of his own horse, opening his arms like he wanted to give the creature a big, friendly bear hug.

"Get away from her." Vaughn's voice boomed across the field. A weird vacuum sensation pulled air and warmth toward him.

Then, in a pressurized snap, a sensation of threat flew out from him and flung her back several feet. She rolled over the ground, collecting mud and snow on her clothes. Vaughn's dark, lethal glance over his shoulder iced her blood.

He turned back to the creature. "Want more, you bastard?"

What kind of man challenged something like this creature? All Mariah wanted was to recover her y-axis enough to stand up and run the heck away from here.

But, sure enough, another rubbery blast of sheer terror exploded out from him, pushing her away again. What in the world? Was Vaughn truly creating an energy wave? How was that even possible?

The thing reared back and howled, becoming smaller in size. Or moving away. Hard to tell. She didn't care, as long as it left them alone.

"Soon," it howled, receding into the tree line. "Not now, but soon you will all be mine."

"Got it. Penciled in on my day planner," Vaughn growled. "Now go screw yourself."

Finally, the nasty creature faded into the forest.

Vaughn spun his horse around. The tight darkness of his expression relaxed, and his brows furrowed beneath his hat. "Mariah? Sweetheart?" he called. "Are you okay?"

She groaned and pressed her hands flat on the ground, working her way up to all fours and then getting shakily to her feet. The knees of her jeans were damp with the snow and mud ground into the fabric. She didn't care how bad she looked. She just wanted to leave this place. Maybe leave the ranch, too, and go far away. She hadn't signed on for this kind of danger when she considered a future with Vaughn.

Stark, white lines bracketed his eyes. "Grab my hand. Now." He reached out and leaned down, moving his foot from the stirrup so she could step up. He swung her up behind him. "Hold on tight."

Didn't have to tell her twice.

Vaughn kicked his horse into a full, terror-fueled run back to the ranch, the mare following. Mariah clung to him with a strong grip as his power sparked and flew out from him in waves. Her arms clenched around his midsection and her face that was pressed into his back reassured him. Calmed him.

Somewhat.

This little incident sure answered his earlier question. What woman wanted a relationship with a mentally unstable, alcoholic, transient, possible adulterer dragging around a suitcase full of guilt who, oh by the way, had a goddamned cloud demon, or whatever the hell that thing was, threatening him and anyone he hung around with?

As Vaughn galloped up to the main ranch, Garrison ran to open the gate. Farther away, Kerr and Eric bolted out of the house.

"Shelby said something had happened," Garrison called out.

"Fucking monster tried to kill Mariah."

"Son of a bitch."

Vaughn grimaced against the blistering headache. "Just help her down, would you?"

"You bet." As Vaughn unlatched her death grip from around his waist, Garrison tugged Mariah off the horse and eased her to the ground, keeping an arm around her.

Damn it all if Vaughn's power didn't resent his brother touching her. This power, this entire situation, was out of control on so many different levels.

Leaping off the horse, Vaughn then swung her up into his arms and rubbed his cheek against her forehead. "Mariah, it'll be all right."

No answer.

He strode into the house, ice pumping through his veins. The pounding in his chest matched the rhythm of her rattling teeth. She had to be okay.

He eased her into a kitchen chair. Her pupils had gone pinpoint, her eyes wide and lips pale.

"Does anything hurt? What about when you fell?" He chafed her cold hands.

In a jagged, cog-wheeling motion, she shook her head. "What was th-that thing?"

"We don't know, but it wants to destroy us. Shit. Once I know you're all right, I'm taking you home, okay?"

With Odie close behind, Ruth appeared and quickly checked Mariah over. "She's in shock, but her condition is improving. I don't believe anything's broken. Probably some bruises."

Vaughn's own body ached for any injury Mariah had sustained.

"What the hell are we supposed to do?" Garrison gritted out.

Shelby entered on crutches, wincing. She must be receiving a hell of an emotional blast from everyone around her.

Ruth pushed to her feet, studying each of the siblings. "Is this thing what you shot at the other day?"

"Yes, ma'am. We said it was a bear, but it was a…creature. It's also what attacked Shelby and Eric," Vaughn added.

Ruth and Odie exchanged a glance.

"Old news." Garrison smacked the table with his fist. Mariah jumped. "Sorry," he muttered.

Vaughn stood next to her, resting his hand on her upper back, needing the constant connection. He shook his head, trying to clear the static that had affected his hearing since he pushed that thing away. He had to concentrate to make out what everyone was saying. "It said it wanted all of us," he muttered. "Together."

After a resigned shrug from Odie, Ruth cleared her throat. "Maybe together, you all have the ability to destroy that thing. But together, you all are also vulnerable to attack."

"Holy catch-22, Batman. Got any information we can actually use, oh Magic 8 Ball?" Kerr barked what passed for a laugh. Then he stared at the nurse. "Wait a minute. Ruth, it sounds like you know more. Do tell."

She glanced behind her at Odie. "I know things."

Garrison opened his mouth like he wanted to take off the woman's head with his retort, but Shelby interjected, "It's true." Eric hovered while she hobbled over with her crutches and sat down in a chair. "Ruth somehow knew that I could adapt my power to help Eric."

As Vaughn scooted a chair over and sat, draping and arm around Mariah, his power, pulsing, staked out a ten-foot sphere. Ruth and Odie backed away several steps.

Kerr whipped his head up. "Dude, is that what you meant about your ability changing?" He put an arm up like a shield. "Because you need to stop that crap."

With effort, Vaughn tamped down the urge to push the entire world away from Mariah. "Sorry."

Ruth backed up another few steps, Odie holding her hand.

"Oh no, Ruth, you're not getting away without explaining what you know," Garrison said.

The woman pressed her lips together. Finally, she said, "What I shared with you is based on things I've seen before and conjecture from past research."

Garrison shook his head. "Research? Who the hell researches this kind of stuff? We need more information. Have you seen that thing before?"

"No," she said. "We've just heard about things like this...elsewhere."

A red-faced Garrison took a step toward her.

Odie held up his hand. "Stop, my friend. We don't know anything else, other than whatever's out there is scary."

The Taggarts couldn't strong-arm these two people to spill— they'd simply leave. Then Dad wouldn't have the help he needed.

"Okay, guys. Got it," Vaughn said, studying Mariah's face as her color improved. "Look, we won't take care of that...thing...tonight. In fact, it seems to want all of us together for some reason. It's best if we aren't in the same space. Too much of a temptation for that thing."

"We can't separate, though," Kerr said. "We have to protect the ranch."

Shelby rubbed the bridge of her nose. "How well is that plan working?"

Garrison dropped his fist on the tabletop. "Son of a bitch. He's right. We have to separate."

"Yeah. For now, let's make sure no more than three of us are here at the same time," Vaughn said. "I'm leaving with Mariah and staying with her tonight. You all do what you need to, and we'll caucus tomorrow."

"Got it," Garrison said, scowling over at Ruth.

"Mariah?" Vaughn murmured.

She looked him square in the face. "I'd like to go home," she whispered.

"That's the plan. You okay to walk?" He tugged her to stand, understanding now why Eric hovered next to Shelby. It killed Vaughn to see Mariah hurt and scared, and he'd do anything to prevent that from happening again.

Anything? Yes.

"I'm okay. I'm fine." She pasted a tiny and bland smile on her face as she headed toward the back door, her steps stiff and halting. "Just fine."

Fine? Not even close. He helped pull her coat closed.

If Vaughn had any doubt as to whether Mariah wanted to take on this extra-special bonus pile of crap that accompanied a future with him, no question remained now. She stumbled on the snow-covered gravel, and, prompted by a flare of his ability, he caught her under an elbow before she hit the ground.

She flinched.

In the late afternoon, the sun was setting behind gray clouds. He scanned the ranch property. Nothing out of place now.

But that could change.

If things got worse, Mariah would suffer.

Pausing before he opened the driver's side door of the truck, he centered himself, like he did before a fight. Only he wasn't going into an MMA bout.

What he was going to do tonight would be much harder.

CHAPTER 31

Mariah sat stiffly in the front seat as he maneuvered the pickup down the miles of ranch road, the ride made rougher by the frozen ground. God, it was taking forever to get back to her house.

She glanced at Vaughn and rolled her hands into fists. Damn him for…everything. She bit her lip. Maybe that wasn't completely fair.

Which pissed her off more? The fact that, for a second, she had considered jumping into Vaughn's mess of a life? Or the fact that no human should have as many bad things to deal with as Vaughn did?

And how about the part where he had created some kind of bizarre mind-meld. She hadn't signed on for that.

Peering out the window, she imagined that shadows grew into dark shapes with evil, red dots for eyes. Despite the insulation of her coat, she tucked her chin into the material and shoved her hands into pockets. Damn these shivers. She couldn't seem to warm up.

"More heat?" His voice pierced the silence, making her jump.

"I'm fine."

A muscle jumped on his jaw. "Yeah. Fine. Obviously." His clipped statement popped her like an emotional rubber band on tender skin.

They lapsed into an uneasy quiet, with the rumble of the truck as the background noise.

Man, she picked a winner in Vaughn, hadn't she?

That question made her as sad as the answer.

The worst part was that, sure, he had made some mistakes in the past. No question. But none of what happened today was his fault. None of it.

Could she stick with him, despite his literal demons and the fact that he might still leave town?

Maybe it was better to plan for a future devoid of Vaughn.

The issue wasn't the life-altering sex. It had nothing to do with the fact that she felt safer in his arms than she ever had anywhere else in her entire life. It wasn't that, despite their differences, they fit together like the perfect puzzle pieces.

Heck, they'd only known each other for a week.

But it felt like years.

In only a week, she'd caught glimpses of what it would be like to have a partner who cared for her but also would go to the mat for her. Literally.

Oh God, what was she going to do?

Balling her hands into fists in her coat pockets, she forced herself to take in a long, slow lungful of air, hold it for four seconds, then slowly let it out, using her go-to breathing exercise when stress became unbearable. She cycled through the breaths again, willing her shoulders and back muscles to relax when she exhaled.

He pulled the truck into her driveway.

Shoving the truck door open, she hurried to the porch, unlocked the front door, and paused. The sun was setting, and behind her, Vaughn's face fell into shadow. It would hurt, but she needed time alone to process everything.

"Well, thank you for the ride home."

"You're welcome." He didn't move but instead took up space between Mariah and the entire universe outside the house. Like he wanted to prevent anything from reaching her. Didn't work before, why should it work now?

"Um, so you have a good night," she tried again. Surely he would get the hint.

"I'm not going anywhere. That is," his voice dropped, "if you'll let me stay here with you."

Adrenaline shot through her limbs. "With me? Like last night?"

Heat flared as he met her gaze. "No. I can't imagine you want me that close to you, much less touching you." He chopped a hand through the air, stopping her protest before it left her mouth. "But that thing is still out there, and no way am I leaving you alone."

"But—"

His voice, a low gravelly sound, shredded her. "And as soon as I make sure you will not be hurt because of all my...bad stuff...I'll get out of your hair for good. I know you don't want anything to do with me after all that happened. I can't blame you."

"No, Vaughn. I don't think that."

"Then you're an idiot."

His words landed like a jab to the jaw, and she reeled backward a step. "What?"

"Hey, if you don't want me in your house, I won't argue. I can stay in the truck all night." He rubbed his temple. "But I need to be close."

"Is that you or your mental power talking?"

"Both."

Another shiver hit her, and she motioned him into the living room, flipping on the light. He took off his hat and stood a few inches inside the house but didn't move. The stark expression took her breath away.

No way could she ask him to guard her for the night. "Listen. I don't mind you staying here, but I'm sure I'll be fine."

He barked a laugh. "Fine."

"Yeah, fine."

"You weren't *fine* when that thing reached for you. Hell, you could have broken your neck falling off the back of that horse."

She stepped in front of him. "But I'm okay now."

With a rough knuckle, he brushed her aching jaw where she'd hit the ground. She flinched.

"Obviously."

"I'm not a fragile piece of china, you know."

"Hell yeah, I know you're tough as nails." He shoved his hand through his hair, giving him a wild appearance. "Even the biggest, baddest person in the world might not be able to stand up to whatever was out there tonight."

"That creature wasn't your fault, Vaughn."

"Wasn't it? Maybe not, but it was my fault that it got close enough to hurt you. And you'd better believe I won't make that same mistake again."

Her nerves sparked, irritating her skin, followed by a fleeting headache. "Hey, are you doing that psychic protective thing again?"

"Maybe. Why?"

The pieces fell together. "Because every time you do it, I get a headache. That's why I thought I was getting migraines over the past week. That's so strange."

"Well, let's ice that crappy cake." He entered the house behind her, slammed the door, and then leaned against it, hands rolled into fists and head hanging low. "An even more fucking fabulous side effect. If I leave you alone, you might get hurt. If I'm here with you, my presence will cause you pain. Damn it." He thumped his chest hard, like a bass drum. "I am sorry for everything, Mariah."

A virtual wave broke on top of her, pushing her underwater. "Everything?" she whispered.

"Listen to me." She had to strain to hear him. The words barely escaped his clenched jaw. "I would never trade what we had together last night for anything in the world. But somehow, because of our connection, it puts you square in the crosshairs of god-knows-what. Even worse, the simple act of being near me causes you pain. If anything happens to you, I'm not sure if I could live with myself."

Hot bubbles burst in her head; she blinked back tears. "So you're taking the blame for something you had no control over?"

"Well—

She crossed her arms. "Hush. I'm not done." His mouth gaped open. "When will you get it? You can't control everything that happens in life. You can't dictate someone's feelings. You can't make people behave in a certain way. We have no power over choices that other people make. Hell, I know that as well as anyone, with my past. So get it through your thick skull. None of this is your fault."

"Mariah." It sounded like the word had been ripped from his soul.

Lifting a hand, she shook her head. "Know what? I'm done talking. You want to wallow in self-pity and blame? Be my guest. But don't make me a party to it." She pointed. "In the hall closet, there's bedding for the sofa couch, if you'd like. Take whatever food you want from the fridge and pantry. I'm done for the night."

"But what about…?

"Your past?" she snapped. He reared back. Good. Maybe this gut-wrencher of a chat would shake him out of his self-pity. "You know what? You're right. People make bad decisions. Sometimes they make horrible ones. You can't fix what happened in the past. But you sure as hell can learn from it and become better for it. So, yes,

I'm disappointed by some of your past, but I am judging the man in front of me today. Got it?"

"I'm sor—"

"If you complete that statement, I cannot be held responsible for what I do." She ignored the quirk at a corner of his mouth before she walked away. Spinning back, she pointed at her temple. "And for at least a minute, could you stop whatever the hell you're doing that involves my head? If the Tylenol doesn't fix this headache, you're going to have hell to pay. Now, let me get some rest. I have to work tomorrow."

Slamming the door to her bedroom satisfied her for all of ten seconds, until she sank to the bed and dropped her head in her hands. Never had she said things like that to anyone before. Should she apologize? Not yet.

Let him think about it.

She pulled on pajama pants and a tank top and crawled into her cold, empty bed.

Tomorrow she'd reassess where things stood and decide whether her heart could handle another try at a relationship with Vaughn or not.

CHAPTER 32

Vaughn woke with a start, his temples throbbing, and immediately scanned the living room. "Christ." When had he fallen asleep?

A noise came from her bedroom. Danger. Mariah.

He flew from the couch to her bedroom door, following the pulse of fear that sent his power dials to eleven. Easing the door open, he readied for a fight.

She thrashed on the bed, mumbling, her hair sticking to the sweaty skin of her face. He scanned the room and used the light from his cell phone to check under the bed and in the closet. *Nothing that could hurt her.*

Except him, of course.

He turned to go but couldn't do it. He could not leave her here, alone, scared.

Fuck him. Fuck everything.

He padded in socked feet to the side of the bed and knelt. "Mariah?" He rocked her shoulder until her eyes fluttered open.

"Vaughn?" Her voice cracked. "You're here." The words came from her lips like a prayer, and she clamped her hand down on his wrist. "Please."

"Anything, sweetheart. Please what? I'll do whatever you need me to." Except leave her vulnerable to attack by that creature.

As if she knew exactly how to break him, she whispered, "Stay with me."

"Are you sure that's a good idea?"

"Yes." She guided his hand to her cheek and nuzzled it.

Damp. Her skin wasn't sweaty. Those were goddamned tears. Guilt flayed him alive.

"You…you really want me here? After everything?"

Even with the midnight shadows, he spied her frown. "Unless you're not comfortable being around me…"

"Oh, hell no," he said. "I want to be here more than anywhere in the world."

"Then yes. Please." She tugged on his arm until he crawled over her and slid under the blankets. He rested on his side, head propped on a hand, other arm making a triangle over her torso.

In the low light, the glow of the smooth skin of her chest and neck turned his tongue to sand. How the hell would he get through this night? Damn it, didn't matter. He'd keep his hands off and watch over her if that was required of him.

She sat halfway up, a tank top-covered breast brushing against his arm and making him rethink that vow to maintain his distance. "Vaughn. I need…"

"What? Anything."

"I—" She pressed her lips to his.

For the dumbest second of his life, he froze. He wanted to rip off her clothes and bury himself deep, pushing her over the edge time and again. Nothing tender about the way he wanted her.

But tonight, he needed to be different. He needed to make love to her. Temper his hunger and focus it in a different way. Stroking her mouth with his, he poured gentle care into the kisses.

So the guy who walked right into the fists of opponents and didn't give a crap, the guy who would rather leave town than destroy his brother's life, the guy who wanted to go guns-a-blazing to destroy that demon whatever-it-was…that guy dialed the burner back from boil to simmer.

Her tiny gasps as he worshipped her with his mouth made him want to tithe at the Church of Mariah for the rest of his godforsaken life.

Tomorrow. Tomorrow he'd cut her loose.

Tonight was hers.

Mariah rubbed sandpapery eyes as her alarm buzzed. Snowy dawn gave the room a cool, gray light, and she missed the warmth of snuggling in Vaughn's arms. She stretched muscles that were sore from another night of sheer bliss.

She had floated with him on a cloud of passion and tenderness for hours last night. The gentleness and connection stunned her.

If she had questioned whether she should stick with Vaughn and give their relationship a try, if she had wondered if she could support him as he worked through his serious issues, the morning brought clarity. Everyone had baggage. God, she had her fair share.

It's what you did despite the setbacks that counted.

Was it the earth-tilting sex that made the decision to try for a future with Vaughn? Didn't hurt.

But honestly, it was the man himself. The solid guy who tormented himself about things over which he had no control. The man who put others before his own interests. The man who had gone through hell and come out better on the other side.

She pulled on her pajama pants and a sweatshirt. A flutter of excitement swirled in her belly. She could do this, tell him how she felt. Whatever the future held, they would face it together.

Weightless effervescence propelled her into the living room.

Vaughn stood in front of the living room window, hands gripping the curtain rail, his back to her, his big torso blocking the early dawn light.

"Good morning," she called, eager to sink back into his arms.

He turned, stiff. Mechanical. The hard planes of his face were indistinct in shadow.

Clicking on the lamp next to the couch, she froze. That sensual mouth that had given her unending pleasure last night was now jammed into an unyielding, grim line. That gold-glinting gaze that had curled her toes last night had gone cold, like pyrite in a polluted streambed.

Maybe he was tired. Did he doubt her feelings? Of course. How could he know? She hadn't told him anything yet.

Squaring her shoulders, she approached him. This time, though, proximity to Vaughn didn't create any warmth.

In fact, the temperature dropped ten degrees.

"Feeling better?" he asked, not moving.

"Better?"

"Better than yesterday."

"Sure." She pulled back. "What?"

"I hope I made you feel better." His words came out flat. Dead.

Unable to form words, her mind raced to catch up, leaving her mouth gaping open for too long. "Pardon me?"

He blinked and a flash of intense hunger flipped back to the cold boredom. "You deserved to feel good after the danger I exposed you to yesterday."

"That wasn't why—" Her voice caught. "What happened on the ranch wasn't your fault." She gulped past a hard lump. "Look, I—"

He stopped her with a slash of his hand in the air. "No, let me say this. I had plenty of time to think last night. This…fling—whatever we have here—needs to stop. Now." His statements sliced through her like fiery whip lashes. "It was fun for a while, but let's face reality. There's no future."

"Wait, what?" How she heard him with her heart pounding double time, she didn't know. It was hard to fill her lungs. Nausea crashed into her in churning waves.

His hands balled into fists at his side, but his expression remained etched in granite. "It's for the best. I'm blowing out of town soon anyway. Don't get me wrong. Things were great for a few days. What a stress reliever, huh?" Another pained crease across his brow, then it went ice rink smooth and cold. "You're smoking hot and smart as hell. But let's get real. You don't fit in with my family. I don't fit into your life. This little fling was never meant to be anything serious."

This little…fling? The one time she'd trusted someone with her heart and soul.

And he'd thrown it away like stinky trash.

You don't fit in…

Had she imagined their connection? Had her feelings truly been so one-sided?

Air wouldn't move through her trachea.

He'd made his choice and it didn't involve Mariah. There was no need to say anything more. No need to beg, no counterarguments. This was it. Done and done. She needed to do something about the fist squeezing the hell out of her heart before she passed out.

You don't fit in with my family…

No way. She would not break.

She locked her knees and shoved an invisible ramrod down her spine. His crappy speech sucked, but she would not give him the satisfaction of seeing any reaction.

"All right, then." He dusted his palms together, like he was washing his hands of her. "Glad to see you're okay. My apologies for all that you had to deal with recently. Take care."

With a light step out the front door, he eased the door closed. No slamming, no storming off. No drama.

Nothing.

Which was exactly what they had all along.

A fleeting headache came and went.

The truck engine fired up, headlights throwing lurid shadows on her wall as he backed out of the driveway. Dropping to the carpet on her knees, she curled forward, hand pressed to her chest, mouth open in a silent cry.

CHAPTER 33

The world's biggest asshole slammed the truck door and stomped across the frozen ground and into the kitchen.

As one, Garrison, Kerr, and Odie looked up from their seats at the kitchen table, half-eaten meals in front of them.

"Rough week last night?" Kerr quipped.

"Shut up." Vaughn so wanted to wipe the floor with that know-it-all face. "So, what are you three stooges doing together? Looks like you're plotting world domination."

Garrison groaned. "Fight with Sara this morning."

"I'm facilitating the therapy," Kerr winked. "Want to make it a group session?"

"Have a seat, *mon ami*. We're trying to figure out women," Odie drawled. "We have no leads, no advantage, and no hope of ever solving the puzzle. You got any ideas?"

Vaughn motioned to his rumpled, unshaven, sorry-ass appearance. "Does it appear that I have a clue about women?"

Odie patted the chair next to him, his glass-green eyes disgustingly merry. "You might need something stronger than coffee this morning."

Kerr whistled low.

"That's the last thing I need, trust me." Vaughn slumped into the chair and scrubbed his face. "What's the plan for dealing with the badness stalking our ranch?"

"Way to change the subject, slick," Kerr quipped. "How about fill us in on the woman details first. Why the long face, Trigger?"

Garrison rubbed his own stubbled jaw. "Yeah. You look like you had your ass handed to you."

"In two fists." Vaughn studied his brother, like Garrison might have the answers. Nope. "I'm an idiot."

"Well, we had to endure the story about Garrison's screw-up." Kerr straightened. "Your turn. Inquiring minds want to know."

"Nothing, man. It's nothing."

"You walk in here, almost taking the door off the hinges, and it's nothing?" Kerr pursed his lips. "Not buying it. Welcome to circle-sharing time for the boys. We'll all take turns. You're up."

"I ended things with Mariah this morning."

Silence fell for a few seconds before Kerr leaned back. "Before or after you made a few more O faces with her?" The way Kerr cocked his head to the side, Vaughn's hands itched to strangle his kid brother.

"Fuck off."

"Okey dokey, but I do prefer a little privacy." Kerr grinned, then he sat straight and glared at him. "Holy shit, you really did the nasty first and then broke it off? That's pretty cold, even for a jerk like you."

Vaughn sucked in air and prayed he wouldn't kill Kerr.

Odie lifted a hand. "Maybe we should refocus here."

"Who the hell are you to talk?" Vaughn snapped.

The Cajun chopped his hand through the air. "Listen closely, boys, and maybe one day you'll have a long, meaningful relationship with a beautiful woman who puts up with your stupidity."

Garrison grinned. "Like you?"

He rolled his lips together, the beard and moustache meeting in the middle. "Me? No. I've only known Ruth for a year. A mere blip of time in the grand scheme of the universe, really. But once I figured out that my life meant nothing without her, I pulled my sorry self together in a hurry, before I lost her. You hear me, *mon ami?*" Damn. The guy went from jovial to dead serious in a millisecond.

"What you're saying is, don't make mistakes with a woman," Vaughn muttered. "One, that's impossible. Two, a moron could have figured out that advice."

"Yet here you sit." He sighed. "No, my friend. What I am saying is, when you find the woman who you would die for, the woman who makes you a better person and a hell of a better man,"—resting his thick forearms on the table, Odie propped his hands on the rim of the mug—"if you're smart, then there should be absolutely nothing in the world that prevents you from holding on to her for as long as she will allow you to do so."

Vaughn winced as the man's words, like an arrow, hit a bull's-eye on his heart.

"And your credentials in family counseling are from what university?" Kerr raised orange brows.

Odie shot a tight smile. "My credentials are far more than you'll ever know. Let's just say that I know what it feels like to have someone I love ripped away. I know what it feels like to see someone I love hurt because of my stupid decisions." He pushed away from the table and stood. "You can learn from my mistakes or keep making your own and live with regret for the rest of your life."

"That's the worst *Dear Abby* advice I've ever heard." Kerr rolled his eyes.

"Is it? What will you sacrifice for the person you care about?"

"I don't—" Kerr sputtered. "There's no one."

Garrison shook his head and glared. For a split second, he looked like Dad, giving his sons hell. "There'd better not be. Least of all someone with the last name of Brand."

Odie cut off Kerr's sputtered response. "All that matters is that you don't miss your chance. There aren't a lot of do-overs in this life." His mouth twisted into a grimace, like he had an awful private joke. "And you'll pay dearly for the do-overs you get."

Vaughn didn't like the sound of that sage advice. "Where are you going?"

He rubbed his beard. "To personally thank my wife for sticking with an old, dumb Cajun and to beg her to stay with me for years to come."

"How are you going to do that?" Garrison mumbled.

"For starters, I'll tell her that I'm sorry."

Kerr coughed on coffee. "For what?"

Odie whipped around. "It don' matter, boys. But those two words are a great place to start. *I'm sorry* softens the ladies right up. Putty in your hands. Primes the pump. You don't even have to give her specifics, just bury what little pride you have left and say it." He cut his eyes to Vaughn. "You should try it before the chance is gone." Turning on his heel, he swaggered out of the kitchen.

Vaughn tried hard not to make eye contact with his brothers.

"Damn. I'm a real idiot, huh?" Vaughn moaned.

Garrison pulled out his phone and raised his hand. "Don't bother me. I need to text Sara and hope to God she'll talk to me again." Head down, he typed as he slowly walked out of the kitchen.

"You two are one grovel away from losing your man cards," Kerr said. "So, what are you going to do, Vaughn? Crawl back?"

"She may not talk to me again. I'm not sure what to do."

"Wait. You don't know? Let me get this straight. You have a smart, beautiful woman who, by some miracle, digs you despite your weird brain stuff, sordid history, and caveman complex. Oh, and you're ugly. And you kicked that awesome package to the curb?"

"Fuck." He began to sweat.

"Here you sit, still unable to figure out the right thing to do?"

"Uh…"

"Even a blind man can see that was a boneheaded move. What were you thinking?"

Vaughn tried with two hands to scrub the stupid off his face. "I was thinking it would be good if she didn't get hurt by the insanity going on here."

"So you hurt her…to keep her from being hurt?" Kerr flipped two thumbs up. "Way to go, Romeo."

Vaughn shoved to his feet and grabbed his coat. "Fuck if I know what's the best thing to do in this situation. For now, I'm going to do chores until I'm too exhausted to think about stupid crap like feelings. If I'm lucky, I won't reach for something that has 'proof' on the label." He wet his lips. God, how good would a stiff whiskey taste right now? And the numbness to follow would be wonderful.

"Dude."

"Don't worry. I'll steer clear of the Wild Turkey. For now. Damn it. Even if I beg for forgiveness, I don't know if I can ask her to step into the mess we've got here. When Mr. Text Apology stops groveling and wants to discuss the monster trying to kill our family, let me know. As much as I want to fix this disaster with Mariah, there's a bigger problem waiting out there."

CHAPTER 34

Damn Vaughn Taggart anyway.

And damn herself. For a person who gave out advice all day long, she had a hell of a personal blind spot.

It took all of her energy to focus on each patient in the office today and not make mistakes. But her eyes burned as she tried to read the blurry medical record on the computer. Picking the right doses of medication became dicey. The day dragged along, slower and longer than it ever should.

It wasn't like she had tons to look forward to after work.

God, she had been so stupid.

Which hurt worse: trusting Vaughn and being wrong or trusting *herself* and being wrong?

Moot point. He made a choice and it didn't involve her. Then why did it feel like an ice pick had been driven through her chest?

Get a grip. Do your job. Personal issues needed to wait until after work.

An urgent add-on showed up on the end of her schedule. Izzy Brand.

At 5:45 p.m., Mariah knocked and entered the exam room.

"Hi, Izzy." She forced her upbeat tone.

The woman stared at the floor. "Hi." Her voice came out flat.

"What can I do for you today?" Settling on the rolling stool, Mariah rested her hands on crossed legs and waited.

Izzy shoved her golden blonde hair away from her face. Tears shimmered in her stunning blue eyes, underscored with dark circles.

The woman's lower lip trembled. "Do you…um, do you have something I could take so I don't care about my life?"

Whoa. Mariah leaned forward, medical radar on high alert. "Could you explain that a little more?"

No words emerged for thirty seconds. Izzy brushed at the tears with the heel of her hand, and Mariah offered a box of Kleenex. "It's like I can't take the stress with my mom, my family, and everything anymore. Life. Right now."

"Do you feel like you want to harm yourself or someone else?" Oh, God. Was this vibrant, pleasant woman suicidal?

"No. I wouldn't do anything like that." She sniffed and crumpled a tissue in her hand. "It's that…there's no end in sight. I'm doing most of the work to help Mom. And that's okay. I mean, she's my mom and all. I understand that she's got a difficult medical condition where complications happen. It's not her fault. Then my brother, Hank, disappeared not long after he went off the rails. Now people in town look at me like I'm bad, too. I can't handle the judgment, especially from people I—"

"What?"

"Nothing." She blew her nose. "Now Wyatt and Tommy are bossing me around."

"Are they threatening you?"

"No. Not really. Just being mean."

"Mean, how?"

"You know how brothers are, right?"

Mariah nodded, but truly, Kevin had never, ever been mean to her.

Izzy touched her damp cheek. "Their comments to me are cruel, like why can't I do more to help around the house and why am I so nosy about their business. Good grief. I'm twenty-six years old. Time for my own life, right? But every time I get fed up and think about moving out, the guilt about Mom stops me. My brothers make me feel like, if I leave, Mom'll die." She whispered, "It's like I'm trapped."

"Trapped?"

"Sometimes, yes." A grim smile flickered across her face. "No matter what I do, it's the wrong answer. And I don't understand this other thing going on." She leaned forward, elbows on her worn winter pants. "But there's something else happening. At home."

Mariah tilted her head. "I don't follow."

"When I go home, everything there feels heavy. Depressing. Dark."

A strange shiver worked its way down Mariah's arms. "Are you sure that's not maybe your own mood talking?"

Izzy burst into tears again. "I don't know anymore. I have no idea. Everything I do takes so much effort. It's like every day, I'm waiting for something bad to occur. I can't take it anymore." She sniffed. "You know what I do sometimes? There's a cave near the house. Well, it's about a forty-five-minute walk straight off the back of the house. I even notched some trees to make a path, since I go there so often. Some days, I sit in that cave and dream about living there, alone."

More internal alarms went off in Mariah's head. Izzy was in real distress. "Have you thought about counseling?

"What counselor wants to deal with this mess?"

"That's their job. There are good counselors. They can help."

"You got a counselor who's a saint? Because that's what it's going to take for someone to dig through this mess." Her laugh edged on hysteria and tears, and she took a shuddering breath. "How about that pill so I won't care about my life right now?"

"Um, I'm not sure we specifically have that."

"Sure you do, Doc. Come on, don't hold out on me." A wobbly smile capped the comment. "Anything?"

"Well, how about we start with a low-dose antidepressant, some counseling, and we meet again in a week?"

"That's not a bad idea. It'll give me something to look forward to." She raised her hands when Mariah opened her mouth. "Kidding. Okay, not really."

Mariah stepped out to send the prescription to the local pharmacy. Six p.m. Most staff had gone home. The day was almost done. Thank God.

When she came back in the room, Izzy had her cell phone clutched to her ear, eyes wide. Her chest rose and fell rapidly.

"Okay. Yeah, but is she—?" Izzy shoved her hair back off her face. "All right. I can check on her when I get home." She pursed her lips. "I know it's bad," she snapped into the phone. "That's all we can do." Ending the call, she rubbed her face. "Sorry."

"Everything okay?"

"No. Mom's not doing well."

"Like you mentioned before? How her health is causing you stress?"

"No. Now is different. Tommy said she's having trouble breathing and she's talking out of her mind."

Mariah fingered the stethoscope around her neck. "Can he get her to the hospital? If not, call an ambulance. We'll run some more tests. The pneumonia could be back. Or she could be septic."

"You know Mom. She refused to let the boys call 911. Tommy said she'd only see you, and she won't leave the house."

"What?"

"He's going to try to get her to go to the ER. If she shows up there, would you see her?"

"Sure. I'll be here doing paperwork for another hour or so." Because no way did she want to go to her empty house alone. "If she comes in, I'll see her name pop up on the ER census." No way did Mariah want to make another house call out to the Brand ranch, either.

Izzy rubbed her face. "I don't know if I can handle any more. If Mom dies…Oh, man. Worst of all, Mom's kind of a jerk at times. Must run in the family."

"I don't know about that, Izzy. But, yes, if they can get her to the ER, I'll do what I can to help her."

Izzy's eyes lit up, like this was the first piece of hope she'd heard in ages. "Deal." She sniffed. "I've got another few hours to work at the store tonight. Then I'll stop by the hospital. Hopefully she'll be here. Thank you." She tucked her worn jacket over an arm and exited the exam room.

"Of course."

A little over an hour later, Mariah's stomach rumbled. A few snacks from the break room hadn't made much of a dent in her hunger, and she stared at her desk computer. She sighed and updated the hospital's census. No Mrs. Brand registered or admitted to the ER yet. Mariah could just imagine the effort it would take to get that woman to the hospital.

Finally, she traded her white coat for her wool one and headed for her car.

Tossing her satchel into the front seat, she turned at the sound of a vehicle approaching. For a brief second, her heart leapt.

Not an old ranch truck. Not Vaughn.

The Brand family conversion van rattled to a stop. Mariah glanced in the window. Looked like Tommy at the wheel. He cracked open the passenger-side window.

"Izzy said you might check on Mom."

Not exactly. "In the ER."

A jerk of his head in the shadows. "She won't go. Can you talk sense into her?"

No depth to his words. Wooden. A chill worked through her. Something was off.

Behind him, the silhouette of a figure.

Crap. Mariah blew on her hands to warm them.

Tommy motioned her to the side of the vehicle.

Mariah pulled the door open and stepped up. The folded gate hit her at waist height.

Tommy stared straight ahead. The car was still running.

The figure in the chair turned. From the shadow of the vehicle, Wyatt lunged at Mariah and wrapped her in his meaty arms, muffling her scream. As he dragged her into the van, he kicked the door closed with his booted foot. "Go." It took no effort for him to keep her from moving.

She worked her face out of his stuffy, stale shirt. "This is illegal!" she screamed, her heart pounding double time. Another time, with a vehicle screeching up to Mariah and Kevin as they ran over red-dusted roads, overlaid this scenario. Caught. Trapped. No. Not this time. She would fight. "Let me go! Stop it," Mariah commanded him as she twisted her head to look at him.

A weird red glow came and went in Wyatt's eyes, like the guy was possessed. "Then you need to behave. If you get out of line, Doc, we're taking it out on Mom."

"What?" Air came in and out of Mariah's mouth, but no other words followed. Her head spun. No way could she be in the middle of a kidnapping. This had to be a bad dream.

Think. Come up with a plan. Play along or, or...placate them.

"Fine, I'll cooperate. What's this about?" She craned her neck toward the front seat. "Tommy, you're the sheriff—what's the deal?" She held off on reminding them that they were committing a felony. Pretty sure all parties had clarity on that item, and if sworn law enforcement officials didn't care, then...Damn it.

Tommy kept his hands planted on the wheel and head locked forward. It was like he was in a trance or something.

Had Izzy known what her brothers were planning?

Before she could sort through the possibilities, more waves of memories crashed over Mariah's mind, drowning her. That hot, confined plywood room. The men outside the door with guns. The image of her brother's swollen and bruised face after their first escape attempt.

Bile burned its way up her throat, but she forced it back down and concentrated on staying calm. At least with her head turned, she wouldn't suffocate in the musty flannel of Wyatt's shirt. Man, could he try to bathe at least once a week?

Could Vaughn pick up on her danger?

What were the rules with his psychic power when he broke up with the object of his protection? Damn it. Tears stung.

Quit it. Concentrate on coming up with options.

Instead, she went numb, closed herself off from everything that was happening. It was like she floated separate from her body. She couldn't deal; she just went very, very still. Sounds and light faded in and out. All the activity detached, and she watched, like an audience member, while the bizarre events unfolded. She had little connection to the terror inside the car.

After some length of time—a minute or forty, who knew?—dimly, as if the audience member rubbed her eyes and wondered if she had nodded off, Mariah focused on the sensations around her. She felt the rumble of the road change to what felt more like the chip-seal. Then another fifteen minutes later, Tommy steered the vehicle onto a bumpy road. Each rut and divot rammed the undercarriage of the van against her tailbone. As they traveled what she assumed was the Brand ranch access road, the air turned thick. Oppressive.

Taking a breath took effort.

A blanket of *wrong* wrapped around her. There might be some truth to Izzy's sensations here on the ranch.

If Mariah concentrated hard enough she could convince herself that something terrifying lurked in the woods.

Waiting.

Something bigger. Darker. Worse than Tommy and Wyatt.

Shadows flickered over the car windows, just like all those times she'd watched the tiny gap between door and casing in that awful room back in Utah. Flick. A shadow of her captor. Another flick, and he walked the other way. Breathing became difficult.

The minivan rolled to a stop outside the main house. The Brand house. Numbness fled, chased by an ice-water splash of stark reality.

Every instinct screamed at her to run and fight. Wyatt cranked down his vice-like, unfriendly hug until her ribs creaked.

"Honey, we're home." Wyatt snickered as he pushed down the ramp and hauled Mariah out of the minivan. His grip on her upper arm squeezed hard enough that her hand went numb, even through the coat.

She heard no other sounds besides the scrapes of feet and vehicle doors opening and closing. Gravel crunched under booted feet.

Nothing else moved, not even a breeze through pine boughs.

Wrong. This was so wrong.

She dragged her feet and tripped, banging her knees on the porch boards. The last thing she wanted to do was enter this house.

Wyatt yanked her up, wrenching her arm. "Won't you come in?"

CHAPTER 35

E xhausted from his attempts to physically exercise the stupid out of his body all day, Vaughn settled on taking a cold shower that evening. Maybe he could finish the purge by scouring the bad decision-making off of his skin. Then he'd figure out what to do about Mariah.

What he had done to her went beyond wrong. He thunked his head against the tile and stayed in that position for several minutes, the chilly spray pinging off his back.

He would crawl back to her, but that was no guarantee of success.

First, though, he needed to check on Dad. Then he could confront his mistakes head on.

After drying off, he pulled on clean clothes and went down to the kitchen. With Ruth and Odie hovering nearby, Dad leaned on his walker as he cooked a simple dinner. Vaughn didn't care if they called the activity "occupational therapy"—he called it a damned miracle.

Zach, Garrison's son, flitted around them like a deranged hummingbird. The running monologue from the kid numbed Vaughn's brain.

"Hi, Uncle Vaughn!" His nephew waved.

Vaughn gave a half-hearted wave and surreptitiously studied Zach. No evidence of strange behavior. Maybe Garrison would get his wish and the development of an ability would skip a generation.

"Where's your dad?" He tousled Zach's dark red hair.

"In the living room, reading with Ms. Lopez."

If Sara had returned, then Garrison must have eaten a bucketful of crow.

Vaughn could take some lessons.

"Hi, son." One side of his dad's mouth didn't move, so the smile came out crooked, but happiness glowed in his watery blue eyes. Vaughn wanted to hug him but didn't want to break his dad's concentration.

"How's it going?"

Dad clanked a plate. "Pretty good." His voice came out slurred but understandable. Improved, even, over the past few days. Amazing.

"I'll say. He's doing great." Odie waggled his brows. "We'll have him cooking proper gumbo soon. I don't know how you people can live without okra here at the end of the Earth."

Vaughn squeezed his dad's shoulder. "Way to go. Dinner smells great."

"It's because I'm helping!" Zach reminded him.

"Sssecret ingredient." Dad pointed a spatula toward his grandson.

"What's the time for dinner?" Vaughn asked, unwilling to examine the knot that had formed in his throat.

Ruth leaned a hip against the counter but kept his dad in her line of sight. "Soon. Around seven, give or take. Your brothers and sister are waiting for you in the living room."

Family meeting. Great. Just what he didn't want.

"Shouldn't you go as well, *chérie*?" Odie asked.

"Shush," she said.

Yes, why would Ruth want to attend a family meeting? "Do you have something to add regarding the creature we're up against?" Vaughn asked.

She flicked a glance at Odie and shook her head. "As I mentioned yesterday, we've heard stories over the years."

"Stories?"

"People experiencing…similar things as you have described."

Now if that wasn't an evasive answer. "If you know anything that might help…"

"I'll be along in a few minutes," she mumbled.

With no energy left to crack the enigma that was Ruth, Vaughn turned and headed to the living room.

Shelby sat in the recliner, her feet up. An elastic bandage wound over her lower leg and around the metal posts that joined a vertical rod holding her fractured leg together. God, what she'd gone through. If only he'd gotten there sooner.

Eric hovered next to the chair, arms crossed over his chest like some oversized bouncer.

Garrison sat on the couch next to Sara. When she made a move to get up, he asked her to stay. Guess she was part of the family now. Whatever spat those two had was long forgotten, given the sappy expressions they shot each other.

And then there was Kerr, perched in the reading chair, back straight, staring into space like his nightmares danced right in front of him.

Vaughn tucked himself next to the other end of the fireplace mantel and settled in for an unpleasant evening.

"Thought we weren't supposed to be in the same place at the same time?" Vaughn muttered.

Shelby nodded. "We're leaving as soon as our family conference is done."

Garrison raised his hand. "Here's the deal."

Way to command the stage.

His brother rubbed his jaw. "We have crazy neighbors who are clearly becoming more unstable. Hank Brand tried to kill members of our family, and has since gone missing. No one has any leads where he went." His jaw muscle jumped until Sara twined her fingers with his. "Wyatt Brand then stepped up to fill the shoes Hank left behind. And creepy cousin Linc who, from Vaughn's description, is as nutty as the rest of them, dangerous, and a loose cannon to boot, may be part of the mix."

"And what about that creature out there?" Vaughn asked.

"That, too. What's worked against that thing thus far?" Garrison asked.

"We're having a meeting about how to beat it, so obviously nothing has worked yet." Vaughn's nerves prickled. His power reached out beyond the ranch, searching. Like it wanted to draw his attention. Not this time. He'd had enough of his damned power altering his brain waves.

"Garrison and I yelled at it and it went away," Shelby offered. "Then when it tried to kill Eric, I somehow turned my ability into a heat shield and held it off."

"But you almost died," Eric growled.

Vaughn rubbed a palm against his chin. "Garrison shot it. And I pushed that thing away when my power shifted. Not sure if I have another gear, but I'm willing to try." Vaughn flinched like he'd been slapped by an invisible hand. "Damn it."

"What?" Kerr asked.

"No idea. Weird," he said, rubbing his cheek. "Must be because I'm tired." He rolled his neck, an ache in his head increasing.

"So what, then? We have a black blob that wants to kill us." Garrison shook his head. "Anywhere else, that would be ridiculous, but in our world, when added to the neighbors who are sabotaging us, that thing really becomes the cherry on top of a shit sundae." He put his arm around Sara, tucking her in closer to him.

"Shouldn't we focus on the neighbors?" Kerr asked.

"You'd like that, wouldn't you?" Garrison snapped. "A certain neighbor, maybe?"

Kerr flushed red, then lifted his hands. "Bro. Easy, there. Throwing stones in glass houses and crap like that."

"Come on, guys, back off." Shelby pinched the bridge of her nose while Eric glowered at all of them. "My filter is still not 100 percent. I can't stop all the emotions smacking into me."

"Sorry," they mumbled.

"Son of a bitch," Garrison cursed. "So what do we do with that fire-breathing cloud monster that wants to destroy all of us?"

Silence.

"You either stand together and take the risk of failure or success. Or try to survive, but remain apart." Ruth stood at the doorway to the living room. Her face appeared sculpted from stone. Odie hovered behind her shoulder.

"Speak clearly," Garrison snapped.

"The thing wants the four of you together." Her eyes seemed to sink into her head, giving her a tired, haunted expression. "I've…heard of such things before."

Vaughn studied her poker face until her gaze wavered. First time the façade had cracked. "You've more than heard of these things, haven't you?" A twinge flitted across his temple. Damn it.

She blinked. "Doesn't matter. What matters is that you must be at your strongest and in control of your powers when you confront that thing. That time isn't now. Not yet."

Garrison whipped his head around. "How do you know details about our powers?"

"Truly, I don't know all that you are able to do," Ruth said. "But I'm convinced that if you pool your gifts, when the time is right, you can destroy the creature."

"If we can't?" Shelby asked.

"Your destruction will provide the foundation, the fuel, for something truly evil."

Kerr rubbed his leg. "Well, that's super good news."

"Until you are all strong enough," she flicked her eyes to Shelby, "you need to stay separate. That thing will wait to attack when you're all together."

Garrison glared at her. "Seriously, I'm done with the oracle act. Spill." He thunked a fist on his palm. "I've had enough. You're not leaving until you explain how you know these things."

Silence. The wind blew. A shutter creaked.

No one exhaled.

Ruth and Odie could have been carved in marble, so still did they stand.

She bit her lip and glanced at Odie. "We are very old."

"Like in your forties?" Kerr quipped.

No one laughed.

Ruth swallowed. "I'm actually your great-great many times great-grandmother."

"—the fuck?" Vaughn said.

Everyone started talking at once.

Garrison barked, "Wait a minute. Hold on. Just hold on." He stared at Ruth.

"Don't, Gar. You promised," Shelby breathed.

He stood and faced Ruth across the room. His hands rolled into fists as he stared at her.

Odie stepped in front of his wife. "Don't what?"

With a hoarse cry, Ruth rubbed her temples.

"Quit it, my friend." Odie physically held up his wife for a solid twenty seconds.

Garrison winced. "It's done." Tight lines formed next to his grim mouth. "I don't know how it's true, but she's not lying."

"You would doubt her?" The Cajun didn't let go.

"He needed to do it," Ruth murmured, no longer sagging against her husband. "You know it's true. We're hundreds of years old."

No reason to doubt it. Lie-detecting brother had checked.

"Distant relative, why are you here? And how is it possible for you to be this old?" Garrison asked.

A weird echo, like a scream in the distance, made Vaughn wince and whip his head to the side. He checked the room. No one else appeared to hear anything. He rubbed his temples again to try to sweep away the growing headache. The back of his head prickled. Was his power activating? Shit. Why? He tried to relax by taking a few slow breaths.

"It's a really long story. But I'm here now to help you all," Ruth said.

Shelby stared at the door. "Help us defeat that thing? Then you know what it is."

"Not exactly. We have some guesses. And we're not yet certain how you can destroy it. We've never seen anything quite like what you've described."

Kerr leaned back in his seat. "That's remarkably unhelpful. Could you go back to the centuries-old part?"

"Yes, in a moment." She sighed. "I know that this information is not helpful. That's why we didn't want to say anything until we had more details."

Garrison snorted. "Still don't buy the story. And it would have made more sense at the interview last week to lead with the part about centuries-old distant relations—not to mention information on a monster stalking the family."

"Well, the monster part did come later. And I'm sorry to have withheld that background. All I know for sure is that you do not yet want to be together. You're not ready. Once you can all fight, then…"

"Then what? We become bait—" Vaughn grabbed his head and leaned against the mantel, his legs wobbling beneath him. What the hell? Without his consciously releasing it, his power had popped out like a damn parachute from his mind, then collapsed inward into infinite gravity, sucking him in.

Then exploded outward again.

"What's going—oh, no!" Shelby cried, holding up her hands to defend herself.

Eric leaned in front of her, as if he could protect her from the bad emotions flying out of Vaughn's exploding head.

"Man, dude," Kerr leaned back in the chair. "I even felt that through my connection with Shelby."

Shelby tucked deeper into Eric's arms.

Something familiar and horrible rained back down on Vaughn's conscious brain. His power pulsed, searching, desperate to surround…

Mariah.

Oh, shit.

CHAPTER 36

Despite the chill in the Brands' house, sweat prickled between Mariah's breasts. The thud of her pulse echoed Wyatt's footsteps as he paced, firearm in hand, in front of her chair. She held her breath.

Linc grinned from the couch. "This is great, huh?"

"Shut up," Wyatt growled.

The impact of the shotgun butt on the table made every nerve in Mariah's body jump. *Stay calm. Don't give them anything to retaliate against.*

She had really been kidnapped.

Again.

This time, though, she was getting out of here on the first try. And alive, by God.

Step one, negotiate. "Guys, let me go back to the hospital. I won't say anything about what happened. It was…a misunderstanding. Right?"

Linc did a suggestive swagger with his thumbs pointed at his chest, then licked his meaty lips, and Mariah threw up a little in her mouth. "No misunderstanding. I, for one, am glad you're here. We didn't get to spend much time together at the fight."

She concentrated on staying upright. The shaking had escalated from a tremor to a full body shudder. Everything about this situation was so wrong. The rough pine floor and wood paneling in this house generated flashbacks that battered her from all sides. When would the beatings start?

Breathe. Think. Do not give in to the panic.

"So what do we get to do with…her?" Linc pointed to Mariah.

Wyatt's slow grin contained zero happiness. Red glinted in his eyes. Not normal. Had to be possessed. "She's bait so we can screw those Taggarts over real good. It's part of the Great One's plan."

Mariah pushed to her feet. She couldn't take this insanity anymore. "That's it. I'm done here."

With a whip-like move, Wyatt's grip bit into her upper arm. The muzzle of the gun rested under her chin. "I don't think so."

Through a motionless jaw, she whispered, "You'll be arrested for this, Wyatt."

"Only if anyone says anything." He smacked his lips. "Or if there's any evidence left to find."

The edges of her visual field dimmed. Her heart beat too quickly. She couldn't breathe. The scent of moldy wood made her stomach cramp.

Tommy piped up, his irises flashing from blank to briefly red. A whiff of sharp scent, like a match strike, drifted past her. She was dealing with much more than a crime here. "Good news. The sheriff witnessed this scene. Nothing to see here."

She bit her lip. This could not be happening. But if they needed bait, maybe she could buy time.

She tucked her hands in the coat pockets and wrapped her fingers around the cell phone.

Maybe she could get a message out.

Wyatt dragged her toward the hallway. "Why don't you go check on our mom while you're here. Although, I'd say she's pretty relaxed right about now."

"What?"

"Once you're in her room, sit there and be quiet."

Mariah froze. Walk deeper into this house?

"Go!" he bellowed, his voice echoing in a strange reverberation that spiked jolts through her spine. "If you try to leave, we'll hurt our mom."

Linc snickered. "And I know how to find your brother, Doc. A bantamweight can't stand up against a heavyweight."

Mariah froze. It was Utah all over again. Sweat prickled her chest.

"Linc, take her phone and car keys."

"Good idea." The fighter groped in her pocket, with far too much extra touching. Mariah's stomach churned. "Want me to destroy her phone?" he asked.

"Not yet. We may need it to send our message."

"Yeah." Linc waved at her. "Get out of here. We have revenge to plan. I get dibs on Vaughn. He owes me."

Mariah forced her legs to carry her out of the living room and down the hall.

Wyatt's gravelly voice drifted to her. "Not me. I'm going for low-hanging fruit. Kerr's easy. He can't run."

Gasping, Mariah ducked into Mrs. Brand's room. A bedside lamp gave off sickly, yellow light.

Oh, no. This room also had wood walls. A thick odor of musty pine made it hard to breathe.

Mrs. Brand opened an eye. "What're you doin' here?" Her words slid out, slurred.

"Are you okay?" Mariah asked. At least she could focus on treating a patient. Do something useful. Anchor herself to reality.

"Mmmph." The woman drifted back to sleep. The hiss of oxygen and her light snore produced the only sounds in the room.

Mariah gently shook the woman's shoulder, but nothing happened. She frowned as she checked the bottles at the bedside. Medication for her multiple sclerosis, an antibiotic, some blood pressure medication, and inhalers. Nothing that would...ah, a bottle of lorazepam. She shook the bottle. Two tablets left from the twenty prescribed a few days ago. That explained the stupor. Was the woman going to be okay?

Mariah paced, her head whipping to the door at any external sound. Only the low voices of the three nuts filtered back to the room.

Leave and Mrs. Brand might be hurt. Along with Mariah.

Stay and the entire Taggart clan might be hurt. Along with Mariah.

Where was Izzy? Mariah checked the bedside clock: 7:45 p.m. Even if she waited another hour or so for Izzy to return, there was no guarantee the woman could help. Worse, involving Izzy might put her in danger as well.

Sweat trickled down her back.

Heavy footsteps transmitted through the floorboards.

No way was she staying here. She'd go for help and send someone to check on Mrs. Brand. But Mariah couldn't call for help here, trapped. She picked up the landline phone on the nightstand. No ring tone.

What she really wanted to do was curl up in the fetal position and wish this nightmare away.

Quietly, she began systematically going through the room. The window had a retrofitted lock on it. Unlikely they kept a key in here. But a window lock hadn't stopped Mariah years ago. She had defeated that lock with a metal brad and a paperclip back then. And a lot of desperation.

The dresser top held a few boxes. Some earrings but the posts weren't long enough. A brush. How about bobby pins?

Nothing. Damn.

Moving to the closet, she fished around until a harsh squeak stopped her.

Metal hanger.

Metal.

Keeping an eye on the soundly sleeping Mrs. Brand, Mariah fished out the hanger, winter pants, and boots. Opening a few dresser drawers, she found woolen socks and gloves. She wasn't picky on sizes. Anything was better than the current work clothes she wore, because by God she *was* getting out of this place.

A door slammed. She didn't move.

A few low voices continued, presumably from the living room. The ever-present hiss of oxygen provided background sound.

Quickly donning the extra layers, she took two hangers and bent one into a longer piece and pinched an end to push up the lock pins. She pressed the wire of the other hanger into a narrow loop to turn the lock itself.

The lock was at waist height on the sill. With trembling fingers, she used those memories of her escape in Utah and went to work placing the narrow loop into the lock as a lever for the other metal piece. The wire thickness barely fit. But it fit.

Click.

Plink.

Click.

She turned the lock. Nothing.

Sweat rolled down her temple, tickling her cheek. Air rasped in and out of her lungs.

The voices continued. When would they come back?

Forcing her hands to stop shaking, she rolled her shoulders. Not only would she make it out of this hellish place and find her way across wilderness to safety, she would call for help for Mrs. Brand, and then she would let the Taggarts know about the extent the Brand guys wanted to hurt them.

She readjusted the hanger pieces.

The light metal in the lock made tiny *scritches* in the quiet night. Who was it that had left the house? Would they be out here, waiting for her?

She'd deal with that issue later. For now, escape.

A slight movement of her hand, and there, she felt the bent tip of the long piece of metal push up the farthest pin. Easing the metal back, she pressed the second pin, then the third. One more to go.

Footsteps echoed down the hallway.

Last one.

Clink.

Scared to move, in case the whole thing slipped, she paused. Then, with a slow and steady twist, she turned the lock.

The window lock popped open.

CHAPTER 37

Vaughn staggered in a circle, like he'd unloaded a gallon of brandy into his gut. "Where is she?" A vice grip cranked down on his brain. Remaining upright had turned into a hell of a chore.

He stopped fighting and his knees gave out, dropping him to the floor.

Shelby gasped for air in the chair as she pinched her nose. "Dude, stop."

"Quit hurting her," Eric growled.

Vaughn held his head in two hands, as if he could keep it from exploding. "I'm trying."

Desperate. The power wanted—needed—to find Mariah. Needed Vaughn to protect her.

Was she hurt? He tried to use his power to try and locate her, but the damned mental ability couldn't tell direction.

Maybe this was the reason his power had shifted. So he could help Mariah when she was in danger.

He glanced up. Ruth's wide-eyed expression iced his blood. Underneath, though, there was more. Like she understood how he felt. Like she'd experienced something similar herself. He rubbed the goose bumps on his arms. He'd deal with Mrs. Sphinx later.

Another wave of pain hit him. His ability stretched his mind, reached out farther than he thought possible, pulling him in all directions with its clawing need to find her. He lifted his head out of his hands and met the horrified stares around him.

"Find her," he said, the words tearing out of him.

No one moved.

"Please, Shel." Still on his knees, he turned toward his sister. "I'm begging you."

Eric knelt and got in his face. "No. No way are you doing that to her. She's barely recovered from a damned coma. We don't know what using her power will do to her."

"I know. Shit." The words ripped out of the back of Vaughn's raw throat.

"It's okay." Shelby motioned Eric back. "I get it. When someone I loved was in danger, there was nothing I wouldn't do to help them."

"Geezus—" Eric bit off as he stood up.

Shelby's deadly expression made him bump back against the wall in a huff.

"Let me try," she said.

Garrison stood up. "Just don't go all the way into Mariah's head. That nearly killed you the last time you tried it on someone."

She rolled her eyes. "Trust me when I say you don't have to remind me."

Another blast of agony shot urgency through Vaughn's skull and he groaned. "Shit. Hurry."

"Okay, then. Help me up, sunshine," Shelby said.

Eric clenched his hands into fists, but as soon as she tried to stand on her own, he was right there at her side.

Ruth clutched the wall near the entrance to the living room.

Shelby pinched the bridge of her nose and closed her eyes. With the hardware on her leg, movement took extra effort and extra time that Mariah might not have. Slowly, Shelby rotated until she stopped, facing the back of the house. "She's that way."

"Wait. Her house, the hospital, and town are all over there," Vaughn protested, pointing in the opposite direction.

She raised her orange brows. "And I'm telling you she's that way."

He shook his head, trying to shake sense into what she was saying. "Nothing's out in that direction, except forest and…"

The blood drained to his feet.

"The Brand ranch," Kerr spat.

"Damn it."

"Well, let's go." Garrison pushed to his feet, grim set to his mouth. "With Shelby, we'll keep a bead on Mariah."

"The hell you will." Eric helped Shelby to sit again. Her face had gone white, either from the pain of standing or the effort it took to force her over-taxed radar.

"I can go," she mumbled.

"Sorry, no. Not happening." He crossed his arms. "And you all better not ask her, or I won't be responsible for what I do. She has a freaking broken leg and was in a coma not a week ago. And you're seriously considering sending her out there into potential danger? Forget it."

Ruth's voice came out icy and smooth. "He's right. Do not go together. Not all four of you. As I said, don't go until you're ready to confront it once and for all." Her hazel and gold eyes unfocused, like she peered far beyond every last one of them and saw their souls.

Vaughn ground his teeth. "I don't have time for riddles, Great-Grandma. Time's ticking."

Ruth paused, then shook her head. "One of you must stay back."

"Okay, okay, I'm staying. Problem solved," Shelby said.

Garrison rubbed his jaw. "Don't we need you for the radar?"

"Not if we're just going to the Brand ranch. We all know where that is." Vaughn danced from foot to foot. Damn it, he needed to get moving. Mariah was somewhere out there. In danger.

"What if she's not there?" Garrison asked. "Shelby can tell direction, not distance."

Vaughn pressed the heels of his hands to his burning eyes. "First of all, that's the most likely place where she is. Second of all, if she has left there, Shelby can tell us if the direction changed. We can track her."

Garrison shook his head. "Lots of variables. And no phone coverage out there."

At the same time, Kerr and Shelby's heads swiveled toward each other.

"Got it," they said together.

"We're 'lost and found,' remember?" Shelby grinned.

Kerr winked. "Twin brain!"

"Talk English!" Vaughn roared.

"I'll work with the maps while you are heading out," she said. "Should be able to get you a feature or location to aim toward, even if it's not the Brand ranch."

Kerr pointed a thumb toward his sister. "And she can nudge me in the right direction."

"With our link!" Shelby finished.

"You know this how?" Garrison scowled.

"Dude, how do you think we always won at capture the flag and hide and seek?" Kerr tipped his chin. "Teamwork."

Eric looked like he'd eaten a lemon. "But your brain, Shelby."

"Like it can get worse."

"Uh, that's not the right answer," he muttered.

"It's going to have to work. And if it hurts you, Shelby, you have to break the connection and stop using your ability. We can go back to old-fashioned tracking. And rely on the fact that Kerr can't get lost." Garrison studied Vaughn's face. "We'll get her back, big brother."

"So what's the game plan?" Vaughn struggled to focus.

"Storm the castle." Kerr grinned at the horrified expressions. "What? Sounds good to me. Tell me a location. I'll get us there."

His ability didn't allow him to find a person like Shelby's power did. But Kerr was right—he couldn't get lost. As long as he had an end point, he could spin in circles yet somehow find the place. Great plan, as long as Mariah was at the place they homed in on.

Vaughn clapped his hands together. "Let's go."

"Wait." Ruth's clear voice sliced through the energized air, stopping them all cold. She tilted her head, like she detected a scent. "Be ready for that creature. It's out there."

"Done. What else?" Garrison motioned to her.

She opened her mouth, then shut it. "That's all."

"I just bet," Vaughn muttered.

Eric stepped forward. "Want help?"

"No. Stay here and keep everyone else safe," Garrison said.

"I can come with you," Odie appeared next to Ruth and slid his arm around her waist.

"No," she said.

"Yes, *cher*. I will add my strength to theirs."

Her eyes went wide. "But you're no longer im—"

"Impressively good looking as you? *Mon dieu*, it's a cross you must bear, being around someone as hideous as me." His beard framed a rakish smile, and he kissed her on the forehead. "Well, gentlemen. What are we waiting for?"

Ruth's smooth face went marble pale as she backed out of the living room. "I'll get Zach and Mr. Taggart sorted out for the evening."

Garrison brushed a kiss over Sara's lips. "Be safe, please."

Urgency drove Vaughn. In no time, they had the horses saddled and moving in the direction Kerr indicated. If the end point changed, they had only Shelby's ability to redirect them. A few miles into the National Forest, the cell phone signals wouldn't work well enough, even to get a text out.

CHAPTER 38

Mariah shoved one foot in front of the other in the six-plus inches of snow, the crunch of the ground and whistling wind through the trees keeping poor company. After tumbling out of the window five feet down into the snow, she'd rubbed out her footprints with her gloved hands as she backed across the too-exposed open area surrounding the Brands' house. Once she had reached the trees, she gave a sigh of relief.

Hopefully, the extra blanket she'd added for Mrs. Brand would keep the woman warm enough with the open window.

But now where to go?

Izzy's words from today's appointment drifted back to her: *There's a cave near the house. Well, it's about a forty-five minute walk straight off the back of the house. I even notched some trees to make a path, since I go there so often.*

Mariah turned and spotted the back of the house, then drew an invisible line into the forest and edged over in that direction. Tree notches?

She searched, patting tree trunks in the moonlight. Wasting time. Someone would find her if she stuck around this place. She should be running away from here.

But where?

Couldn't go back toward the county road. She'd have to pass too close to the Brand house, and besides, that would be the first place anyone would look for someone escaping.

Chances were, if they found her, they wouldn't be nearly as hospitable.

The other direction was nothing but National Forest for miles and miles. If she got lost, no one might ever find her.

Notches. Please let there be notches. Give me a direction. Anything.

Her hand drifted over a trunk. An irregular piece of bark was missing, the wood gleaming in the moonlight.

She sagged against the tree.

Peering into the forest, she saw another notch, about ten feet ahead. Her breath puffed out, visible in the unfortunately clear night. The clouds had given way to moonlight that now streamed through the trees and dappled the ground, illuminating her location for anyone searching for her. Her legs burned as she kept bending down to obscure her tracks. Progress was so slow. Her heart thudded as she looked for the next marked tree deeper into the forest.

What would be waiting for her? She looked over her shoulder. That cloud monster still lurked out here, somewhere. No Vaughn here to protect her this time. Her pace picked up as imaginary fingers danced up her neck. Her breath came out too quickly. Her vision grayed.

Stop. Break the task down into pieces. First and most important step: get as far away from the Brand family as possible. Next step: survive the night. Simple enough.

Already, the suffocating, heavy sense of despair and darkness had lifted. What was she, twenty or thirty minutes away from the ranch? No idea; she didn't have her phone.

She stumbled going up a small ravine. *Careful.* The worst thing that could happen would be to get injured.

Actually, no. That wasn't the worst thing that could happen.

When she glanced behind her, a shadow danced in the corner of her field of vision. Were those red glowing dots coming from the depths of the forest? She paused, listening. No sound other than the snow-muffled tinkle of a small stream at the bottom of the steep hillside and the thudding of her pulse in her head.

What would the Brands do when they realized she had escaped? If they caught her?

Nothing good.

A choking sensation clogged her throat. *Stop it.* Time to focus all her energy on staying alive right now. *Find the next notch.*

It took too long this time. Panic clawed its way up her throat— and she found the next trail marker.

Her thighs burned as she trudged farther into the mountains. Every so often, she used a pine branch to obscure her footprints behind her.

But lack of tracks also meant anyone trying to help her couldn't find her. A hysterical bubble of laughter threatened to erupt. No one knew she was even out here to help her. Oh, God.

Cold nipped at her nose.

Izzy had said forty-five minutes of walking. Probably took longer in the dark, trying to find the path. But it would be easy to find the cave, right? Mariah prayed that Izzy had stocked her escape from the world with at least a blanket.

Keep following the notches.

Reaching back to brush the tracks away, she stopped, sweat chilling on her forehead.

From the bottom of the steep hill she had just climbed, Wyatt's grinding voice floated back up to her.

"The tracks end here. She has to be close."

"What are you gonna do to her?" Linc, that jerk.

"Everything."

Sound faded as her head swam.

She eyed the top of the hill. About fifteen feet ahead was another notch gleaming in bark. If she could reach there without the men seeing her, she might have a chance.

The internal rat-a-tat of her heart provided a beat to drive her feet faster. Her legs screamed to stop slogging through the deep snow. Fighting the urge to flat-out run, she erased her trail as best she could.

Damn the moonlight. If she could see the shadowy forms of the men, then they could see her against the moonlit sky. Her stomach muscles clenched.

Wouldn't it be nice to have someone like Vaughn here right about now?

Moot point. The only way she would get out of this bad situation was to do it herself.

She crested the hill and came close to passing out with relief.

A forest road stretched to her right and left was snow-covered and trackless. Across the road was another tree notch.

"She's up there!"

CHAPTER 39

Vaughn checked his cell phone again. Close to 9:00 p.m. No signal now that they'd reached the hills.

What if Kerr was wrong about the location? What if Shelby couldn't stay in contact with him to adjust direction?

Just like Shelby always located the person she sought, Kerr never got lost. Ever. Vaughn sent a brief prayer that his younger siblings wouldn't lose their mojo tonight. Already, Kerr had adjusted direction once based on urging from Shelby.

Even if they reached a location, they had no guarantee that Mariah would be alive.

What if the Brands got to her first?

Shit. He tightened his hands until the horse snorted. Loosening his grip, he peered into the forest. If anything happened to Mariah, he would personally dismember anyone responsible. Plain and simple.

His power surged again, wanting him to move faster.

Something had just happened to increase the danger to her. Did that mean she was still alive? Hurt? What? Damn his stupid power, it was acting like a directionless stagecoach driver, whipping the team into a frenzy but without a clue as to which direction to go.

He wiped sweat off his upper lip.

"Stay calm, my friend." Odie kneed his horse to draw even with his. "We'll find your lady. You must trust the process. Your brother and sister can do this."

Vaughn ground his molars until his jaw ached. "It's hard to know that she's out there, alone, in danger."

After a pause, Odie studied him with ancient eyes. "I know precisely what you mean."

"What do—?"

Kerr lifted his arm up with a fist, military style, and they all stopped.

As they reached a forest road cut, Garrison whispered, "Anything?"

"We go on foot from here," Kerr said. "Keep it quiet. I thought I heard something."

"How close are we?" Vaughn's gut twisted into a snarl of knots.

"Close. Tie 'em up, bro." As soon as their horses were secured, Kerr motioned to them as he walked into the forest. "Footprints," he whispered.

Multiple sets.

Something edged into the periphery of Vaughn's vision. Dark and light. Shadow and movement. He peered into the woods. Nothing visible. Every nerve went on screaming alert, making his skin crawl. "There's something out here, guys."

"I feel it, too." Garrison's jaw had gone rock-hard under the shadow of his hat brim.

"Keep going, we're almost there," Kerr whispered.

Another fifteen minutes of bushwhacking up and down draws, jumping small streams, and they reached a cliff edge. Vaughn braced against the headache and reached out with his power. Nothing distinct, but the mental ability pulsed again. She was close. Still alive. He hoped.

But in serious danger.

Frigid air scythed in and out of his lungs.

As they came to a high point, Kerr held up his fisted hand again. Everyone stopped. He pointed.

There, a hundred feet ahead of them, two dark figures scrambled over the edge.

His power all but dragged Vaughn forward. Mariah. Those men had to be tracking her.

"Stop, man. I'll go in first, undetected," Kerr said. "You know, with my little trick?" He pulled off his duster and hat and set them on the ground.

Garrison crossed his arms. "Can you get in there, make sure she's safe, and then stay hidden for five minutes?"

"Of course." After a grimace, the edges of Kerr's body blurred. His rarely-used ability to disappear manifested as he faded from sight. Invisible steps crunched away from them.

Odie murmured, "*Mon dieu.* Impressive."

Waiting nearly killed Vaughn, but after what seemed like forever, Garrison finally gave the okay to move, and Vaughn and Odie paced right with him to the cliff edge. Following the tracks, they navigated a steep, thin path down to a four-foot wide ledge jutting out from the sheer rock. Below that: another fifty feet of fresh air.

Vaughn's overactive imagination fed him an image of Mariah's broken form at the bottom of that drop. His stomach muscles tightened. Kerr had better reach her before those bastards did.

The crisp, frigid air crystallized his decision: If Vaughn got her out of here alive, not only would he beg for her forgiveness, he'd spend every day of his natural life atoning for being dumb enough to let her go.

If his bad decision hadn't already cost Mariah her life.

They crept along the ledge, and sure enough, a dark opening into the rock loomed out of the shadows. Footprints, large and small, tracked into the cave. Vaughn's heart stopped.

Flickers of light, then voices and shouts filtered out of the cave.

"Careful with guns in there, guys," Garrison muttered. "No collateral damage."

Collateral damage. Mariah.

CHAPTER 40

Huddled in the entrance of the cave, Mariah shook like a quaking aspen in a stiff breeze. Despite her wool coat and borrowed snow pants, the hard rock conducted cold straight into her butt. Scant light from the moon trickled in to her location. Behind her, darkness yawned. Waiting. Tempting her to retreat there. Warning her what might await.

Maybe there were worse things than the guys who tracked her.

Voices and the scuff of booted feet triggered a flurry of palpitations in her chest. She glanced up. Her tracks were plainly visible leading into the cave.

She edged back into the darkness, running her gloved hand along the rough rock wall. With each step, she probed back with her foot to make sure solid ground remained underneath her. Wyatt and Linc's voices echoed louder.

A nasty chuckle made her skin crawl.

Oh, God.

Scooting another few feet back into the depths, she crouched behind a rock just as a flashlight beam swept the cave. Despite the freezing temperature, sweat dampened her skin. She was trapped. Again.

"Where is she? Not like she could go far."

"No idea. Wanna go in there?" Linc asked.

"Not particularly." Wyatt hocked and spat. "But yeah, we need to find her. Forget using her as bait. She's too much trouble. We'll make her an example of what happens when a Taggart goes up against us. The Great One will be pleased with our efforts."

No, no, no. Lack of oxygen made her head spin. This could not be happening.

Before she could scramble away, a warm, strong hand clamped over her mouth. Her scream fizzled out as an arm around her chest squeezed hard.

"It's Kerr Taggart. Don't move." His friendly whisper was the sweetest music she'd ever heard.

At her nod he moved his hand away from her mouth and patted her on the shoulder.

How had he gotten in here without anyone seeing him? Heck, how did he know where to find her?

"Vaughn's on his way," he murmured, a ghost of sound in the darkness behind her. "You'll be okay. Promise."

Every muscle in her body went limp.

"I'm going to draw them away," he said. "When they pass by, you need to run for the entrance. Got it?"

"You sure?" she whispered.

"Yup."

She had questions, but now wasn't the time to figure out how they'd found her. How Kerr had entered the cave in front of the men, undetected.

A reassuring squeeze of her arm, and he was gone. From the depths of the cave, the sound of scrapes and crunches bounced in all directions.

"What was that?" Wyatt's light swung in wild arcs over the cave walls.

She peeked behind her. Nothing visible in the area illuminated by their flashlights.

She remained crouched behind the rock, her gloved hands pressed against the rough stone.

"That's gotta be her. Let's go." Wyatt kept his flashlight beam fixed on the recesses of the cave and stormed toward the sounds.

Linc trailed right behind him. Two wretched peas in a pod.

At the dust kicked up, she barely stifled a sneeze.

"What was that?"

The flashlight beam skimmed three inches above her hiding spot.

She crouched into the tiniest ball possible.

More rock sounds came from farther into the cave, and the light slid back to the depths.

Another few feet, and they'd be past her position.

She held her breath.

Wyatt and Linc snickered as they stalked their presumed prize at the back of the cave.

Three feet away from her.

Two feet.

One.

They drew even with her position, within a foot of where she crouched. She shook with effort to tuck her head and curl into a small, rocklike shape. If they so much as turned their heads in her direction...

With three more steps, they were past her position.

Keeping her hand on the rock, she eased out of her hiding place. The beams of light shone forward, but Wyatt and Linc were only a few feet away. She struggled to make her ragged breathing soft and even.

Now fully exposed to view, she remained low, thighs burning as she duck-walked toward the entrance of the cave.

Her pulse pounded, too fast. She wasn't getting enough air. Her legs quivered and burned.

Ten, maybe fifteen more feet. Had to keep going.

She lost her balance, and stumbled. Harsh, bright light spiraled around, pinning her like a moth on a spider web.

"What the—? She's right there!"

Damn it. With a sob lodged in her throat, Mariah pushed to her feet and sprinted for the entrance. Just as she hit the opening where moonlight cast the world in an eerie, gray glow, a massive figure loomed in front of her.

A scream bubbled out of her throat as iron bands of muscle clamped around her. She swung out over the cliff edge.

The scent of familiar shaving cream anchored her as surely as the warm arms that pulled her back to reality. Vaughn. Here. She sagged as he tucked her next to him.

And then he faced Wyatt and Linc as they emerged from the cave.

The ledge they were all standing on was narrow. Four feet wide. Would only allow two people to stand side by side. And beyond the ledge was empty space for who knew how many feet down.

She peeked back over her shoulder and, in the moonlight, made out Garrison's grim expression and Odie's oddly reassuring smile.

Kerr was still somewhere inside that cave.

"Taggart." The sound of a gun safety being released...she crushed Vaughn's jacket in her gloved hands.

"Garrison, please move her away from here," Vaughn's voice rumbled through her forehead she had pressed to his back.

No, she couldn't let go of him.

A hand tugged on her upper arm. "Come on. Please," Garrison muttered, urging her away from Vaughn. "Odie, you got her? I'm going to help my brother. Here. Hold my hat."

"Absolutely." A warm, almost fatherly, arm went around her. "Don't worry, *ami*. The boys will take care of things."

Mariah's knees locked as the two brutes faced Vaughn and Garrison.

"Seems like a fair fight to me." Wyatt's laugh scraped like dead tree branches against a glass pane.

"Put down the fucking gun and maybe I won't call you a wimp." Vaughn glanced back and stepped to one side, blocking any clear shot at Mariah.

"Once we've dealt with you Taggarts, we can finish our business with Dr. Mariah."

"The hell you'll ever touch her again."

"You have no idea what you're messing with," Wyatt growled, eyes flashing red. Mariah reared back at the wave of hot sulfur that blasted past her. Odie kept a solid grip on her arm.

"Neither do you, sweetie pie." The voice came from the mouth of the cave, and suddenly the gun flew out of Wyatt's hand and off the cliff.

"What the hell was that?" Wyatt spun and swatted at empty space, then stumbled.

A shrug, then Wyatt ran straight at Vaughn.

When they hit the ground and rolled, Mariah leapt forward, reaching out to Vaughn. Odie pulled her back to a safe distance. Punches flew faster than she could follow.

Unlike in the octagon, this fight had no rules.

But it had an outcome.

Her heart stopped when Wyatt caught Vaughn across the face with an elbow.

On the far side of the ledge, Kerr suddenly appeared out of nowhere behind Linc, nailing the guy in his kidney with several solid punches.

Linc spun, swinging at Kerr, but Vaughn's little brother ducked and disappeared. Disappeared. She squinted. Linc staggered close to the brink of the ledge and howled. Garrison tried to get past Vaughn and Wyatt, who were locked in a brutal pummeling match, but couldn't pass.

"Leave her alone," Vaughn panted, driving Wyatt back with several blows. "And leave my family alone."

Wyatt shook the blow off like he'd been hit with foam, not a hard fist. "You cannot win." His voice reverberated off the rocks in an eerie echo that seemed to get louder the more the sound bounced around. "We need one more. And then we will have all of the Taggart family."

"The hell."

"Exactly." Wyatt's teeth gleamed in the moonlight before he tackled Vaughn.

Mariah gasped.

Vaughn's head landed on…empty space over the cliff edge.

Her palms sweated.

Kerr reappeared and danced around Linc as best he could. Linc shot forward with a jab, sending Kerr sprawling on the ground. Garrison caught an opening, leapt around Vaughn and plowed into Linc's midsection. Then the two brothers worked together to level the big fighter.

After a solid minute of relentless punishment from both Taggart brothers, Linc lay on his side, air rasping in and out. Garrison and Kerr stood over him, their postures daring Linc to get up.

Vaughn rolled Wyatt under him but couldn't get a good angle to punch. Wyatt's hands kept moving, darting blows to Vaughn's torso and face. Screams and yowls flowed out of Wyatt and grew until they became louder than a police siren. Mariah clapped her hands over her ears.

"You. Cannot. Win." He spat blood, his voice ringing. Gravel and frozen clods of dirt rained down on them from the hillside above. "We cannot be destroyed. The Great One is coming. Soon. You'll see."

Vaughn locked his hands around Wyatt's thick throat. "Know what? I don't care about your future plans. You just need to stay away from me"—he slammed the man's head into the ground— "my family"—another slam—"and the woman I love." Wyatt's eyes rolled back in his head.

Mariah's heart stopped.

Pushing up and away from a limp Wyatt, Vaughn turned and stalked toward her as she leaned against the cliff wall. In the moonlight, the shadows poured over his face, casting his features into skeletal hollows.

Vaughn stood in front of her, facing away from the drop-off.

Wyatt lunged.

The seconds in Mariah's life slowed down.

His power. Could Vaughn still sense danger to himself?

Wyatt's massive fist was aimed right at Vaughn.

A feral grin ghosted across Vaughn's face, and he dodged out of the way then gave the guy a push to change momentum.

Wyatt flew over the edge of the cliff with a howl that abruptly stopped.

Without a backward glance, Vaughn rotated to Mariah, pressing her into the wall behind her. He braced his arms on either side of her head.

"Damn it. I thought I'd lost you," he breathed.

In front of the cave entrance, Linc groaned and pushed to his knees.

Kerr piped up, "Bro, can you do the smoochie make up bit later? I'm tired of hitting this asshole." He pointed. "Stay down, already."

Garrison did the honors, kicking Linc in the ribs. The man crumpled to the ground again in a sloppy heap.

Vaughn brushed his lips over her forehead. "We're leaving."

The tingle from being in physical contact with him brought stinging tears to her eyes. She didn't even mind the dull headache that accompanied the sensation of safety.

Anywhere. She'd hike with him for hours if it meant getting away from Wyatt and Linc.

Wyatt. The cliff. She craned her head around Vaughn's big shoulders. Should she help? She had taken the Hippocratic Oath, after all.

"Leave him. Linc can take care of it," Vaughn muttered.

On second thought, maybe the oath didn't count when the patient tried to kill the doctor.

Vaughn guided her up the narrow path of the cliff. She panted, scrambling on the snow-dusted rock.

She slipped. No way would she come this far, relive her personal nightmares, and escape Wyatt and Linc only to slide off this cliff. Forget that.

Vaughn grabbed her and pulled her up the steep track. Odie gripped her ankle to stabilize her foothold and helped from below. Garrison and Kerr brought up the rear of their group.

Keeping her hand in his, Vaughn hurried across the stark, moonlit, gray landscape. Snow melted in her hair, chilling her to the bone.

She didn't care. Vaughn was here.

She was safe.

They were both alive.

A sliver of brighter gray appeared through the trees. The forest road she had crossed over earlier. Her legs turned to Jell-O. Thank God.

"Almost to the horses," he said. "What the—?"

A yell lodged in her throat as a black figure loomed out from the trees.

CHAPTER 41

Higher than Everest one minute, bottom of the ocean the next. Vaughn should have known they weren't out of danger yet.

His power sparked into a virtual ice pick and lodged in his skull.

That damned creature rose out of nowhere and turned those nasty, red eyes on Mariah, and Vaughn's ability went crazy.

Mixed curses heralded his brothers' and Odie's arrival.

The voice that came from the creature, a scream blended with an animal howl, scorched Vaughn's ears. Tucking Mariah in to his side, Vaughn turned so his body protected her. His power pushed outward, no longer a rubbery bubble but a harder one, driven by pure rage and fear for her life.

Fuck this. No way would he save her from the Brand bastards only to have this bullshit, whatever the hell it was, hurt her. Not today. Not ever.

"You have tried to take my minion from me," the thing howled.

"If you mean the fucker who kidnapped her and tried to kill her, then yes, you bet we did," Vaughn snarled.

The nothingness expanded, soaking blackness into blackness. "You have failed. We are too strong."

Vaughn was beyond caring. "And by 'we' you mean…?"

"*Mon dieu*, don't ask it questions, my friend." Odie inhaled.

The thing turned to the Cajun. "You?" An inferno-whistle breath of sulfur blasted out of the thing. "I should have killed you when I had the chance."

What the actual fuck? Odie knew the creature? They had a *history*?

"But you did not. Now look at you, a disgusting shadow of what you used to be." Odie was baiting it. Why?

"Is *she* with you?" the thing howled, red ember eyes casting around the forest.

"No idea who you're talking about," Odie replied, his tone casual but his stance rigid. Vaughn had to give the Cajun props for sheer balls.

"No matter. I will destroy her legacy once and for all." The glowing red orbs scanned the group. "Where is the last one?"

"What?" Garrison choked out.

"There is one more of the legacy missing. I must have them all." Snow melted into acrid liquid as thick clouds of sulfur billowed underneath the thing. "No matter." A finger of the black cloud elongated and reached toward Mariah. "Time for you all to know my power. I will destroy this paltry human now."

"No!" Vaughn yelled.

"You cannot stop me."

"The hell I can't."

As the blackness brushed over Mariah's skin, she screamed and grabbed at her neck.

The scent of her burnt flesh seared Vaughn's nose.

He released all conscious constraint of his gift and let it suck up layer after layer of power, cram it into a ball, and extend it out over her. Damn it, his head was going to fly apart.

Concentrate.

This time, he jammed virtual spikes on the outer portion of the thick sphere, because why the hell not? He ignored his own protection and instead ensured that his power covered Mariah. His head throbbed, but damned if she would be hurt any more by that thing.

The creature kept pushing against the invisible barrier, but Mariah's screams receded into a gasp as she sagged into Vaughn's chest. Safe. For now.

Another abrupt change in his power threw his mind from accelerate into annihilate. No longer did his ability want to protect. Now it wanted blood. It wanted revenge.

Time to feed his gift with exactly what it craved. Time to fully *become* danger.

Those previous encounters were rehearsal.

Not caring what it did to his mind or body, he spread out his arms and blanked his mind, gritting his teeth as he let go of control. No longer did Vaughn fight his power's insistence to transform him into a weapon.

The enlarging force grew around him and pushed outward. Virtual crystals in the sphere grew into long spikes fixed into the surface, each crystal a spear of pure hatred for the thing.

No one messed with Vaughn's family.

No one messed with Mariah.

That creature wanted his soul? Fine. Vaughn would give him every last drop.

With interest.

A pulsing surge of energy rose from the soles of his feet, moving through his body and building power, growing until it became a roaring tidal wave of rage, threatening to consume him, funneling everything he had into the spears. He could control it but just barely.

Vaughn's ears rang, and all sound around him disappeared as his ability approached critical mass.

The suspended spears quivered, sticking out of the virtual sphere.

Somehow he held it back, every muscle in his body shaking with the effort to remain upright.

"Get back, you guys," he gritted out. His voice sounded like he was in a thick barrel.

"Why?" Garrison panted.

"Fucking do it. Get behind a tree or something. Now!" No way to aim this mess. He could only hope he wouldn't wipe everyone out when he let it fly.

It was time. He pushed Mariah toward his brothers and stared down the red-eyed bastard.

Putting every last ounce of hatred for that creature into the virtual ball of fury, he lengthened the spikes.

And…

Like a cannon firing in all directions, the sphere exploded outward, blasting spears into the creature.

A howl—an air raid drill, wild animal, and fire engine mashed together—expelled from his head. Vaughn would make that monster pay for hurting Mariah, and he didn't give one single fuck what the effort cost him personally.

Fireworks blasted across his field of vision and boomed in his ears.

The creature screamed again. "You will not prevail. The legacy will be my first feast when I enter this human world. Count the days until my dominion upon the Earth begins anew."

"Count this, bastard." A second migraine-inducing wave of rage flooded his senses, and he gave himself over to the ability once more. "One." The bubble reformed, bigger and stronger this time. "Two." The crystal shards held steady, vibrating and ready to go.

Time stopped.

He had fully become danger. He would protect what was his.

"Three, fucker." A horrible blast came from him, sucking him dry.

The screech stopped.

Nothing.

No sound. No movement. Nothing.

Mariah? Was she alive?

He shook his head. Still had goddamned stars dancing in his vision. His hearing was screwed up, too, like cotton got stuck in his ears. He bent over. Whatever. He was getting her out of here. Now.

When he staggered forward and went down on a knee, Mariah appeared. He locked onto her arm and dragged her down. He couldn't seem to release his grip on her.

Damn it.

"What the hell did you do?" Garrison ran up. His voice sounded a million miles away. Tinny. Muffled.

"Power. Changed," Vaughn gritted out as he grabbed his head with his free hand. "Holy crap." He forced himself to let go of Mariah before he hurt her. "Sorry."

"Can you walk?" Garrison grabbed him under the armpit.

"Ease up there." Vaughn wobbled. "I'm a little weak. Can't hear real well." He rubbed his ear. Warm, iron-scented wetness dripped down his neck. He wiped his fingers on his jeans. Later. He'd deal with the fallout later.

Mariah's fingers were feather light as she ran them over his face. Best feeling in the universe. "You're bleeding from your ears. What can I do? Do you need anything?" Her voice barely reached him, but he still heard it. Sweetest thing he'd ever heard.

He took her face in his shaking hands. "I need you to be okay." He kissed her hard enough to scrape teeth. The heat from her soft lips gave him an extra burst of adrenaline he didn't know he still possessed. He sat up straighter.

Kerr cleared his throat as he looped a hand under Vaughn's other arm. "Bro. Again. I know it's quite the debate: escape black blob of evil versus swap spit with pretty doctor." He sucked a tooth. "Hate to be the adult once more, but we should get the hell out of this place before something else tries to kill us."

Vaughn leaned against both his brothers. "Let's go. Odie, can you help Mariah?"

"With pleasure."

"Don't get too handsy with her, man," he growled. Shit, Vaughn needed to be in contact with her. Needed it more than air.

Odie's chuckle was seen rather than heard. "Not to worry. I'm spoken for."

Vaughn leaned on Garrison while their motley group limped through the forest to the horses.

"Are we close?" Garrison gritted out. "Delicate flower here weighs a ton."

"Head more to the left, and we'll be at the horses in a few minutes," Kerr said. "Not that you need to hear this, but I'd hurry. Stuff feels spooky out here."

"So says Mr. Obvious," Garrison agreed.

After another minute, Vaughn's legs became more stable. The ringing continued, but at least his ears had stopped bleeding.

All he wanted was Mariah next to him.

He clambered onto his horse. He turned and extended his hand; she hesitated. Then with a boost from Garrison, she settled behind Vaughn.

The moment her arms clamped around his midsection felt like heaven.

CHAPTER 42

Mariah relaxed, her cheek against Vaughn's back, absorbing the heat that radiated from him, even through his leather coat. From hips to chest she molded to him and felt each muscle's movement as he shifted in the saddle, guiding the horse in a canter down the forest road.

Once they reached the woods again, the horses slowed to a walk in the snowy, uneven terrain.

Even though they'd put distance behind them, she kept checking over her shoulder, expecting to see a wild-eyed Wyatt or leering Linc. Or that terrifying thing that had touched her. Rubbing her neck, she winced at the raw skin.

"How are you doing back there?" Vaughn's delicious voice rolled through her bones, and it felt like home.

Her chest ached. "I'm okay."

It would be so hard to walk away after being this close to him again.

But she wouldn't fight. He had his world back in New York. He had his family. No way could she ask him to give that up for her. He had made his decision.

And she wouldn't compromise. She needed a long-term relationship, not a few weeks' fling. He needed to be certain of his intentions. As much as it hurt, the final decision would be best for both of them.

But why then had Vaughn come for her?

More to the point, how did he know that she was even missing? Or where to find her?

He'd said he loved her. Well, that complicated his declaration of never wanting to see her again. And he might still leave town, which took him off of her personal relationship "must have" list.

Damn his leather and shaving cream scent. Damn the knowledge that, in his arms, she was safe. Damn the way his muscles tightened and shifted next to her own skin, screwing with her heart and mind and body in the worst possible way.

At the sight of the ranch lights in the distance, a sob bubbled up. Whether the tears came from relief or impending loss, she didn't have the energy to analyze.

Vaughn guided the horse through the gate and to the barn. Light snow fell, buffering all the sounds around them. The windows of the house glowed, a welcoming beacon in the freezing night.

Garrison dismounted and hurried over to help her down. Her legs wobbled as they hit solid ground. Was it exhaustion?

Or was it because she no longer rested against a guy who infused her with strength?

In a flash, Vaughn was next to her, enveloping her in a tight embrace as he lifted her.

"God, you almost died," he ground out. Her bones creaked under his grasp, but no way would she would complain.

When she could breathe, she locked eyes with him. "How did you know where I was?"

"I just knew you were in danger and I had to find you. I needed you to be safe."

"But where do we go from here? It's clear we don't have a future together."

He pressed his mouth into a hard line. Half of his face was visible in the light from the ranch house. "I'm a total idiot."

"That's not really an answer to the question."

"Can you forgive me?"

"For what? You just saved my life."

"For what I said to you this morning."

"You made your opinion clear about us. I can respect that."

He lowered her to the ground. "I never said I was a smart guy when it came to women."

The cold seeped in under her clothes, and she wrapped her arms over her chest, trying to still the shivers.

"No more standing out here," he said, tugging her toward the house. "Let's get you inside. I need to explain some things to you, if you will give me a little time."

Eric held open the back door, with Ruth and Sara peering out from behind him.

Ruth sucked in a breath and in no time had Mariah seated at the table, salve applied and an ice pack pressed to the burned area on her neck. She wiped away the dried blood from under Vaughn's ears.

"How's Odie?" Ruth asked, her gaze flicking to the back door.

"Fine. Garrison and Kerr, too." Vaughn gave a thumbs up.

Sara rested a hand over her chest and leaned against the counter.

"Uh, guys. Some privacy?" Vaughn muttered.

The women filed out of the kitchen, but Kerr entered a few seconds later, his eyes glued to his cell phone. He glanced up. "If you're about to have a serious conversation or private canoodle-fest, know that Garrison and Odie are still in the barn and will be through any minute, breaking whatever magical reunion you might have planned. Just sayin'."

"Thanks." Vaughn rested his knuckles on the table, then pushed away and paced the kitchen.

Mariah mustered the energy to stuff her gloves in pockets and shrug out of her coat. He took it from her and hung it on the peg inside the back door.

"Do you want some water or something to eat?" His low voice melted her bones.

She shook her head.

Vaughn. Being helpful.

Emptiness sucked at her insides as she waited.

She had nothing left in the emotional tanks.

Sure enough, a minute later, an exhausted Garrison beelined through the kitchen toward the living room.

Odie, no less purposeful, entered and paused only to wink at her.

Happy voices rose and fell from the living room, and the tense set of Vaughn's shoulders relaxed.

Because everyone in his family was safe. Reunited with their loved ones.

His family.

Family. Where he belonged. Where he fit in.

She set the bag of ice down and rested her forehead on her palm.

It was a mistake, spending any more time here than she needed to.

She bit her lip and motioned to the kitchen. "I don't want to overstay my welcome here, but I have no way to get back to my house."

"Got it." His words hit her like sharp pinpricks of sleet. "I'll take you wherever you need to go."

Did she read a double entendre in there? A tease? Another mean twist of the proverbial knife in her chest.

She pushed back from the table.

He rested his warm palm on her hand. She went still.

"Wait." He took a big breath. "I meant what I said a few minutes ago. Mariah, I'm so sorry." Holding up a hand when she opened her mouth, he continued, "I thought saying that crap this morning, cutting you loose, would protect you. I couldn't have been more wrong." He rubbed his chin. "And I hurt you in the worst possible way. Have I mentioned that I'm sorry?"

"No need." The air caught in her throat and she had to clear it. "But there was truth in what you said. I get it. You have a life elsewhere. I understand why things wouldn't work out with us. There are things I need, too."

"About that…"

She slipped her hand away from his and pushed the ice pack around on the table with a tinkle of cubes. "You know what you need in your life." She sucked in a good, solid breath and met his eyes, like this conversation wasn't already a MasterClass in emotional torture. "Well, I know what I need in my future. I need a long-term and stable relationship. Someone who wants me for who I am. I compromised before. I'm not compromising again."

"Damn," he breathed.

Memorizing the rugged lines of his face, she sighed. "And no way would I ask you to give up what's important to you."

He reached over and squeezed her hand again. "You're asking me what's important?" The bark of his laugh didn't make it to his hard, serious expression.

"In a manner of speaking. But I think I've got the gist."

"Do you even understand what happened tonight?"

It hurt to swallow past the lump in her throat. Did he really want to dissect the whole mess? "Um, I had a front row seat to both the kidnapping, rescue, and attack, so…yes."

"No. I meant do you understand what tonight meant? About what's important to me." He rubbed the dried blood under an ear. "Look, my life in New York is good. No question. I have a lot going for me there."

Just like that, the elevator floor dropped out from under her. She pressed her free hand against the solid wood tabletop. Anything to steady her.

He leaned forward, startling her. "You know what's even more important than all that stuff back east?"

"No."

"This family. The people inside this house."

"Of course. They're your family."

He brushed a thumb over her lips. "Please wait. I wasn't finished." His Adam's apple bobbed. "There's more. It's you, Mariah."

"What are you saying?"

"You're going to make me work for this one, aren't you?" He barked a harsh laugh. "Look, here are all my cards, on the table. Do what you want with them."

She froze.

"I want you," he said. "You're what's most important to me. You, Mariah. More than money, more than my career back in the big city, more than fighting."

"Vaughn?" She exhaled the question.

"I want you more than all of those things. Do you think"—he hesitated, glancing at her then away—"that there's ever a chance of any future?"

"With you?"

"Ouch."

The invisible weight on her shoulders lifted by degrees. "Clarifying because of this morning and all."

"Good point." He scooted closer and leaned forward, elbows on his knees. When he tilted his head to look at her, they were at the same level. "We have a hell of a good connection, wouldn't you say?"

"Of course." Her eyelids prickled. "I care about you. But I won't ask you to change. And I won't change the person I am. I won't be hurt like that again."

"Shit, no. I would never do anything to hurt you."

"Contradict yourself much?"

"Okay, I deserved that." He laced her fingers with his in a loose hold. "I'm no good at figuring out the right thing to say. But if you felt anything…deeper…when we were together, would you consider trying again? Start fresh."

Her heart stumbled. Before she threw confetti, she needed to make sure she understood exactly what he was saying. "So you mean…"

"I want you. Mariah West," his words stuttered out. "Exactly the woman in front of me. In my life. In a relationship. And one day, maybe you'll give me a chance at something long term. You deserve a solid guy, and I want to be that guy. I'll stick around long term, too. But we'll take baby steps now."

"Even with what you said about my not fitting in, not being what you wanted?"

Leaning back, he raked fingers through his hair. "I am the dumbest fuck to ever walk this Earth. Lying was no way to start a good thing with you, but that's what I did. And I did it for a good reason, thinking a lie would protect you." Grabbing her hands again with both of his, he brushed his warm lips over her knuckles. "I'd like to spend a great deal of time making up for the stupid stuff I said."

It took a solid ten seconds to breathe again. She studied his battered but earnest face.

Her heart sped up several beats. "Got any ideas on how to make it up?"

The flash of his grin sent a shiver down her back and lower into her pelvis. "I'd like to start with my mouth. If that's okay." When she nodded, he leaned in and stroked her lips with his, sending little sparks of happiness over her skin. "Then I'd add my hands and touch every inch of your body."

"Sounds like a good next step."

Pulling back, he took her face in his hands. "What I said this morning. It was a lie. Truth is, you fit here perfectly, Mariah. My family thinks you're great, and they're right. I…I'm falling in love with you. You make me want to sand off my rough edges, be a better man, reset my roots here in Copper River. Or wherever you are. I want a chance with *you*." He tilted his chin toward the door. "And I know there's some scary stuff out there trying to hurt us. It would be totally reasonable if you walked away from the insanity here."

"I don't scare that easily anymore," she breathed.

"Damn straight. You're one of the toughest people I've ever met. And you can kick ass. But I also want to be the man to protect you. That's not my weird power talking, that's me."

She leaned against the solid palm caressing her cheek. "Oh my God, Vaughn. I fell in love with you the first time you stood up to Wyatt Brand then turned around and cleaned up the spilled coffee."

Closing the space between them, she straddled his lap and hooked her hands behind his neck. She and Vaughn fit together perfectly.

As those hard arms snaked tightly around her, his voice reverberated through her chest. "I'm not sure I can ever get enough of you."

"And you're the strongest man I know, inside and out. When I'm with you, I feel safe, and you're right, it's not just your power. It's you, Vaughn."

His chest rose and fell, more quickly. "Do you know what I'd like to do to you tonight?"

"Tuck me into bed so I can rest? Hiking all night in the snow is hard work."

"Not quite."

"Fill out yet another police report?"

He groaned. "Okay, yeah, we need to do that, too."

She nuzzled her lips against his neck. "Was there something else?"

"Well, I was thinking about a few other things." He whispered details into her ear until her toes curled. When he finished, he nipped her earlobe.

"That's not the worst plan ever." She smiled against his mouth before running her tongue over his lips. He growled and pulled her hips against his hard groin.

When he came up for air, he eased her back and grinned. "Let's get out of here. I have hours of serious apologizing to do." He slid a rough hand under her shirt and stroked her back.

"Sounds good." Shivering, she took in his determined expression. "Vaughn. Are things going to be okay? With that creature out there?"

Gold glinted in the depths of his dark eyes, utterly focused on her. "I don't know how, but we'll figure something out. The Taggarts stick together. Somehow, we're going to be okay. And I will keep you safe. I promise you that." He kissed her again. Then he stood and helped her to do the same. But he didn't break their contact. "Let's take care of business, then I plan to take you back to your place and tuck you into your bed like you've never been…tucked…before. If I'm lucky, you'll let me tuck you in for many nights to come."

Holding his hand, she felt confident enough to walk on air. "That sounds like a great plan for our future."

The End

THE
HELL'S VALLEY
SERIES

Legacy of Lies
Legacy Lost
Legacy of Danger
Legacy Found

*Turn the page for an
excerpt from*

LEGACY
FOUND

Hell's Valley
Book Four

Jillian David

Nothing said *hey, just making sure you're okay* like trespassing and stalking in the middle of the night.

In retrospect, maybe Kerr's plan had a few weak spots.

He hung by his gloved fingers on a windowsill of the Brand ranch. Damned house looked like a series of afterthoughts and second-guesses. Nothing fit. Nothing felt right either, but the sensation had nothing to do with architectural design, or lack thereof. No, when he had gotten close to the main compound, it felt like his body weighed fifty pounds more, which made this crime even more challenging as he was literally hung out to dry. His toes cramped as he balanced on the upended ten-gallon bucket.

Would it kill these people to lower the windows or build on less of a slanted piece of land where the windows were equally close the ground on all walls of the house? Not that he could ever file a formal protest.

Praying that he had the right room, he propped his chin on the sill between his hands and didn't move a muscle. Izzy's pale face filled the glass. A hand covered her mouth, her eyes opened wide.

Now what?

Okay, yes, definitely his plan had a few weak spots.

Like how she blinded him with a flashlight beam. Ouch. He squinted and grinned for all he was worth. Even tried to wave without falling on his ass. See? Nothing wrong. Just another day, lurking in people's windows.

If she didn't shut that mag light off, not only would his retinas burst into flames, but someone would see him. Like whoever slammed the front door and now crunched through snow nearby. Crap.

The second that person rounded the corner of the house, they would see Kerr, dangling like tasty bait. No time to run. Nowhere to go.

Trapped again, this time by his stupid choices.

The crunching squeaks of dry snow compressing under boots grew louder.

Kerr closed his eyes and prayed he could trust her. Clamping his teeth together, he braced against the inevitable headache. His vision went filmy, like several layers of plastic wrap covered his eyes. Blinking against the stab in his temple, he clung to the windowsill. One foot still tiptoed on the bucket. With effort, he held the fade effect until he was completely invisible.

She pressed a hand against the pane, head whipping from side to side. She turned the flashlight off and shook it.

As much as he wanted to reveal himself to her and stop the pounding headache, he had to maintain the disappearing act for a little longer.

God, the heaviness in the air here—how did she stand it? Like breathing underwater. Even the typical ranch sounds of cattle and horses reached his ears in a muted way, like the animals didn't dare to make any noise. Just like at the Taggart ranch, no more dogs ran around here, either. A tendril of sulfur irritated his sinuses and made him glance back over his shoulder, expecting to see that bastard evil creature that had been terrorizing his family.

No cloud monster tonight, only Linc. With a clomping stride, the big man emerged from the side of the house, no more than ten feet away from Kerr's precarious position. Kerr would recognize that jughead anywhere. Linc, the guy who tried to kill Vaughn in the octagon last week. If that Linc got hold of Kerr, he'd become the fighter's personal hand puppet. Shit.

At least tonight Frankenjerk marched with a determined step to the large metal Quonset-style garage on the other side of the main compound. Dude didn't glance to either side. No pause in that stiff stride until the metal man door closed behind him. Long may the asshole stay away. Kerr wished frostbite on the guy, but no way would he be that lucky in eliminating a nasty Brand family member.

Waiting a few more seconds, Kerr finally exhaled and let go of the fade, nearly losing his grip when the headache receded from ice pick to dull throb.

Izzy's wide eyes locked onto him.

That damned light blinded him again.

He flinched and waggled gloved fingers. His arms burned.

"Hi, Iz."

———◆———

LEGACY FOUND

available in print and ebook

Jillian David lives near the end of the Earth with her nut of a husband and several bossy cats. To escape the sometimes-stressful world of the rural physician, she writes while on call and in her free time. She enjoys taking realistic settings and adding a twist of "what if." Running or hiking on local trails often promotes plot development.

Follow Jillian:

Website blog at www.jilliandavid.net

Twitter at @jilliandavid13

Facebook at https://www.facebook.com/authorjilliandavid